———————— ★ ————————

The volume of blood Sperry had lost stunned me. I couldn't tell whether he'd been shot, stabbed, or skinned alive—just that it hadn't happened where he died. A smear of blood wove around the desk across the avocado shag rug like a slug trail. That dried blood was darker than what still saturated his shirt.

The trial-watchers in the press always commented on how incongruous Sperry's aging face looked with his boyishly small, springy body. But the Alfred E. Newman grin he'd flashed in life now drooped like Drew's old drawers. And the apple cheeks that had glowed with spirit—the kind the bartender pours, I suspected, but it came across as merry—looked as pale as kindergarten paste.

In his final moments, Vince Sperry, such a character in life, looked like a sad old man shocked by all the blood on his T-shirt.

———————— ★ ————————

"...a real page-turner."

—*Library Journal*

"The plot is entertaining."

—*Harriet Klausner*

Previously published Worldwide Mystery title by
KRIS NERI

REVENGE OF THE GYPSY QUEEN

DEM BONES'
REVENGE

Kris Neri

W⊕RLDWIDE®

TORONTO • NEW YORK • LONDON
AMSTERDAM • PARIS • SYDNEY • HAMBURG
STOCKHOLM • ATHENS • TOKYO • MILAN
MADRID • WARSAW • BUDAPEST • AUCKLAND

To Judy and Joe, dear friends, who shared it all.

DEM BONES' REVENGE

A Worldwide Mystery/August 2003

First published by Rainbow Books, Inc.

ISBN 0-373-26466-6

Those who cannot remember the past,
are condemned to repeat it.
       —George Santayana

Nobody loves me but my mother,
and she could be jiving, too.
       —B. B. King

Acknowledgments

I'm rich because I have so many generous, supportive friends. My deepest gratitude goes to:

- Judy and Joe Miller, who gave the "baby" its "shower," and to whom this book is dedicated;

- Gayle and Don Triolo, for hosting an enchanting book party for me at the Santa Lucia Preserve;

- Jamie Wallace, for designing my beautiful website;

- Terry Baker, of The Mystery Annex in Venice, California, and Linda Bivens, of Crime Time Books in Pasadena, California, for planning and hosting my magical, memorable book-launch parties;

- Bob and Debbie Levine, for their beautiful cake;

- Gayle McGary Partlow and Gayle Pfaught, for giving my book and signing schedule such fabulous coverage in *Ransom Notes;*

- Barbara Lakey, publisher of *Futures,* for the spectacular coverage she gave my book's publication in her magazine;

- Alexis and Tom Powers, who rallied much support for my signings;

- Gay Toltl-Kinman, who brought me to speak to her Soroptimist friends;

- Kathy Ptacek, publisher of *Gila Queen's Guide to the Markets,* and Margo Power, editor of *Murderous Intent Mystery Magazine,* for the promotional opportunities they gave me;

- Priscilla English, Lisa Seidman, and Mae Woods, editors of *Murder by Thirteen,* for choosing "L.A. Justice";

- The whine & dine gang: Susan Casmier, Claire Carmichael McNab, Gayle Partlow and Judy Smith, for all their encouragement;

- Kathleen Beaver, for giving me the lowdown on law firms;

- Ron Armstrong, for teaching me about bones;

- Serita Stevens, for answering my medical questions;

- Margery Cooper Flax, for lending me her name;

- Cathy Gallagher, the mystery guide for About.com, and Geraldine Galentree, editor of *Cozies, Capers & Crimes,* for their encouragement;

- My sisters and brothers in the Los Angeles chapter of Sisters in Crime, for their unparalleled support and the enthusiasm with which they embraced my first book;

- My sisters in the Central Coast chapter of Sisters in Crime, for always treating me like one of their own;

- My friends in the AOL mystery community and our wonderful HOSTs, especially Sherrill, Jacquelynn, and Pat;

- My cyber-pals on the Short Mystery Fiction Society digest, The Mystery Writers Forum, the Sisters in Crime digest and the readers of DorothyL;

- My tea-sipping friends who share the power of the purple;

- Betty Wright and Betsy Lampé, of Rainbow Books, Inc., who believed in both me and Tracy, and who made it all possible;

- and especially, my husband, Joe, for sharing the thrill of it all.

ONE

"I'm ready for my close-up now…Dr. Freud."

"YOU DO SEE I have no choice, don't you, Tracy?" the breathy voice said over the phone. "I have to kill you."

From where I stood, anyone who could ask that question didn't care how I saw it. Only six a.m., and this was already shaping up to be a day enshrined in hell.

"Without the changes to *Deadly Shadows* we require, I'll have to reject the book and kill your series," my editor, Carolyn, murmured from her superior perch as Senior Editor at Perkins & Pimm, Publishers.

Kill the Tessa Graham Mystery Series? Cold rose through my bare feet from the chilly oak parquet of my study floor, as hot air from the heating vent hit my head. The room spun around me. But my only thought was how much I hated Carolyn's voice. An editor's speech should resonate with the bold assurance a writer needs to cling to, not sound like she was working a sex line.

"Huh?" I stammered eloquently. "I don't get it."

I really didn't. My only doubt when writing *Deadly Shadows* was whether I'd raised the bar too high to hit it again. If Carolyn didn't agree, why had she given me that generous advance after reading the opening chapters? Would they want that money back? Hah! They were gonna have to catch me first.

"We'll need those changes by Wednesday," she concluded.

"You mean next Wednesday, right?" This was Monday.

"No, *this* Wednesday." That hooker voice took on the brisk disapproval my third grade teacher always used when she justified putting a gag on me. Carolyn promised to fax a list of each and every place where the book fell short of her expectations. Ever gracious, she used a dial tone to say good-bye.

My head kept spinning, and this time, it wasn't the heat. *Deadly Shadows* was a good book, dammit. There had to be a way around this. I'd find it, too—as soon as my brain kicked in. If morning was really meant to be the best time of the day, they'd have scheduled it later, when I was awake enough to appreciate it.

I padded to the short bookcase below the window and hovered over the fax, only to be accosted by another angry voice.

"Tracy, what did you *do* with my tie?" My aggrieved husband, Drew, glared at me from the doorway.

Maintaining his customary lawyerish dignity took some doing—all Drew wore was an unbuttoned blue oxford shirt and a pair of dingy Jockey shorts, so baggy they'd morphed into boxers. The sight of those hunky pecs peaking through the stiff, button-down shirt almost thawed the freeze my editor's remarks had left in me. Only the dimples I loved were nowhere in evidence on Drew's chiseled face, and today his normally warm golden-brown eyes weren't taking any prisoners. Didn't anyone love me anymore?

"Where's my tie?" Drew roared, as if the fate of the world depended on it.

He had more than one tie. Hell, he had dozens. He meant his *lucky* tie, though Drew was too anal to admit to superstition. He'd worn that navy-and-maroon tie and those worn-out undies on the first day of every trial he'd ever won. But never had as much been riding on them as in the plagiarism suit beginning today.

Literary conflicts weren't Drew's specialty. He'd been roped into this case at the client's insistence. Stacking the deck still higher was the fact that Drew's client, whose claims were probably true, seemed an oily bastard, while the cheating plaintiff was a loveable old codger the jury could easily take to its heart. If Drew didn't find a way around those obstacles, he could kiss good-bye to making senior partner at Slaughter, Cohen, Rather, Word & Dragger, Attorneys-at-Law.

I started to reassure Drew, only that was when the fax began spitting out the bitch's poison. "That's from Carolyn. She's a heartbeat away from dropping my series."

"Babe, no…" Warmth flooded Drew's eyes. He came over and cupped my face in his hands, as if he intended to comfort me. Instead, he sprayed morning breath up my nose by shouting, "You wouldn't be in a bind now if you hadn't spent your whole advance on that stupid truck. Who in Los Angeles drives a pickup?"

Everyone who didn't drive an SUV.

"You only bought that boat so your mother would stop making you drive her places."

"Not true. I love my truck."

The fax kept spitting out pages. Jeez, were they paying her by the word? Too pissed to look at that road map to the end of my life, I let the sheets fall into toxic curls on the wooden floor.

"Why couldn't you have kept your Jeep, Tracy?" Drew complained. "Your mother didn't like that, either."

But she was starting to.

The fax finally ended. Fortunately, the doorbell rang before I succumbed to temptation and stomped those nasty paper curls into dust.

As I pushed past him, Drew yelled, "Wait. My tie?"

"Relax, Drew. I sent it to the cleaners."

He flapped his arms like a dodo bird. "You what? I have to go into court on an area of law that I know nothing about and—"

"It's in the cleaner bag in your closet," I shouted over my shoulder. If he got any tighter, I was gonna need a nap.

The doorbell rang again. On the living room sofa, the big lump under my ecru down comforter shifted irritably. Drew's eyes traveled pointedly from it to me, punctuating another cause of tension between us. The movement caused a salt-and-pepper haystack to peek from the top, pillow-hair that belonged to Drew's Uncle Philly. I'd met him a couple of months before and invited him to visit us. It was probably a coincidence that as the visit stretched, our cozy condo seemed to compress. Especially after Philly's things filled every available inch of free space.

I stubbed my toe on one of the open suitcases that overflowed across the floor like a salesman's sample cases—if the salesman represented Goodwill. When I stopped to rub my toe, Drew rushed to block my path to the door.

"Tracy, tell me the truth," he said in a hoarse whisper. "Have we adopted Philly?"

"Just till we find his real mom and dad."

"The last time I saw his mom, I was still riding a skateboard, and they were lowering Grandma into the ground."

"So you don't think that's her at the door?"

He threw up his arms and stalked off toward the bedroom.

While I limped to the door, I plastered my most innocent expression on my face. Too many of our callers lately were neighbors to whom Philly had peddled the deal-of-a-lifetime. Best to be prepared. Since my robe's sash had found the secret door in the washer that half my socks used to gain their freedom, I clutched it closed and eased the door open a crack.

Not an irate neighbor, after all. But not good news, either. "Hey, Trace, time to start the closets," Randy Barlow said.

I sometimes thought Randy Barlow, the thirtyish man filling the hall outside my door, had been put together from leftover parts like some benign Frankenstein. Where were the genetic safeguards against combining the soft body of a gigantic Pillsbury Doughboy, with the sun-bleached hair and leathery skin of a surfer, and burning black eyes that Rasputin would have killed for?

"What are you doing here, Randy? You said you'd come Wednesday at ten." Probably the exact time my publisher's axe would fall. How prophetic was that?

"Me, I didn't tell you nothin'. You know my mom does my scheduling. She said to come Monday at six."

Randy's baggy painter pants were spattered with red paint and smeared with Navaho White. He lumbered past me through my tiny foyer, carrying his carpentry tools and scuffing his feet against my slick parquet. I wondered how a guy that clumsy stayed on a surfboard, but regular wipe-outs might account for what didn't seem to be included between Randy's ears.

"Randy, I talked to you last night, remember? You said your mom was out. You know this wasn't the time we agreed on."

He dropped his tools—as a native Californian, I could say with certainty the floor shook like a 3.2 temblor. "Yeah, well, later I got a call about another job I gotta start then."

Why is it contractors think that because they choose to live in denial, you're willing to share their demented roost? Not that Randy was a licensed contractor. He was just a handyman my mother strong-armed me into hiring to free up closet space for Philly.

When Drew realized something else had been added to the mix, his blood pressure would shoot so high his head could blow like Old Faithful. But I remembered another contractor rule before I threw Randy out: Once you let them go, you never get them back.

"Okay, but start with the hall closet and stay away from Drew," I warned.

The fax rang again. I groaned, but I should have expected it. Not only couldn't Carolyn talk like a normal adult, she couldn't send a complete fax in one try. How many pages were there? Outrage rose in me like a mushroom cloud.

Drew stormed into the room. His shirt was buttoned now and cinched with his lucky tie. But shirt tails peaked through his open fly. "Tracy, that lunkhead punched through my closet wall—"

The lunkhead followed on his heels. "It's gonna cost you extra to fix it, too. It ain't my fault your walls are so thin you can't tap 'em to find the studs."

Drew gave his glorious, wavy, light-brown hair an indignant shake. "Tap them? Is that what you call—"

Man, this was the last trial of the century I'd get up for. "Holy freakin' Labor Day!" I threw my arms out like a weather vane. "Drew, finish dressing—Randy, go to the hall closet."

The extent of my frustration must have been clear; they both left my sight, and that was all I cared about. Is it always so nutty at this hour? Reason enough to sleep through...

The telephone rang. I snatched the cordless from where it nested among Philly's pipe paraphernalia on the walnut end table at the side of the couch. "What?" I growled into it.

The dulcet tones of movie star Martha Collins' voice filled my ear. "And a lovely good morning to you, too, darling."

You know that throaty voice as well as I do. It's the one that thrills you on the silver screen, the voice you consider synonymous with sex and glamour, the one that entices you from the radio to buy overpriced cat food. For me, it's different—since that's the voice that has harassed me since the minute I was born.

"This isn't a good time, Mother," I said firmly.

I raked my fingers through the blonde crow's nest that had formed on my head during sleep. Even at that hour, Mother probably looked like the quintessential Hollywood goddess—chic, icy blonde and drop-dead gorgeous. To say our standards differ is the understatement of the millennium.

"You're certainly testy this morning, young lady. If you had to face all the early movie calls I have, you'd manage it better."

She always forgets I was there. I remembered how well she handled toddling out the door before the sun came up; that's how I learned so many swear words.

"What do you want, Mother?"

"I want my cutie-pie son-in-law to come and get me."

Just because she hated my truck, she had no right pestering Drew. "Have you forgotten? He's starting a critical trial today?"

"The way you talk about it, how could I? He's helping the Swampland Production *père et fils* prove they didn't steal that boondoggle '06 script. Imagine being proud of writing something so bloated. Four hours? It took San Francisco less time to recover from the 1906 earthquake."

"That's *Marsh*land Productions," I corrected, unfairly so. Since the Marshland duo seemed part of the Hollywood minority she didn't know, she'd absorbed her opinion from me.

"Whatever. Don't worry, darling. They won't be courting today," she said.

Elsewhere in the condo, I heard the soft sounds of a sledgehammer crashing through another wall. Mother made me hire that dolt. I lit into her.

"*Courting,* Mother? I love it when you use technical terms."

"You want technical, Tracy? Fine," Mother snapped. "The police think I killed the plaintiff in Drew's case. How's *that* for technical?"

TWO

"It's Showtime," Hargrove Pictures, 1946: Introducing Martha Collins as Sue and Angelique Barlow as the Second Girl.

Outside a barn, a crowd of teenagers examine the storm-ravaged remains of a parade float.

SECOND GIRL
How can we raise enough money to fix the float now?
How can we make things right?

SUE
I know, gang! We'll put on a show.

SOME DAYS YOU GET the bear, others...well, you'd better like the idea of being served with some fava beans and a nice Chianti. My publisher's ultimatum ticked away at my life like a time bomb—but Drew and I were on our way to the Hollywood home of the late Vince Sperry, with whose bloody remains the cops had found my mother. If we ever made it there, that is.

I jabbed my finger at the vast opening in the lane before the hood of Drew's sedate brown Volvo sedan. "See that space? That's nature's way of telling you to move ahead."

He pursed his lips in consideration, but lacking the thirty-four car-lengths Drew requires for safety, he scarcely budged. I wanted to belt him.

Clueless, he glanced my way and asked, "You're upset about your mother, aren't you?"

"Don't be silly," I snapped. "Why would you say that?"

"You always criticize my driving when you're worried."

That couldn't be true. I wasn't worried, not really. Drew just drove like my Aunt Fanny—and she'd spent the last five years in a coma.

Still, it wasn't like Mother to cry uncle. That woman can talk her way out of a bear trap. And nobody could seriously regard her as a murder suspect. While she prided herself on breaking most of life's rules, she'd never included the one that forbids bumping off cute old guys who file bogus lawsuits.

With a weary sigh I said to Drew, "I wish we could have tracked my dad down." I had called the Del Mar horse ranch he'd visited, only to be told he left without saying where he was going.

"It's funny Alec didn't let you know he was leaving the ranch. He may like to keep Martha guessing, but not you."

My thought as well, but I wouldn't admit it. "How do we know, Drew? Maybe we've never tried to track him down while he's been on the move. Once he lands, he'll let us know."

Or we'd have something else to worry about. Why did my parents persist in trying to run my life when they were so bad at managing their own?

Drew took the Barham Boulevard exit to Cahuenga instead of taking the freeway to Highland. He muttered something about surface streets moving faster, but I knew better. Along that stretch of road was a body shop housing a big, silver vehicle that looked like a space ship, which must have been built for some cheapie sci-fi flick. You'd think Drew would get enough of that showbiz crap from my parents, but seeing movie memorabilia in unexpected places was the part about La-La Land that still tickled him. I didn't care how he went as long as he kept moving. Why was it taking so long?

When Cahuenga curved into Highland, where the darkened marquee of the Hollywood Bowl rolled by on the left, I motioned for Drew to move over a lane.

"I'm signaling, Tracy." He glared into the rearview mirror at a car that blocked him out of that lane.

That's what happens when you let other drivers in on your plans. Fortunately, he had me along to flip that driver the universal symbol of displeasure.

I glanced at Drew's profile. The taut lines of that handsome face held such strength. Mother always called him "our designated adult." Now me, I generally wished he would let loose and surprise me. But I was starting to hope it wouldn't be today.

"Did you take care of everything at the office?" I asked.

Drew gave a tight nod. "One of the senior partners called the judge at home. She's continuing the case till things shake out. And I talked to the opposing council before he left for the office. But I couldn't reach Benny Butler Marsh."

I could never hear the words *Benny Butler Marsh* without that echo effect they use in the opening credits to announce all Marshland Productions and *Benny Butler Marsh—Benny Butler Marsh—Benny Butler Marsh* films. That was one of the reasons why I never liked Drew's client—no one deserves his own echo.

A possible division in Drew's loyalty occurred to me; I approached it obliquely. "Benny'll turn cartwheels when he learns the case is kaput. Once you get the injunction lifted on the picture's release, Marshland Productions should be in Fat City."

"The case isn't necessarily over, Tracy. I'd expect Sperry's estate to continue with it. Though without Sperry around to testify how Benny plagiarized his script, they don't have a prayer." Drew shrugged. "Benny says they're not hurting now."

Right. Marshland Productions had sunk three hundred million into a story the History Channel could cover for five bucks, and Benny not only didn't feel the pinch, he could afford for its release to be held up while they duked out the ownership.

Benny was the one who should have been found with Sperry's body—he had the motive. Couldn't the police see that? What possible connection could Mother have to that plagiarism suit?

We cruised down Franklin, passing pristine old buildings that echoed Hollywood's past glory, alongside rundown dumps that reflected its present. We were still close enough to spit on Hollywood's Walk of Fame where Sleaze struts its stuff these days.

"But with the case winding down, Benny won't care that you'll be helping Mother. I mean, there's no conflict, right?"

Drew sighed. "Why does everyone force me into areas beyond my expertise? Tracy, you know I'm not a trial lawyer."

"I see. You'll represent Benny Butler Marsh—Benny Butler Marsh—Benny Butler Marsh—"

"Stop with the echo already!" Drew demanded. "You really don't know when to quit, do you?"

Anything worth doing is worth overdoing—that's my motto.

Drew took a left on Beachwood and headed up into the hills to what had been Sperry's home for thirty-odd years. They kept the better real estate there. Pseudo-Tudor, California-Spanish, ultramodern statements and charming cottages, all wedged into the sides of hills or teetering on the tops of them.

"Whatever Mother's entangled in today won't get to

court," I predicted. "She just needs someone to protect her from herself. She certainly didn't kill that man, and you know it."

Drew seemed to be biting the inside of his cheek. "Honey, I love Martha, but you have to admit she doesn't have much impulse control. How can you be certain she wouldn't kill Sperry?"

I didn't say she *wouldn't* kill him, I said she *didn't*. Big difference. Drew approached my family with the same trepidation brought to high explosives—and I didn't mean that in a good way.

"Tracy? I asked why you're so sure—"

"She doesn't know him, Drew."

At a three-way stop on Beachwood, a stupid little sign read: *Welcome Home, Hollywoodland. Now Slow Down and Relax.* Maybe Sperry hadn't been murdered after all, maybe he just read that sign too often and took relaxation to the max.

Growing exasperated, Drew asked, "And you know that…how?"

"Because I don't know him, and she forces all her friends on me. Besides, she knew you were representing the other side on Sperry's claim. Wouldn't she have told you? She loves doling out her insider dirt."

"Tracy, your mother was found at Sperry's house this morning—*with the body*."

"It happens." Hadn't he learned anything from reading my books?

Now Drew seemed to be gnawing *through* his cheek. So that was how he wanted to play it. I grabbed my purse from the floor and pawed around in it till I found my cell phone. Dead again. One of these days I had to remember to charge that thing.

I grabbed the door handle as if I intended to yank it open. "Let me out here. I'll find a pay phone." I wasn't so nuts that I'd jump from a moving vehicle, but somehow, my husband didn't know that. We nearly had a head-on when Drew lurched across the seat to keep me from leaping to my death. Jeez, he makes it so easy.

"If I promise that your mother will be protected—not by me but a good criminal attorney—will you swear to stay out of it?" He shook his head; those ash brown waves fell perfectly into place. How does he do that? "Look who I'm asking to swear. You'll say anything, then do whatever you want anyway."

So he'd finally figured that out. I wasn't sure I liked the edge it gave him in our relationship.

"This time I mean it," I insisted. "I won't get involved."

Drew snorted.

"I won't!" I wailed. "I have a deadline, remember?"

Drew nodded, but skeptically. What is it about me? I can always sell a lie, but the truth? Forget about it.

We turned onto Forest Hills Drive, Sperry's street, but we were still a few turns from his house. Parking's a bitch in the best of times on those narrow hillside streets, but now the cars and crowds spilled into intersections like toothpaste from a tube. Drew wedged the Volvo just outside the mouth of Forest Hills, between a driveway and a blue-and-yellow Channel Seven TV news van.

The media was there in force, judging by the orange cords that snaked up the hill. So was about half the city. Nothing like a circus to bring the jury pool for an L.A. trial.

Drew encouraged me to run around the crowds. In my new shoes? Fat chance. He might be able to trot uphill in his stodgy oxblood wingtips, but I sure couldn't pull it off in high heels. I don't often wear heels and hose, much to Mother's dismay. Let's face it, when your mother looks like a miniature *Vogue* model, you gotta go in a different direction. But I'd started thinking that maybe eating, sleeping and breathing in the same pair of sweats was taking the slob bit too far. Besides, I went all out on things to wear for Drew's big day in court, and no matter where this day took us, I was gonna wear them. Dress, $150. Shoes, $89. Seeing your mother sent up the river… priceless.

While weaving our way through the crowd, a stout woman wearing a faded, flowered housecoat and pink-foam hair rollers stopped me. "Hey, I know you. You're somebody, ain't ya?"

That recognition was what I'd be losing if I didn't find a way around my editor's unreasonable demands. I savored the morsel of fame as never before, preening for the woman.

"I'm a bestselling author," I said, selling the exaggeration with the full set of choppers my dental hygienist had polished only days before.

"Nah, that's not it." The woman snorted. "Are you kidding, honey? Who reads?"

Inwardly, I groaned. She was picking up on my resemblance to Mother. Though I was a touch taller and my hair more golden than Mother's ash blonde and my eyes a warmer blue—my similarity to her was striking, even to me. Especially now that we both wore our hair in chin-length bobs, mine straight and hers wavy. After a lifetime of people commenting on the resemblance, you'd think it would cease to piss me off.

The woman looked over my shoulder. "D'ya know what's going on up there?"

"Why don't you check your newspaper? Maybe you can figure it out from the *pictures*." Drew dragged me off before I could tell her what I really thought.

The crowds thickened the closer we came to the crime scene, but the hill finally leveled out. By the time I caught my breath, we'd hit the yellow cop tape. The police had cordoned off an area that extended past the homes on either side of Sperry's. Or what I assumed to be Sperry's, judging by the law enforcement types swarming over it.

While the houses rose from minuscule plots of land, they were all big homes with forever views. But while Sperry's neighbors had afforded their gracious old dowagers the care they deserved, his place looked like it should be carted off to the dump. What remained of the faded white paint was peeling; much of it had worn all the way down to the bare sidings. Someone had attacked the trim during the last decade, but the work had stopped after no more than a quarter of the fascia had been changed from faded blue to bright green. Grass was sparse on the tiny strip of barren lawn that claimed more caked dirt than the surface of the moon. Yet weeds thrived nicely through the cracks in the narrow concrete driveway.

That's where Mother's tan Mercedes was haphazardly parked.

Drew tried to signal the uniformed cop patrolling the perimeter. But my eyes were drawn to the deep porch framing the front of the house, where my mother stood.

I had to admit the old girl still looked good. Despite the efforts of rotating teams of Beverly Hills plastic surgeons working 'round the clock, the lines of that haunting face no longer held up to the same standards of perfection when projected on a thirty-foot screen. But I liked it better for its seasoning. Whereas it once held such an aura of mystery, that face now seemed to project unexpected strength and a wealth of understanding. Amazing, really—the woman was no deeper than paint on a wall.

Mother gave the silvery blonde tresses dipping over her forehead that sexy signature toss. Men a third of her age found their eyes drawn to it. When you've got it, you've got it—and she still had it by the bushel. She wore her royal blue Chanel suit this morning, the one she prefers for her talk show appearances. The color transforms her deep blue eyes to violet. That jacket was so good, it hung perfectly, even though she stood with her hands behind her back.

My heart gave an involuntary twinge when I realized she wasn't *holding* her hands behind her back—they were handcuffed there. Did they really think she was going to bolt?

Her face looked tighter than usual, like after her last lift. Mother was clearly scared, but by what? Surely not the cops. While anyone else might find it alarming to be suspected of murder, it took more than a little skirmish with the LAPD to ruffle Mother's feathers. This could be worse than I thought. I got a sudden case of the willies.

Drew tapped his well-shod foot in frustration while he sought unsuccessfully to attract the attention of the baby-faced cop patrolling the perimeter. "Look at that? He's avoiding me."

"You want his attention?" I said with a sigh. "Duck under the tape. See how fast the rookie notices."

I tried to demonstrate, but Drew held me back. He scanned the bustling crime scene for a more agreeable cop to call to our rescue, but his face froze at the sight of someone in that crowd.

"No! Why him? Why did it have to be him?"

Shaken by Drew's groans, I followed his gaze to a man who seemed to have been transported from the streets of Miami, circa 1985. The sleeves of his turquoise knockoff Versace jacket were rolled to the elbow, while gold chains and a clump of chest hair danced over the neckline of a silk singlet the color of a Tequila Sunrise. To the beat of the coins he jingled in his pocket, he strutted between a dusty red Mazda RX-7 and the porch with a cocky flair. He sported such a Caribbean look, such an eighties feel, I found myself humming Jimmy Buffett's "Jolly Mon" to the beat of his walk. The respite proved comforting, since I was finding it continually harder to lay my hands on my own shaker of salt.

Remembering the depth of Drew's dismay, I asked with a nervous giggle, "Who's that keeping Sonny Crockett alive?"

Drew glanced nervously back down the street to where he'd parked the Volvo, as if he were considering making his escape. With a sigh he said, "My guess would be—the detective in charge."

According to Drew, Sonny, a.k.a. Detective Tag Schuller, glommed onto that look during the *Miami Vice* heyday and hadn't been seen in anything else since.

I did the math; he must have been in high school then. How wonderful to know at fifteen what you'll wear for the rest of your life—assuming you didn't mind being bored to death. "So he's a clown, huh? No one takes him seriously?"

"Think again, babe. Schuller's conviction rate is one of the best in the LAPD. It's said he doesn't care how he accomplishes it, either."

I frowned. "You sure know a lot for a guy who's not a trial lawyer."

"That's the point. If I've heard of him, everyone has. Believe me, Trace, if Martha has anything to hide, she better just get fitted now for a jailhouse jumpsuit."

Discarding pretense, I finally admitted to myself how scared I was for Mother. But what could she possibly have to hide?

THREE

"Mother Knows All," Hargrove Pictures, 1947: Starring Lorna Halliday as Mother and Martha Collins as Janet.

JANET
Oh, Mother, you don't understand. Young people do things differently today.

MOTHER
Darling, times may change, but a mother always knows what's in her child's heart.

They hug until the crisis passes.

WHILE DREW'S chilly warning echoed in my mind, I watched Schuller drag Mother back into the house. Time to quit playing by the rules—I ducked under the tape. When Drew caught up to me, the game-playing rookie had already agreed to take us to Schuller. Would Drew never learn from the fine example I set for him?

The rookie led us up the steps and through the open doorway. The house featured grand, old-fashioned parlors on both sides of a central corridor. The smaller one on the right must have served as Sperry's den. Cherry bookcases, mostly empty, filled two walls, and a desk and cabinets in cherry lined another wall. While heavily scratched today, some good workmanship had gone into those pieces that looked as if they'd been built decades before.

The dead guy on the floor, however, was probably a recent addition.

The volume of blood Sperry had lost stunned me. I couldn't tell whether he'd been shot, stabbed, or skinned alive—just that it hadn't happened where he died. A smear of blood wove around the desk across the avocado shag rug like a slug trail. That dried blood was darker than what still saturated his shirt.

The trial-watchers in the press always commented on how incongruous Sperry's aging face looked with his boyishly small, springy body. No spring now, though he'd gone out dressed like a kid in his usual tight jeans and black basketball sneakers. But the Alfred E. Newman grin he'd flashed in life now drooped like Drew's old drawers. And the apple cheeks that had glowed with spirit—the kind the bartender pours, I suspected, but it came across as merry—looked as pale as kindergarten paste.

In his final moments, Vince Sperry, such a character in life, looked like a sad old man shocked by all the blood on his T-shirt.

THE ROOKIE DEPOSITED us in a screened-in porch at the rear of the house to wait for Schuller. With its Mission-style oak chairs and floral cushions, that must have been a gracious setting once. But the patterned cushions had faded to the point where they were only colored in spirit, and the furniture looked more like kindling. So much dust had collected on the brick floor that with each breeze it drifted like snow.

I positioned myself just inside the doorway where I was least likely to brush against those filthy surfaces. Fastidious Drew seemed not to notice the dirt. He stood staring through one of the screen panels, absently stroking his lucky tie.

Detective Schuller charged down the hall toward me, hands thrust into his pockets and shaking his coins in a sharp, distinctive beat. The sound of Springsteen's "Born to Run" flowed into my mind. This was great. If Mother stayed in trouble, I'd get to revisit all my favorite hits of the eighties without needing to watch those late-night TV commercials.

Close up, Schuller's eyes were as rich a turquoise as his suit. Color contacts, no doubt—did he have a pair to match everything he owned? His highlighted brown hair was slicked back in a style some men wore when Schuller invented himself, and he'd fossilized it with gel. But bitter grooves between his eyebrows injected too much reality into his retro presence.

He greeted us with a brusque nod before his take-no-prisoners mask broke into a nasty grin. "Gotta tell you, Counselor, your client's looking at one in the arm."

One in the arm? What was that? Street lingo? Finally, it hit me—he meant a lethal injection. For *finding* a body?

Schuller's prediction didn't seem to upset Drew that much, and Mother exasperates him way less than me. Drew chuckled with amused tolerance and shifted into his courtroom demeanor. Though he keeps protesting it's not his natural environment, Drew goes to court regularly, though usually to argue estate matters. The last time was when he set up a conservancy for Jolly Marsh, father of Benny Butler Marsh and one of the executive producers of the embattled '06, though in name only since Jolly's brain became Cream of Wheat. If only Drew could see himself in trial turbo-drive. I'd never seen him take a false step in that mode.

Cocking his hip, Drew drawled, "Don't count on it, Detective. Remember, she's not only innocent, she's Martha Collins."

Nothing like making your first blunder a big one. Something Drew said caused Schuller's facial grooves to contract, making his bushy brown eyebrows collide like thunderclouds.

"That don't cut no ice with me, pal. She had no business calling you after she called us," Schuller said.

Mother's celebrity seemed to anger him. Had she said something thoughtless? She's usually quite kind to people she hasn't given birth to. I considered Schuller's getup. Was looking like a TV cop his second career choice, maybe after *being* a TV cop? I focused on his speech. With that outfit, I expected to hear the rhythm of the Caribbean or at least the drawl of the Keys, but all I heard was standard Van Nuys, California. Local boy reinvents himself and still fails to make good. Whose rejection was my mother paying for?

But Schuller's anger had made him careless. Drew's lips twitched with amusement. "She called you...? Do most killers do that?" he asked of Schuller.

Schuller admitted Mother had reported discovering the body to 911, though only moments before the cops arrived. That brought us to the pesky fact that she was there at all. Apparently, she insisted she'd come to visit as part of a charitable activity one of her acquaintances had organized. It called for old Hollywood legends to spend time with some of their contemporaries who weren't as fortunate. There is a tradition in the industry of taking care of those who have fallen on hard times, but this visitation variation was new to me. So was Mother's charitable impulse.

Schuller showed us a scrap of paper in a Ziploc bag. Mother had scrawled Sperry's name and address at the top. Below it, the name and room number of an old second banana, Gloria Harney, had been added in pencil; hastily, it seemed to me. Gloria was one of Mother's oldest friends. Since she lived at the Motion Picture Country Home in the West Valley, she would be a logical candidate for such a charity. Only Mother visited her regularly anyway. Not as a good deed, but because Gloria dished the dirt better than anybody.

"She claims she never met the victim; he was just assigned to her by the broad who set up this visiting thing. But she says she asked for Harney to be put on her list 'cuz she goes there anyhow,'' Schuller admitted, now that Drew had pierced his armor.

That sounded like Mother's kind of charity.

Drew leaned casually against the outer wall of the house, apparently oblivious to the dust it would leave on the sleeve of his expensive grey suit. ''What is it that you don't believe about a simple act of kindness, Detective Schuller? She knows you'll check with the woman who established the visitation schedule.''

Schuller thrust his hands back into his pockets like a pouting third-grader. ''Lotta good that'll do. These people all stick together.''

His funk was well-founded. Mother had markers she could call in all over town.

''Besides, that don't explain why she was carrying,'' Schuller went on in a happier tone. He began jingling change.

''She was armed?'' Drew blurted.

Jeez, couldn't she have left the firepower home for once? She claims to carry that gun for protection against stalkers. Hah! She'd pay people to stalk her. That gun appeared only when I started writing murder mysteries.

Drew asked, ''Was it fired?''

Schuller answered with a grudging shrug. The clanging change went silent. It looked as if they didn't have anything on her other than being at the wrong place at the worst possible time. Hell, she specialized in that.

When Drew asked to see her, a nasty look skittered across Schuller's turquoise eyes. There was no doubt in my mind he intended to make her pay for whatever status she enjoyed to the extent that he could get away with it.

Schuller scuffed his sockless loafers along the hall's threadbare green shag when he went to wherever he had stashed Mother. On their return, he kept a hand clasped around one of her fragile arms, still cuffed behind her. Her shoulders had to be in agony. But Mother held her head high and faced the ordeal with dignified strength.

For once, her portrayal of the martyred heroine moved me. I longed to throw my arms around her, to use the huge, pear-shaped diamond ring Dad had given her to cut those cuffs from her wrists.

Mother came to a stop in the doorway. Her misty blue eyes rested on me, her only child. It was going to be one of those bonding moments we'd always look back on. I just hoped she wouldn't say anything too mushy before Schuller.

With a frail smile, she said, "Tracy, don't you understand English? I told you to send Drew, not *bring* him. I have nothing to say to you."

Why couldn't I have been raised by wolves?

SHE KICKED ME OUT! I stood in the hall and glared at the closed porch door. Someone had better spill his guts about this later, or Drew's life wasn't going to be worth living.

Schuller had returned to Sperry's den, and cops and crime scene techs buzzed all over the place. But nobody seemed the least concerned about me. Ooh! A chance to snoop. Nudging open a door along the hall with my elbow, I passed into a room beyond the kitchen where Sperry must have watched TV. A vinyl recliner, the color of French's mustard and accented by silver duct tape, dominated one corner. Across the room a 36-inch stereo television tee-tered on a rusted, wrought-iron patio table. Old issues of *TV Guide* filled a hutch built into one of the knotty pine walls. Clearly the nerve center of the house, this room seemed marginally cleaner than the rest of the place, like maybe Sperry had dusted it a few times in the last decade. But perhaps it was just the cool breeze blowing in through the open window that relieved the grimy odor permeating everything.

A universal remote rested on the arm of the recliner. Though the traces of black dust on some surfaces seemed to indicate fingerprinting had been completed in this room, I took a used tissue from my purse and pressed a button on the remote with the clean end. Numbers lit up on the cable box that rested on the floor under the table, and I heard the sound of groaning before the screen came to life. The Smut Channel. Sperry didn't seem to have much money, but he had enough for the good stuff. I punched off the television and looked around.

Faded black-and-white photos hung askew on the grooved wooden walls. I didn't recognize anyone in the candid shots taken behind the scenes on movie sets, but the subjects all wore the clothes of the forties, fifties and sixties. Nothing later. Did Sperry stop working when he was in his forties? Pretty young to retire, especially when money didn't seem plentiful. He claimed to have written the '06 screenplay only during the last couple of years. What had he done for decades?

In one shot, a younger Sperry in hippie garb leaned over the shoulder of a dark, intense man Central Casting might have classified as a Latin-lover type, even if he didn't look Hispanic. Black Irish maybe. A couple of children played in the foreground.

Did Sperry have kids? Probably visitors to the set. A rat-faced little boy of eight or so sat cross-legged on the floor with his hands hidden in his lap, while a rapturous look filled his face. Too young to whack off, the little creep must have been pulling the wings off flies—he looked the type. The other child was a girl, an out-of-focus blonde toddler. The little blur of motion must have been a handful; the camera had caught her as she bashed the boy over the head with her doll.

A commotion in the hall drew me away from the photos; I stepped from the TV room to see what it was. The Coroner's crew was removing the body, now encased in a black bag. I followed the gurney to the front yard and watched as they loaded it into a van.

The sound of shaking coins announced Schuller's approach. Didn't this clown ever need to sneak up on anyone? I took the twitch around his mouth to be an attempt at pleasantry, though it looked more like a warning he needed to barf.

"I hear you're a writer. What do you write?" Schuller asked.

I told him.

"Books!" he said with an exaggerated guffaw.

No question, I was getting out of this racket just in time.

I noticed the look of expectancy in his face and played a hunch. "What do you write, Detective?"

In three quick jumps, Schuller leaped to the RX-7, threw the door open and yanked something from under the seat. After he returned to my side, he deposited a screenplay in my hands with a flourish. I tried to keep a straight face. Only in L.A. Given its curling corners and coffee stains, the screenplay looked like it had been kicking around for a while.

"Death Walks the Beat," I read from the cover page. "Catchy title. Does that mean the cop did it?"

Schuller growled like a junkyard dog. "Don't be so literal." He kicked the crusty surface of the ground with his black loafer. "How come your mom's production company don't read screenplays?"

I nearly cracked up over the idea that my mother might own a production company. If she were the executive producer, who would give in to her star tantrums? But I didn't intend to tell Schuller that—my mama didn't raise no dummies. Of course, as late as she started, she only had time for one turn at bat.

Schuller rocked back and forth, seemingly in expectation of my opening gambit. What was I doing? Hadn't I promised Drew and, more importantly—myself, that I wouldn't get involved? Mother didn't want my help; she made that clear. But it would take so little to save the old girl some dignity.

"She gave up on finding something good. There's a lot of crap out there." Maybe even some right in my hands. "I bet she'd agree to give this a fair read...*if* she were free to leave today."

Schuller gave one eyelid a vigorous rub, and change began to jingle. "You trying to bribe me, cookie?"

"Wouldn't dream of it." Not by that name, anyway.

We engaged in some negotiation. Schuller insisted that Mother take a gunshot residue test and account for her whereabouts over a twelve-hour period. It had to mean Sperry had been shot. But shooting doesn't take twelve hours—why was that important? If the test result proved negative, she'd be released in my custody. In return, she'd read his script. Who would call that a bribe?

I held my breath—would he go for it? Relief came with his grudging nod, though not without conditions.

"I'm warning you, sugar. You fuck with me and your old lady's gonna pay for it." Grinning with venomous glee, Schuller flashed me the chance to study his yellow eyeteeth. "Soft old broad like her, some little chippie's bound to knife her."

We couldn't have that. If anyone got to bump her off, it had better be me.

FOUR

"Always a Bridesmaid," Hargrove Pictures, 1948: Starring Lane Chandler as Johnny and Martha Collins as Beth.

Outside a chapel, a bride in a pastel suit returns a corsage to a soldier in uniform.

BETH
Gosh, I'm sorry, Johnny, but I can't marry you. Before I become a wife, I need to take a journey of self-discovery.

JOHNNY
Aw, heck, Beth. Where will it lead?

I UNLOCKED MY CONDO door and hurled it open. "Bite me," I said to my companion.

"Shouldn't that be 'Bite me, *Mother*'?" she asked, unoffended. "All I said was that you wouldn't be having these publishing problems if you agreed to ghostwrite *my* book instead."

I couldn't leave her in my dust. The door to the coat closet was half open, and Philly stood next to it, blocking my emotional charge into the living room.

"You're writing your life's story, Martha?" Pilly's cheeks flushed to a brilliant scarlet, and once his glowing blue-green eyes landed on Mother, they never budged.

"Finding Sperry's body and that test you took at the cop shop will make a great chapter."

Only because she passed her gunshot residue test. I'd called Philly from the police station to tell him everything was okay. Or okay enough for now—she'd proven she hadn't shot anyone. As for Schuller's inexplicable but relentless interest in her...

Never deal with reality today, when, if you're lucky, it'll disappear in a flash tomorrow—that was *truly* my motto.

Randy's voice chimed in from the closet, echoing as if from the bottom of a well. "Old news. Everybody knows about Martha's book."

Then everybody accepted a falsehood. Mother's proposed book would never be realized. It was just another attempt to muscle into my territory.

The well Randy spoke from proved to be the one he had cut into the wall of my coat closet. He'd pulled the insulation out and now had his head stuck in the hole.

Philly remained fixed in my path, seemingly unaware that we were all still bunched in that tiny entry. "I'd buy a book about your life, Martha."

Some surprise. If Mother asked him to run naked through sprinklers, he'd do it. In January. In the Yukon.

I couldn't stay angry with that cheerful old cherub. Philly always made me laugh. It wasn't just that the coarse hair sticking out in little points all over his head was a little funny looking, the old codger had the youngest spirit and most engaging smile of anyone I knew. Since he'd met my mother, the voltage in that smile sent it off the charts.

The object of his affection adjusted the jazzy taupe tie she'd bought for him and gave his lapel an intimate pat. "I'm glad you took my advice and switched to a blue shirt, Philly," Mother said. "It makes this suit look so smart."

Philly's old brown-tweed suit, like everything he owned, looked like something the homeless would donate to charity. The way my married mother pursued that poor slob was so cute, I wanted to stick my finger down my throat.

"Mother, if you really want your life story written, why don't you get Logan Wayne to write it?" I tried to inch around Philly, but someone must have glued his dusty shoes to the floor.

"Who?" she asked.

"You know, that pompous twit at USC, teaches film survey classes. He's always calling me to ask about you."

"Oh, darling, that man is such a bore."

Tell me about it.

"Tracy, it would be much more fun if you wrote it."

Not for everyone.

Randy emerged from the hole in my closet, crowding our gathering spot even more. I started to ask what the deal was with all the holes; he hadn't made this much of a mess when he worked on Mother's place. But I didn't want to know.

Randy greeted Mother showbiz style with air kisses; the affectation looked silly on the big lug. I'd rejected the ways of her reality-challenged world, while he embraced them. Of course, Randy hadn't experienced the life of a celebrity child as I had. His ailing mother, Angelique, just hung on to her celebrity friends, begging them to throw her bit parts when her health was good—and now to get building jobs for Randy.

Philly still looked like a deer thrilled to be caught in headlights. When he began absently patting his pockets, as he did when he wanted his pipe, I seized the opportunity to escape that little group by offering to find his smoking gear. Who knows? Maybe Randy did us a favor. While I adored the smell of Flying Dutchman, Philly's favorite tobacco, Drew didn't want him smoking in the condo. Philly could smoke with his head stuck in our closet holes—a perfect modification for our evolving lifestyle.

Pushing the closet door out of my way, I gently eased

Philly aside—but stopped no more than a few feet into my living room. How can I describe what I saw? Pale peach walls, tasteful walnut furniture, a brown marble fireplace—and every item we owned still lying where the tornado that must have struck had tossed them.

Mother came up behind me and wrinkled her small, straight nose. "Tracy, you need a maid."

My hand brushed against something soft in the stack before me. My new mocha cashmere, tossed along with a bunch of other sweaters on a pile of towels. "Yeah, I'll get right on that when my next book tanks. Like I could afford to pay a maid."

Mother sidled close to my ear. "There's a telephone number everyone in Beverly Hills is talking about. You order a servant you can keep forever for little more than a few years' salary. I heard about it from Rico, my hairdresser."

As I reeled away from her into a pile of skiwear, I shook my head. "Please, tell me I'm adopted."

She lifted one exquisitely arched eyebrow ala Queen Victoria when not amused.

"Mother, you're talking about *buying people*."

"Don't blame me, darling. I haven't bought any."

"Only because Yolanda would kill you before she'd let you fire her." I was thrilled when Mother had finally found Yolanda, a housekeeper who could give as good as she got, only the little witch gave it to me, too.

I waved my arm at a precariously stacked collection of photo albums that a whisper could have sent tumbling. "Randy, what is this?"

Philly rushed to my side. "Now, don't you worry, honey. I've got everything under control."

It reassured me no end to know they had a reason for demolishing my scant grasp on order. At least they thought to hang Drew's suits and shirts from various points on the wall units next to the fireplace. My things were buried in huge hills in the few spots not taken up by Philly's luggage.

"Randy's designs for the closets wouldn't work," Philly said. "But don't worry, kid, I'm working with the boy now."

That was like the blind giving the blind a museum tour. Drew was going to blow his stack when he saw this mess, but if it kept them busy, I didn't care. I kicked my shoes onto a pile of clothes across the room. I could get to like living like this.

People say I gravitate to chaos anyway. Not true, really. Well, maybe I was hopelessly addicted to change. But, mostly, it's that the eye of a hurricane is the safest spot. Except for Hurricane Martha—she keeps shifting her eye.

"Now you'll *have* to take me to Bistro Fleur de Vigne." She made a break for the door.

We had argued all the way home from the Hollywood Police Station about whether we could have lunch at the only restaurant she considers acceptable in the San Fernando Valley, my home in the less-trendy part of L.A. She and I argued, that is. Drew just stared through the windshield in deflated silence. She has that effect on people.

I ran behind her, slipping in my stockings on the few exposed areas left on the parquet floor. She had no idea how much trouble she was in, nor what I had to promise to buy her a reprieve. The kicker was that neither she nor Drew recognized their obligation to clue me in on their little powwow on Sperry's porch.

Now she was getting away. I leaped into the air, going into the tackle I'd once used on the boys in touch football—when their touching got too specific. I landed comfortably on a pile of sweaters and grabbed her ankles, welding her to that spot.

Some days, you do get the bear.

I ASKED PHILLY to make her some lunch. "Mother wouldn't know what to do in a kitchen," I added with an acid bite.

She shot me a black look, but she followed along behind him. The days she accepts defeat—they're what I live for. Even though my own stomach roared at its lack of content, I'd had enough company for one day. I sought refuge in my study.

My eyes fell to the floor where I had left the pages of my editor's fax. They were gone now. Philly had haphazardly stacked them under a brass paperweight on one side of the icy-blue Mac on my desk. I hiked up my dress and sat cross-legged on my desk chair, fidgeting till the lumpy, blood-red seat cushion conformed to my contours. Home.

Before I could get too comfortable, I heard the scuffing approach of Randy's steps. I looked up at him expectantly.

"You had a couple of calls, Trace." He scratched his shaggy blonde head. "But I can't remember one of them."

Talk about Elvis leaving the building.

His face brightened. "I know the other one. It was from Charlotte, your mother-in-law."

That call he couldn't have forgotten? Charlotte probably wanted to grouse about the latest shame my mother had brought to her stuffy New York family. It was going to be tricky answering the phone for a while—Charlotte was persistent. Maybe I'd let Randy screen my calls. If she talked to him enough, it would cure her of the need to improve me.

Randy wandered away, and I turned back to my desk, where a yellow legal pad sat perched conspicuously on the keyboard tray. For a messy guy, Philly's printing was so neat, I recognized it instantly. I wasn't sure I wanted to read what he'd written there, however.

Drew had kept his uncle's existence secret from me for years. Even when I finally met his mother's brother, Drew hid the fact that Philly made his way in the world by conning people. Drew loved his uncle in spite of his taste for easy money; I loved him because of it. That the cheerful sprite could defy his stuffy upbringing and find such a colorful outlet for his natural skills made him my kind of guy. Only now he was operating in my backyard. I couldn't let him really cheat people—not the ones who knew where I lived anyway. My solution was to find another outlet for his misfit creativity. But so far, the precise outlet eluded me.

Jeez, if I let this unexpected conventional streak grow in me, I'd be indistinguishable from Drew.

When I studied Philly's pad, I found he hadn't been working on either the draft of a begging letter or diagramming one of his elaborate schemes. He'd been redesigning my closet organization plans, and his ideas were better than anything Randy or I devised. Maybe I had found an outlet for Philly after all.

Wait! Putting together a con-man and a contractor? Talk about a license to steal.

"Drew's right—I am becoming Philly's mother," I muttered aloud. No fair. Who made me the grown-up?

My reference to the dreaded maternal noun seemed to draw Mother. She announced her presence with a martyred sigh. "Lunch here really won't do. Philly's making an omelet with something poured from a little carton. From what I remember growing up on my daddy's farm, eggs come in a different container." She tossed her wavy blonde hair in such a way as to deny that a sophisticated creature such as she had ever come face-to-face with a chicken.

"You gotta get out more," I said.

So she did need to get out—out of my house. I drew the phone to my ear and dialed a number I'd written on a pink Post-it that morning.

"Who are you calling, darling?"

"Dad." An exaggeration; I was calling the last number I had for him to see if his friend had dug up his new location.

Mother stomped her foot. "Tracy, put the phone down. You might as well know—your father and I are through."

I stopped. "Since when?"

"When he went to Del Mar." She gave my hair a motherly stroke. "We didn't tell you because we didn't want to upset you."

"You never worried about upsetting me when I was two...ten...eighteen." I began marking off their breakups on my fingers but lost count. Yet I'd never considered myself the product of a broken home, since somehow Mother and Dad always were always together. When they were married, when they were divorced—and even, let's face it, when they were married to other people. "I don't take your other marriages seriously."

Mother smiled enigmatically as she drifted toward the door. "Wait till my next one."

Not again. Before I could mourn the loss of a family situation that put the *fun* in dysfunctional, an awful thought occurred to me. Could Mother have been involved with—Sperry? I recalled how incongruous her frou-frou suit looked against that filthy background. I couldn't make that work. But for the first time, I questioned the excuse for her being there.

My hand still curled around the telephone. My fingers itched to pick it up. I bet I could get to the bottom of this with just a few calls. No, no, no! If this star-visitation scam were part of some web she'd spun, she could stay caught in it forever. That I had to babysit her till I could hand her off to Dad, or the next guy in her queue, was bad enough.

The temptation I felt was merely my avoidance of that fax. Once my eyes fixed on it, I found Philly had been busy there as well. Not only had he put the sheets in order, he'd written comments in the margins. "Rocks in her head," one said. "She calls herself an editor?" read another. "Bottom line, kiddo," he'd written on the last page, "you put a lot more of yourself in this book, and that demands a better class of place. She did you a favor by threatening to give you the boot.''

Right. Man, I hate that real life is so—real. Used to be a writer with a good track record who got pushed from one house could easily land at another. In today's cutthroat world of publication, when a writer is heard to have turned in an unacceptable manuscript, she might as well eat her mother's gun.

Was Philly right? Had I put too much of myself into the book? How could that be a bad thing?

Deadly Shadows was a departure from the first four books in the Tessa Graham series. The idea had come to me in a dream. Instead of tripping over a body, as Tessa usually did, I decided she would try to free one of her students from a stalker's harassment. Only for much of the book, Tessa wouldn't be able to confirm there really was a stalker. That forced her student to cope with both Tessa's growing disbelief and her stalker's more aggressive tactics.

That the idea came to me nearly complete in every detail had seemed like an omen at the time. So many wonderful things come to me in dreams that I never questioned it. Once I designed the most perfect house in my sleep, known since as "the dream house." Year after year in dreamland, wings would be added, room upon room, in ways no builder would sanction. I loved the hodgepodge place so much, I'd probably always hunt for its real-life equivalent. But that was why I trusted any idea that came in a dream. Only now my book's origin felt like a practical joke.

On my desk was a tomato-red mug with *Deadly Shadows* printed in white lettering. I always had a mug made with my working title. Dammit, I loved that book—I didn't want to change a word. But my truck had its uses, too, and the bank was picky about getting paid. I cradled the mug in my hands, then hurled it at the wall, where it shattered in pieces on the floor.

"That'll cost you extra!" Randy shouted.

BFD. If this room hadn't been off-limits to him, Randy'd see there were dents all over its walls. Fortunately, they make you order those mugs by the case. I reached under the desk well where I stored the box of *Deadly Shadows* mugs, just as Mother appeared again in the doorway.

"You know, darling, you should let me treat you to a new house. You wouldn't have to worry about a little closet space."

I'd rather French-kiss a dog. "Then you'd really feel entitled to run my life."

When Drew made senior partner, we'd buy our own new house. Until then, I rationalized that I'd hate any place that wasn't the dream house, anyway. Real life was so vastly overrated.

My hand groped through empty pockets in the mug box. Apparently, I'd thrown more mugs than I'd realized; there were only a few remaining. I pulled one from the box and placed it in its revered spot on the pseudo-oak Formica desktop.

"As if I—" Mother's eyes fixed on the mug. "What's that?"

"The title of my book. Why?"

"The one that won't see daylight?"

Nothing like shattering more of your child's illusions. She took the mug in her well-manicured hands. Watching her, I almost thought I saw her hands tremble. The day's events must have upset her more than she let on.

Philly rushed into the room with a dustpan and mop, like Rosie on "The Jetsons". He began sweeping the pieces as he'd already done several times during his stay with us.

Mother watched in silence. A bit of her customary mockery invaded the smile that raised one side of her full crimson lips. "I may be the least domestic person here, but does anyone else smell something burning?"

Philly sniffed. "Shit!" He rushed toward the kitchen.

With a sigh, I glanced at Mother and silently surrendered to her demand to go out to lunch. She didn't return my look. Still gripping the mug, she raised her arm over her head—and hurled it at the wall. Hers shattered into far more pieces than mine had.

"Extra!" Randy shouted.

I was so stunned, I didn't react. I didn't remind her it was my right to throw those things. Her pose—when her arm was poised over her head—it reminded me of something. I just couldn't say what. But the memory of whatever it was hooked something deep inside and sent a chill clear through me.

FIVE

WHILE PHILLY SOAKED the scorched omelet pan, I went to
the garage alone. But when I pulled around the front of
the building to pick them up, Mother balked at riding in
the truck. Did she think I'd be driving a Rolls Royce I
hot-wired for her comfort? By rights, she should be transported in a straightjacket.

"Mother, get into the car!" I shot out each word with
the force of machine gun fire.

Since I had double-parked, cars full of angry drivers
stacked up behind me. But it takes more than some honk-
ing to make my mother budge.

"If I saw a *car*, I'd be happy to get into it. All I see is a big, black rhinoceros.'' With arms crossed over her chest, she cocked a hip against the rhino's passenger door.

The driver of a green Jag screeched past, pausing long enough to insult my origins. Like that wasn't obvious.

''Mother, I'll make a deal with you. Climb in here, and I'll consider ghosting your autobiography.'' When pigs fly out my butt.

She accepted, nodding regally. But from the sly glance she gave me, I knew the book was as much a crock as I suspected. Philly beamed at the arrangement like he scored a finder's fee.

With a gallant bow, Philly offered to help Mother into the front seat. Ignoring his gesture, she threw open the rear door, and, after hiking up her skirt high enough to make the drivers behind us glad they waited for the show, she climbed into the back seat of the cab, next to a box of my latest books that I keep there.

By leaving the front for Philly, don't think she was displaying deference to his Y-chromosome. Mother didn't defer to anyone, especially not those attached to her leash by the heart. She operated on the principle that in any encounter, there's a winner and a loser, and she'd fight to the death for the superior spot. The lengths to which she'd take it became evident when I told them to buckle up. Philly complied; Mother refused to wrinkle her suit.

And some dense souls wonder why I don't have kids.

With a wave of apology to the caravan behind us, we headed down the hill, where I slipped behind a FedEx truck to join the traffic worm—inching down Ventura Boulevard.

Even though my oversized, black purse crowded the floor at Philly's feet, he wasn't about to be robbed of all his comfort. He lowered the back of the buff-leather bucket seat and adjusted the lumbar control. For a man who could live happily in a cardboard box, he sure knew what to do with the bells and whistles as he came across them. When the heat in the seat cushion reached his comfort level, Philly sighed with contentment.

He pulled his stained old Meerschaum pipe from his side pocket and lit it. Between fragrant puffs, he said, ''Great truck, Trace. All you need now is a dog in back.''

A dog. Why hadn't I thought about that? One that would slobber on my passengers. I glanced into the rearview mirror to imagine seeing a doggie face there—only my eyes connected with Mother's, reminding me why that wasn't a good idea.

''No pets,'' I said. ''You hit a sore spot, Philly.''

''Yeah? How come?''

''Maybe you should ask my mother.''

Deep blue eyes, wide with innocence, met mine in the mirror. ''Darling, I can't imagine what you mean. If you're not an animal lover, it's not my fault.''

Right.

To distance herself from this conversation, Mother raked her hair away from her face. There was something about the way she held her arm that drove any thought of a comeback from my mind. She leaned forward in her seat. ''Tracy, have you thought about what you'll order at the Bistro?''

The image in the mirror reminded me of how Mother had looked when she threw my mug. But what memory had that snagged?

''I want the driest martini this side of the Sahara,'' she said with feeling. ''And maybe the lobster salad. How about you?''

The connection finally fell into place—and it hit me like a tidal wave. I think I muttered something noncommittal to Mother, but maybe not. I pawed through the truck's center console till I spotted the curly wire of the cigarette lighter charger for my cell phone at the bottom and yanked it to the surface.

I held it out to Philly. "Do you know how to connect this thing?"

Philly gave his head an amused shake, causing his grey hair to quiver like meringue. "I don't know about you, kid. If you can't work a cell phone adapter, you don't belong in this town."

With a hand clutched to her heart, Mother fell back against the seat cushion. "My deepest sorrow. I don't know where I went wrong." A performance worthy of an Academy Award.

Philly had finished connecting the adapter when I pulled up before Bistro Fleur de Vigne, *the* place to be seen on this side of the hill, as we, in these parts, describe the Santa Monica Mountains. The valet attendant, a ponytailed Latino man in a magenta vest, opened the passenger door. He greeted Philly graciously, but shot me a dirty look when he helped Mother from the back seat. As if I made her squeeze back there—that was her way of turning me into her chauffeur. He came around to my side and waited for me to unlock my seatbelt. He tossed a pointed glance to the space behind mine in the valet lane, where another car had pulled in. I didn't budge.

"Darling, aren't you coming?" Mother asked plaintively.

Good question. Hadn't I known the answer since I asked Philly to hook up the phone?

"Something wrong, kid?" Philly said.

What could be wrong? Sure, I was a slave to my insatiable curiosity, but what was wrong with that?

I pulled my door shut. "The book's deadline—you know, it's coming up fast." No lie, just not germane. "Why don't you two have lunch on your own. Call me at the condo when you're finished, and I'll come for you."

"We'll miss you, dear," Mother said. She beamed when she said it, possibly as sick of me as I was of her.

As soon as they reached the sidewalk, I shot out of there,

turning on the phone even as I peeled rubber. I wasn't a total feeb when it came to high-tech gadgetry; I knew how to forward my calls from my home phone to the cellular. Mother would never know I hadn't returned to the condo.

Okay, so I really couldn't contain my curiosity. That didn't mean I was getting involved, just satisfying myself on one teeny point. However I justified it, I *had* to get another look at that photograph in Sperry's house.

ON THE WAY TO Hollywood, I considered how I was going to get back into that house. If the cops were still there, I was in Luck City. I still had Schuller's screenplay stuffed in my bag. I'd either tell him I wanted to discuss it, or I'd flash it for any other cop who had taken his place. No matter. I can talk my way into or out of anything—that's in the genes.

The spectators had cleared from Forest Hills Drive. Onto the next circus. So had the police, it seemed. I turned into a cul de sac down the road from Sperry's place, where the houses backed up against his block. Once I'd parked, I grabbed a book from the box behind my seat and approached the first house. With a little luck, no one would be home, and I'd be able to cut through to Sperry's yard. With a little less luck, I might sell a book.

No one answered the bell. I glanced at the other homes. Not a single curtain fluttered at the windows of any nosy neighbors. Practically an invitation.

At the side gate, I shouted, "Anybody home?" Like maybe a pack of vicious dogs?

When no one growled back, I slipped through the gate to the back of the house. No real backyard in that terrain, just a pretty little patio of Mexican tiles that butted up against the hill. I hadn't been looking forward to climbing that bluff, but these nice folks had made stairs from railroad ties and cut terraces into the hillside in case I wanted to check out the view. I just skipped to the top and slipped through the low bushes that separated Sperry's house from the one below it.

Sperry's place enjoyed a smidge more land than his neighbor. But as his yard hadn't seen water since the ice age, not much grew there. Except for the marijuana patch hidden behind a hedge alongside the porch. It thrived beautifully. We all have our priorities.

The police had gone; their seal was affixed to the rear door of the screened-in porch. I pressed at one of the screen sections to see how much pressure it would take to break through. But I remembered the open window in the TV room. Would they have been careless enough to leave that open? This was L.A., after all.

I misjudged the fuzz. It wasn't wide open, but the wood was too warped to close completely. The window was too high for me to climb through, especially in a dress. Fortunately, there were a bunch of garbage cans there. I had to unsettle a colony of critters, but one can was the perfect height.

I stuffed the book I still carried into my purse and tossed it through the window. It hit with a thud—good thing the house was empty. Taking one last precaution, I removed one of the gold pierced hoops I put through my earlobes that morning and slipped it into my pocket. Then I leaned through the open window, bending over the sill at the waist. Just a little shimmying, and I would tumble right to the floor. What could go wrong?

Nothing much…until I smashed into my husband's shins.

BUSTED.

"Are you really incapable of giving an honest answer?" Drew shouted, stomping his feet so hard, he sent up clouds of dust from that filthy shag carpet "You swore you wouldn't get involved."

Now that's the trouble with telling the truth. You tweak

it a bit, and all they notice is the change. A good, consistent lie right from the start beats it every time.

"Apart from the way it's disrupted my schedule, I couldn't care less about this murder," I insisted, rushing into my earring excuse. When I saw his anger abating, I went on the attack. "That doesn't explain why you're here."

He shook a set of keys. "I happen to have a key. Now that he knows his case is through, Sperry's lawyer has become cooperative, hoping we'll settle for enough to pay his bill."

I noticed he answered *how* he came to be there, not *why*. He also must have broken the police seal on the front door when he used that key. Mr. Officer-of-the-Court shaving corners finer than I did? They say couples become more alike over time, but Drew was moving too fast in my direction for this to be good.

I suggested we look for my earring in the hall. Drew stepped aside for me to pass, dammit, denying me a moment alone with those photos. I meandered down the corridor, combing the floor for something in my pocket. No matter how slowly I walked, however, Drew fell farther behind.

Finally, he stopped and said, "Trace, there's been a development."

Holy freakin' Mother's Day. No one broke good news like that.

"The Coroner says Sperry was stabbed repeatedly, sometime between eight and eleven last night, and shot around five this morning. That corresponds to the time neighbors reported hearing gunfire."

"He was stabbed *and* shot? That's nuts." I remembered the smear of blood that wound across the room. Poor bastard tried to reach help last night. "Two killers or one incompetent who needed two tries to get it right?"

"That's not clear yet." Drew shrugged. "Or Schuller's not sharing."

For being the latest media darling, a lot of people seemed to want Sperry out of the way.

"It gets worse, babe. We know Martha was here this morning, and she may not be able to establish an alibi for last night."

From where we stood in the hall, I determined that Sperry had once kept cats, but I was rooted to that smelly spot. "Schuller's already tried to establish her alibi?"

"No, that was me," Drew said.

He told me he would hire her another lawyer, but he checked her alibi himself?

"I think her housekeeper, Yolanda, might be playing games. She said she couldn't be sure when Martha was home."

I tapped the wall in frustration; pea-green paint flaked on my hand. "Yolanda doesn't miss a thing that goes on at that house. She and Mother are just fighting about how much vacation time she has coming. She better not pull that crap with Schuller." Fear fluttered in my chest like a butterfly trapped in a jar. "What about Benny Butler Marsh? He had the best reason for wanting Sperry out of the way."

"He said he was working out in his home gym last night, let the voicemail take his calls."

"And this morning?" I demanded.

"Running," Drew said without expression.

"Who knew the tubber was so goddamned fit?"

I paused in the doorway of the room where Sperry had died. There had to be something there to clear her. Despite the debris that filled the rest of the house, this room looked like it hadn't been used for years. A few yellowed paperbacks with lurid covers were stacked in the bookshelves, but there was more empty space in that room than between my contractor's ears. One of those squeezy stressballs sporting a realtor's logo had been plopped on the desk. It had just one three-sided poke in it, as if it had been pushed into the corner of the desk. Well, it didn't look like there had been much stress in Sperry's life, till the end.

Despite all the blood spilled on the carpet, little was spattered on the surrounding surfaces. They were also less dusty than the rest of the house. I threw a quick glance at the ceiling—plenty of blood there. It looked as if someone tried to clean away evidence, but only where he happened to look. Would Mother be that stupid? Would she know how to clean?

Deep in thought, my eyes floated back to the cherry desk…and it's rounded corners. I looked again at the indentation in that stupid green stressball. Now it was starting to look more like the mark a three-carat pear-shaped diamond might make. How many owners of one of those had Sperry entertained lately?

Drew watched me from the doorway. "What are you looking at?"

Diversion time. "Notice anything funny about this place?"

"You mean other than the fact that stuck pigs aren't the only ones who bleed like—stuck pigs?"

Tasteless humor now. He was becoming like me.

I gave the place a quick sweep with my eyes to find something to feed him. "Do you see a computer here? How'd he write the '06 screenplay? With finger paint?"

Drew chuckled. "From where I stand, he didn't write it." He opened a couple of cabinet doors. "There you go, Tracy—he had a typewriter. Writers used them in the Dark Ages."

I came around the desk to check out Drew's find, a toffee-colored Selectric. Despite my dependence on my trusty Mac today, I knew Selectrics well. I still remembered when my parents' secretary showed me how to read Mother's private correspondence straight from the cartridge ribbon. Since I'd already discovered that the key to my school gym padlock worked like a passkey with nearly every small lock I encountered, there wasn't much they could keep from me. But that didn't stop them from trying.

Somewhere on Drew's body, something buzzed. He pulled his tiny matte black cell phone from his inside breast pocket. "Drew Eaton. Hi, Tinker, what did you find?" he asked his assistant.

I debated whether I could slip back to the TV room while he talked, but I didn't want to leave Sperry's den yet. The hillside location played into my hand with its erratic signal-bending.

"Can you hear me now?" Drew shouted. "Wait. I'll try another spot."

He returned to the hall, testing the signal at various points. Once he hit the halfway point, I flipped the top of the Selectric and snatched the cartridge out. Drew would thank me if I found anything on it to help his case. I tried to put it into my purse, but with the book crammed in there along with Schuller's script, it wouldn't fit. I pulled up my dress and stuffed the cartridge into the back of my pantyhose. I'd applied a little surprise back there for Drew—I hoped the cartridge didn't scrape it off. How come Miss Marple never had to worry about stuff like that?

Then, to cover all bases, I snatched the stressball from the desk. If the cops missed the significance of it, too bad. They had their chance. But where to put it? I pressed it between my palms to flatten it and stuffed it into one of the little pockets on my dress. It looked like a hipbone goiter.

"Let me go to the back," Drew shouted.

Yes! He was headed to the porch. As fast as I could move, considering everything stuffed into my clothes, I ran to the TV room. I took a moment to pull the earring from my pocket and placed it half-under the recliner, where we could discover it together. Then I turned to those photos. But in my haste, I couldn't find the right one. All I saw were a lot of strangers mugging for the camera and looking damned stupid to me!

Finally, I hit on the right one: Sperry awash in tie-dye, the man with the fiery dark eyes, the two kids. Ignoring the others, I focused on the baby girl who bopped the boy with her doll. She was a bit out of focus, but I was sure I was right. The way she held her arm was the telling factor. Jeez, maybe it is all in the genes.

The little tyke in Sperry's photo—was me.

SIX

"Star-Maker," Hargrove Pictures, 1950: Starring Martha Collins as Lorna and Alan Garvey as Emile Saffire.

Late night on a Hollywood soundstage. A radiant young woman confronts a tyrannical old man.

EMILE
Leave! I can make a thousand like you. It's me they come to see, my pictures.

LORNA
I'll give you this much: You taught me a star always knows when to make her exit.

Lorna sweeps out, leaving a broken man in her wake.

I BROUGHT TWO FISTS DOWN on the oak front desk at Bistro Fleur de Vigne, shouting to the arrogant host, "You *lost* her?"

His gasp was so athletic, he nearly popped the buttons on his paisley satin vest. But he topped my volume. "I never had her."

A roomful of diners, their cell phones buzzing like a swarm of killer bees, paused in their deals-in-progress to convey the full spectrum of irritation.

I lowered my voice to the level of a fierce stage whisper. "I'm telling you, she was here."

The skinny little twit was shorter than I was, but by

tilting his head back, he managed to look down his long nose at me. "Your mother hasn't dined here since last Friday."

That proved he didn't know Martha Collins from any other lunatic. She never eats on this side of the hill without me, and I wasn't there. I told him as much.

"Of course, I know Miss Collins. I know you, too. She comes in here dressed like a dream, while you look..." Despite my new rust dress, his lip curled. "...different."

Okay, so he did know us. Just when you think things are going your way. I'd stage-managed every detail to perfection at Sperry's house. Wasn't easy, either—that photo floored me. It proved that one of my parents had known Sperry. Who else would have taken me to that set?

Now Mother was missing. No wonder she fought so hard to leave the condo. She must have planned her disappearance from the start. How would she have ditched me if I had come with them? My mind drifted back to that genes thing. If I could have extricated myself—and I could—she could do it in a coma.

I stomped from the restaurant but checked with the valet before I left. He'd been busy parking the car behind mine after I dropped Mother and Philly off and couldn't say where they went.

I climbed into the truck and cranked the engine. Seeing a rare break in both east- and westbound traffic, I made an illegal U-turn and headed home. For the first time in weeks, I wished I had a cigarette. I'd quit months ago—man, had it been a struggle. Now that I'd successfully made it over the hurdle to being a real nonsmoker, I felt myself backsliding. How deep are the roots of our needs?

Philly kept a packet of pipe tobacco in my glove compartment. At a traffic light, I brought the stale pouch of Flying Dutchman to my nose and drew in a deep breath. The tobacco irritated my nostrils. That never happened before. Wouldn't you know? A real nonsmoker at the worst possible time.

Fortunately, I could still eat till I burst. I flung the pouch aside, but the scent lingered in the air, burning my nose, and still making me wish it smelled more like a cigarette.

Cigarette smell...?

I twisted the wheel into another U-turn, this time not in a traffic break. Well, that's why cars have brakes—those drivers leaning on their horns should have thanked me for testing theirs. Weaving more than an Indy car, I raced back toward the restaurant and cut into the delivery alley behind it. At the back door, a dapper man in a tuxedo with only the slightest of spare tires under his magenta cummerbund crushed out a smoke.

After throwing the truck into neutral, I bolted from the cab without turning it off. "Franz, wait!" I called.

Mother's favorite waiter turned to me with no small measure of censure. The only waiter in L.A. without an acting agent, Franz Geller may have lost much of his Austrian accent during his years here, but not his Old World standards. The daughters of prominent guests did not greet the help behind the kitchen door. I wanted to slap him silly for those standards; instead, I acknowledged them with a profound apology.

His greeting expressed his acceptance. "Tracy, my dear, it's always a pleasure." He kissed me grandly on each cheek.

He didn't ask how I knew where to find him, and I wouldn't have told him for the world. But that elegant man always smelled as if he slept in an ashtray. Maybe I wasn't sorry I'd crossed over, after all.

"Franz, I hope you can help me. That jerk at your front desk insists Mother wasn't here today. I know I'm horribly late, but she wouldn't leave without me."

Despite my soft-peddling it, his dark eyes clouded over.

"But your Mother wasn't here today. You know I'd never miss her."

No, he wouldn't. She had truly never entered the joint. I remembered what the host had said.

"Perhaps I entered it in the wrong week in my calendar. Was Mother here last week?"

After a quick search of his memory, Franz's face brightened. "Of course. I was thrilled to see her with him. The parts, they're not too plentiful at Martha's age, eh? This man can do wonders for her career."

Not to mention raising her status in her waiter's eyes. Franz Geller may have retained his courtly ways, but the royalty he served today was strictly Movieland's. Why couldn't he have named her companion?

"Who...?" I asked, as if it didn't mean the world to me.

"Why Benny Butler Marsh!"

I DROVE HOME in a daze. A menace behind the wheel, stopping at green lights, running reds, like I'd never read the DMV manual. Come to think of it, I probably never had. Whatever skills I may have picked up along the way were gone now, edged out by all I had to process.

Mother met with *both* Benny and Sperry? Might she have been trying to affect a compromise between them? A little one-upmanship with Drew to prove she was the Queen of Tinseltown? What could that have to do with her disappearing act at the restaurant? Tell you one thing: If she whacked Sperry, the State was going to have to get in line behind me.

I was so out of it during my drive that I forgot what awaited me at home. The sight of the mess made me want to run away. But I waited too long. It wasn't enough that I had to deal with my own mother's antics—my contractor had now added *his* mother to the picture.

Angelique Barlow spread wide the bell-bottom sleeves

of her lilac crepe dress and swooped down on me like a big purple bird. Well, as much swooping as a woman dragging a portable oxygen container could manage. She'd suffered from smoke inhalation making some low-budget flick, and her lungs had never recovered. Poor Angelique. She was the only one in the company to sign the waiver holding the producer harmless from any accidents that might occur. The apples didn't fall far from Randy's family tree, either. At times I thought I saw flashes of intelligence in Angelique's watery blue eyes, but Mother insisted it was just a trick of the light.

Everybody's favorite party girl hadn't aged well. Angelique still wore her hair in the long feathery style of her youth, but her golden locks were now a brittle platinum blonde. And these days the huge breasts that represented most of her screen appeal, rested on a belly that looked like she swallowed a bowling ball. Too much booze and drugs, too many men, had left her all used up.

For all her apparent frailty, Angelique's hands locked on to my arms and pulled me to her. "Too long, Tracy. It's just been too long. But I'm glad you and my Randy are finally together."

Together? As we Valley Girls used to say in my younger years, gag me with a spoon.

"We're not—" I started to say.

"Come along, honey, and see what the dear boy is doing."

The wheels on her oxygen canister screeched like nails scraped across a blackboard. Couldn't her son oil it? My teeth locked. I only managed to put that sound aside when I noticed the trail Angelique brought me along led straight to my study, a room I forbade Randy to enter. When did I stop running this show?

I found him patching the damage to the wall, rather than adding more. But talk about close calls. Randy held out the most god-awful roll of wallpaper border in gold and Pepto-Bismol pink.

"Tracy, look what Mom brought by. She picked it out for you, see. Won't even let me charge you extra to put it up."

I should have charged her for bringing it into my house. That border would keep me up at night.

"Too generous, Angelique, but I can't let you do that." I yanked the wallpaper from Randy's hand and stuffed it into hers. "Besides, I have a killer deadline. I have to kick you both out."

I took a moment to put my purse and its contents into the study closet. There was a lock on that door, and I'd better start using it.

In the instant that I left her alone, Angelique began banging on my keyboard. "Look, Randy, a computer." To me, she said with a laugh, "Martha once paid for me to go to computer school so I could learn a new trade, you know? But I kept making it crash."

"Then you probably don't want to play with mine." I slipped my arm through Angelique's and led her and the squeaky tank toward the door.

"No time anyway, hon. I gotta take Nan to the free clinic."

With better timing than Angelique ever displayed on the screen, Nan, the homeless woman who shared their home in a Chatsworth trailer park, wandered in. She wore a faded orange sweatshirt and a baggy pair of blue denim overalls. In her callused hand, she clutched a frozen dinner roll she'd taken a bite from.

"Tracy, you've met Nan, haven't you? My stand-in, you know."

I had to bite my tongue to keep from laughing. While ten years older, Nan did bear a superficial resemblance to Angelique, something Angelique had enhanced by lightening her hair to be a closer match to Nan's white hair.

But Angelique didn't need a stand-in. Hollywood is nothing if not elitist; producers believe bit players should do their own standing around.

Nan's pale blue eyes wandered in my direction. "Snorky moon goo duty blue," she said.

Did I mention the woman babbled incomprehensibly? "Yaba-daba-do," I answered. When in Rome...

Mother always referred to Nan as "Angelique's Angelique," assuming her friend wanted to lord over someone else. But the Barlows did seem to take good care of Nan. One of them accompanied her wherever she went. And in her loopy way, Nan appeared equally devoted to her benefactors.

Angelique also seemed to understand her gibberish. "Yeah, Nan, we gotta get going." She threw an anxious glance at a tarnished, but diamond-studded, silver watch I remembered Mother wearing years ago. I knew taking Nan to the clinic depended on adhering to the bus schedule.

I spread my arms wide and pushed them all toward the door.

"At least let Randy clean up from your little tantrum," Angelique said, gesturing vaguely in the direction of a dustpan filled with the remains of two broken mugs. "Bet that brings back memories, huh?"

Sure, we just broke them this morning. Her mind was gone.

I finally succeeded in ushering everyone from my study—when the front door flew open and in walked Philly with a couple of new friends. No sign of his old friend, however, the one in whose company I'd left him at the restaurant.

"How's it going, kid?" Philly greeted me.

He sounded so offhanded, you'd never believe he'd escaped with an almost-felon. But he was a con-man, he should have been able to sell it.

"Trace, meet Lorenzo Perez."

Jabbing a thumb over his shoulder, Philly indicated a wiry Latino man carrying a muddy navy duffel. A match made in bum heaven—finally, someone whose clothes looked worse than Philly's. Gashes slashed through the rubber trim of the poor guy's stained black Reeboks. And while his shoulder carriage was rigid enough to pass a Marine inspection, the plaid flannel shirt he wore had been washed so often that the nap had worn off. But Lorenzo was rich in other ways—he had a dog. Lucky us, he brought it with him.

"Charmed," I said sourly.

"*Que?*" Coffee-colored eyes met mine through a pair of glossy horn-rimmed glasses.

"Lorenzo don't speak much English, kid. He was just standing on the corner waiting for work. Can you beat that?"

Philly must have noticed before today that new immigrants often cluster on corners waiting for employers to stop.

"I thought you could give him a job," Philly went on.

Sure, once they repoed my truck, I'd be in Fat City.

I felt something as hot and moist as dryer exhaust gathering on the side of my calf. The dog was panting at me. No wonder. The mangy Heinz 57 was buried under enough wavy black-and-tan fur to do a yak proud. A reedy tail popped out the back end of the matted coat, while another clump of fur covered all but what looked like a big Old English Sheepdog nose at the front.

"And what's this one's name?" I asked of the scruffy creature.

"...Johnny O'Toole." Philly said.

Strange name from someone who didn't speak English. Maybe the dog picked it himself.

"Look at his eyes—don't they have character?" Philly asked.

I couldn't see them without parting fur that felt as stiff

as Philly's hair. Once I did, a pair of eyes the color of brandy met mine. Deep, soulful eyes that seemed to say, *These people are nuts—let's you and me blow this joint.* Uh-uh. I'd fallen for that line before. No way was this mutt luring me in.

"They look like they belong to an orangutan stuck in a dog suit," I said.

Philly laughed and turned to Lorenzo. "Throw your stuff anywhere, *hijo,* and I'll get us something to eat."

Lorenzo tossed his dirty duffel on my only cashmere sweater. I let Philly's entourage get most of the way through the dining area before putting a stop to the show.

"Uncle Philly, aren't you forgetting something?"

"You look a little strained, kid. Everything okay around here?" Concern creased Philly's forehead, while scores of calculations scampered across his eyes.

"Here—yes. Less so at the Bistro Fleur de Vigne."

Philly slapped his forehead, pushing a clump of hair Due North. "We forgot to call you when we cut outta the Bistro, didn't we? You know me, I don't go for those fancy joints. I talked Martha into going to a little burger joint I know."

A burger joint? My dad could eat in a soup kitchen and act like it was a palace. Mother thinks the Bistro *is* a soup kitchen.

Philly's restless hands fell on a stack of Drew's alligator-crested polo shirts; he folded them while rambling on. "Then your mom remembered another one of them visits she had to make. You know, like the one to Sperry?"

I hoped it wasn't exactly like the one to Sperry. Above the snowy stubble across his chin, Philly's face flushed.

"How did you get to the burger joint?" I asked.

"A cab came by, and Martha flagged it. Lucky, huh? How often do you see cabs cruising around here?"

Almost never. They have to be called.

''Where is she now?'' This person I mortgaged my life to spring.

Philly tossed off a jerky shrug. ''Got me. I figured Martha wanted a long visit. Me and Lorenzo here thumbed our way back.'' He pulled a wrinkled hanky from his pocket and blotted his face. ''Martha should be along anytime.''

In handcuffs, for sure.

Without warning, he shot into the kitchen in a flash, leaving a startled Lorenzo and canine in his dust. I tried to pursue him, but I nearly broke my neck slipping on one of Drew's knit shirts. Once I found my footing, I just pointed Lorenzo in the right direction and fled to my study.

As mad as I was at Philly, that sensation was dwarfed next to what I felt for Mother. It all made sense now. I bet she called for a cab while Philly cleaned the burned pan and I fetched the truck. No wonder she balked at getting into it. The dispatcher must have told her there'd be a delay.

I absently booted up the computer. I still had to come up with something to feed my editor, anything to buy me a little time. I clicked on my word-processing program.

Who was I kidding? I couldn't work as if nothing had happened. I went to the closet for my purse, now spread as wide as the mouth of a shark closing in on dinner. I yanked Schuller's script from it and hurled it to the floor. But my arm slowed when it reached for Sperry's Selectric cartridge.

I spooled out the used section, but there wasn't much written on it. Sperry had changed this cartridge recently. It was infuriatingly incomplete! But what I saw there was bad enough.

''…knows all about Windswept, Martha,'' it read.

Windswept…? The word tickled something in my brain. How did I know it? When the connection wouldn't come, I went back to reading.

"...and I urge you to handle it with the same generosity you've always shown me."

Generosity? That sounded like a payoff.

It ended with, "Your old pal, Vinny."

Her *pal?* Whoa! Talk about lessons in lying. She sure had gotten herself into it this time. When I looked away from that awful message, my gaze fell on the pink Post-It. I dialed my father's last known location.

"Rick, it's Tracy Eaton," I said when the phone was answered. "Have you learned anything about my dad?"

"Yeah, Tracy, I've been meaning to call you. I've asked around, and everyone seems to think Alec went to Mexico, but nobody knows where."

I thanked him and hung up. Why did Dad have to disappear *now?* I remembered Mother's reference to another man. Had Dad left because she was fooling around? His own track record in that area, while a ghost of hers, wasn't spotless, either. I couldn't believe he'd stay away if he knew how deeply she'd dug herself in.

I looked at the computer monitor. Then at the words on the ribbon. Why was I fighting it? Dad was gone, and I was here. What choice did I have? She was the only mother I had—it was too late to break in a new one.

SEVEN

*"Strange Journey," Hargrove Pictures, 1951: Starring
Martha Collins as Lily and Tom Padget as Shale.*

*At the side of her disabled car, a frightened woman backs
away from a dark stranger.*

LILY
*How do you get out of this town? I can't even read
the street signs.*

SHALE
Then you're really not gonna like where they lead.

THERE'S ONE GREAT THING about having a mother who is
at once both loopy and methodical: You may not know
where she's headed, but it's easy to figure how she'll get
there. On this side of the hill, Mother always used Valleywide Taxi, one of a few companies that served the increas-
ing carless population in a city not designed to tread on
foot. Their cabs weren't any less scuzzy than the competition's, but the owner decorated his sooty garage with out-
dated movie posters, many of them Mother's.

And people say she has no standards.

Today's dispatcher proved to be a sturdy woman, with
the face of a bulldog, who wore her steely hair in a pretty
little flip. Deep down, we're all still in high school. Thirty
bucks bought me the location where Mother had been

dropped off, and another ten the promise of a call if she ordered another cab.

I forwarded my home calls to set my cell phone again. Mother would probably make an end run around me, but whether she reached Philly or the dispatcher, she was going to see me.

I wasn't familiar with the street Mother visited, but that didn't worry me. At first. When Dad runs aground, I need a psychic to find him—and if he didn't surface soon, I'd be desperate enough to try one. But Mother moved in more rarefied circles; nothing but the best for The Legend, Martha Collins. Till today, I'd never needed to dig out my old *Thomas Guide* to follow her trail. Now it didn't suffice.

Since my map was at least ten years old, it often failed me in new areas. But the address where Valleywide Cabs had deposited Mother seemed to be in an industrial section south of the Van Nuys Airport. There wasn't any space there to carve out new streets.

I pulled the truck over before an old brick building along a block of structures that all sported "For Lease" signs. Before I could pick up the map, a teenaged boy popped out from a space between two buildings and offered me a seductive grin. I suddenly realized—unless this area attracted really trashy pedestrians—a swarm of hookers had descended on it. Working girls, working boys, working I-wasn't-sures. Jeez, was this place overdue for a sweep by the cops. I sent the kid off with a flip of my hand and buried my face in the map.

There was just one Kenney Avenue, and its numbers didn't reflect the one Mother visited. But it was a stop-and-start street; maybe I hadn't gone far enough east to pick it up again. For the next half-hour, I made countless wrong turns, got stuck in endless dead-ends and learned too many new swear words to count from truck drivers I'd pissed off. Finally, I pulled into the lot of a canvas awning factory to ask for directions.

A frazzled Asian woman in a purple-and-gold Lakers sweatshirt worked at the green-metal front desk. She scarcely looked up from her work when I babbled my request—till I mentioned the address. Her mouse-clicking finger froze and the pink tip of her tongue peaked out the side of her mouth. She didn't need to think about it, either; she just rattled out the directions. It didn't sound far. Nor hard to find—once someone mentioned that part of Kenney Avenue was a parallel street that required a crooked jag north.

I turned to leave. But the woman stopped me, saying, "If you find out what they do there, could you let me know?" She flushed, but her embarrassment wasn't enough to make her back down.

If it mattered that much to her, I thought that she should get off her duff and show me the way. But my own need to know was too strong not to feed another's addiction. I promised I would return and tell her.

Her directions were perfect, though I would never have found the place without them. The continuation of Kenney Avenue wasn't as much a street as a long, winding driveway. On a plot of land behind the airport, someone had constructed a large building of pressed concrete. In another part of town, I might have taken it for a soundstage; here I figured it for a hangar, only there wasn't any access to it from the Van Nuys airport, just from the street.

Van Nuys was strictly for private planes, but its corporate traffic was booming. Perhaps the builder thought he'd sell that hangar to the airport, and they'd remove the fence that separated them. Not a bad idea. But, apparently, that hadn't happened. Since the opening along the side had been reduced to van-size, I assumed it had been converted to a warehouse. Unlike the other area businesses, whose delivery entrances were teeming with workers, this one was shut tightly, and it was deserted.

And *this* was why Mother crept away from one of her favorite restaurants?

I parked the truck where the street dead-ended and stepped from the cab to case the joint. It looked abandoned. The entrance at the front of the building had been carefully boarded up. There were no windows in the whole structure, no entrances at all, apart from the van door along the side, though it looked as if a few skylights had been cut into the high domed roof.

Given the lack of activity, I understood the curiosity of the woman at the awning factory. The offices on the top floor of her building had a direct view of this space. Had she spent her lunches studying it? What had she seen?

No hookers on this piece of property, I noticed. Not a surprise—no traffic, either. Could this have been their clearing house? I never thought the profession to be that organized.

I pressed my ear to the entrance. I thought I heard some muffled sounds inside, but it was too noisy outside to be sure. I raised my fist to knock, just as the phone in my truck buzzed.

I ran back to grab it, barely containing my hope. I had an awful feeling I wasn't going to learn anything here. At worst, I thought, my caller might be Philly, ready to confess.

Why do I persist in using words like worst, without thinking about what they mean. My caller really was the worst, and it wasn't Philly.

Drew had tracked me down.

FORTUNATELY, it didn't occur to him to question whether I'd lost his client. If he asked to speak to her, she was going to have to take the world's longest bathroom break.

"What's that noise?" Drew said. "Aren't you at home? It sounds like you're on a freeway."

No, just a runway. "The windows are open. Randy's working here, remember?"

"Hell." He stewed in a heavy silence. "Benny Butler Marsh wants to meet with us—both of us." Drew's tone implied that he couldn't imagine why Benny wanted me along. My thought, too.

"So set up an appointment. Next year works for me."

"Nice try, Tracy. He wants to meet us *now*. But he says he'll come to our place."

The Benny Butler Marshes of the world didn't come to those who served them. I had a good mind to call Benny's bluff till I remembered the state of my condo. The only place to sit was the bed, and that was *not* a space I wanted to share with Benny. Besides, there was also the pesky fact that I really wasn't there. I remembered where Benny's office was in Studio City and suggested to Drew that we meet in the bar at nearby Bistro Fleur de Vigne. After having yelled at the host, I hoped they'd let me back in.

Once off the phone, I looked back to that menacing concrete fortress. I may not have discovered what drew my mother there, but it wasn't a total loss. With a little luck, her recent luncheon companion might spill why she skipped.

EVEN BEFORE I dropped my truck with the valet at the Bistro, I knew both good news and bad news awaited me there—I just wasn't sure which was which. It looked like Drew hadn't made it yet, but Benny had already arrived. While it's always better to question people out of Drew's inhibiting presence, with Benny I needed a chaperone.

I'd met Benny Butler Marsh before when he threw a celebratory shindig after Drew convinced a judge his father's memory was as solid as Swiss cheese, and it was time for Jolly Marsh's baby boy to take the reins of Marshland Productions and his other holdings. Since I had a book signing that night, I told Drew I'd meet him there.

The glaze over Benny's eyes when he'd opened the door told me he wasn't feeling any pain. But I still wouldn't have guessed that, when he'd asked if he could take my coat, what he really meant was whether he could take me *in* the coat.

Before I could blink, Benny had thrown me into a closet that was so big, I wondered whether he'd designed it as a place to assault his lawyers' wives. While my arms had flailed helplessly in an effort to free myself, my hand landed on a collapsible umbrella. I swung that sucker with all my might, connecting well enough with Benny's head that you'd think I'd practiced the move. I'd hoped he would crash at my feet, but that he staggered unsteadily from the closet without looking back proved to be victory enough.

I figured Drew could kiss goodbye to drawing a paycheck after that. But servicing clients lies outside my helpmate job description. To my surprise, there was never any fallout. Maybe Benny was so out of it that he didn't remember. I never told Drew, so he didn't understand my animosity toward one of his firm's bigger cash cows. Knowing I'd now meet that smarmy perv alone, I didn't hurry when the attendant helped me from my truck.

By guessing from outside the restaurant about which man waited inside, I wasn't playing psychic. I'd driven past the Bistro's valet lot, and I didn't spot Drew's Volvo. No guesses were needed about Benny—the Phoenix had landed there before me and claimed the entire valet lane in front of the restaurant. Not a literal phoenix, of course; nor that city in Arizona, though this one was almost as big. FEENIX was the personalized license plate that graced Benny's white stretch limo.

You probably recognize the allusion from the TV clips. That scene they always show on the news of the actor in '06 railing to the gods above, ''I am the Phoenix—I will rise from the ashes!'' With the injunction blocking its release, that's the only part of the picture I've seen and reason enough to give it a pass. But as bad as the actor comes across spouting those lines, I hate hearing them even more from Benny on his talk-show appearances, though what his delivery lacks in quality, it makes up for in volume.

Dreading the possibility of hearing those lines now, I dragged myself through the Bistro door and into the bar. To my surprise, Drew was there with Benny, ensconced in one of three maroon side chairs gathered around a charcoal marble cocktail table.

After inching my chair closer to Drew's protective side, I whispered, "Where's your car? I didn't see it in the lot."

"It's there," Drew insisted stiffly.

Right. He parked it at the supermarket down the street. Though the Volvo's new-car smell had long since faded, Drew still couldn't bring himself to hand the keys over to a stranger. I wanted to kid him about babying the tin beast, but the stiff set of his jaw stopped me. Drew only became that rigid when pressures overwhelmed him. Besides, making fun of Benny was more fun.

Benny Butler Marsh was the kind of guy who gave all Angelenos a bad name. While Drew sat at attention in that cushy overstuffed chair, Benny stretched out in his as if it were a First Class sleeper seat. Never before had I seen a man with a cell phone pressed to *each* ear, carrying on simultaneous conversations. The jagged, untrimmed fingernails wrapped around those phones provided such an earthy touch.

Most Hollywood hotshots subscribe to the theory that you can never be too thin. They accomplish their enviable leanness by putting in countless hours in their home gyms under the watchful eyes of their slave-driving personal trainers. Or maybe by snorting so many bushels of happy dust that they no longer remember food exists. I had to give Benny credit for waddling to the beat of his own drummer. I'd seen his black silk-knit shirt in the window of a Rodeo Drive shop, only the mannequin hadn't sported such a roll under it that it stretched till its pasty skin showed through. Ironically, there was one part of Benny's body that *needed* some weight; his face was so long and thin, a ferret might claim it as his own. His receding hairline, with freckles the size of quarters dancing across it, made his face look even longer.

Benny shouted final comments into both phones and tossed them onto the cocktail table. His murky eyes found mine, and he leaned over the table as if he intended to kiss me. I eighty-sixed that by thrusting my hand out for a shake. Benny's clammy mitts swallowed it, though he missed scratching my hand with his ragged nails. Otherwise, I would have needed a tetanus shot to survive.

"Trace, how'ya holding up, babe?" Benny went on before I had a chance to tell him. "This shit with your mom is so bogus. I told Drew to forget about my work. I've been, like, on the horn to his bosses, and I'm all, 'You better support him, man, or Benny Butler Marsh is finding himself new shysters.'"

Strictly speaking, Drew wasn't Benny's shyster, but Jolly's. While they seemed virtually the same now, the law drew a distinction. Something Benny never acknowledged. Drew hated that he was forced by the firm's higher-ups to serve on the Marshland Productions' plagiarism team, when his expertise was estate law. Drew bore it well. But to be endlessly pursued by the people you most want to avoid—that has to be the definition of hell.

I might want to remember that the next time I stalk a book reviewer.

Benny's voice whined with such sincerity, I wondered whether I'd misjudged the uneducated boor. As I prepared to dole out one of my rare benefits-of-the-doubt, Benny pulled a pack of cigarettes from the pocket of his pale blue stone-washed jeans and lit one up. Smoking is forbidden in California restaurants. Not that anyone could tell from the cocktail waitress, half-clothed in a burgundy mini-dress. She wiggled over to bestow not one, but two ash-trays on Benny. Two phones, now two ashtrays—was there any doubt this clown sported Hollywood's requisite two faces?

Sure, I'd longed for a cigarette myself earlier today, and maybe I still did. What can I say? Benny rubbed me the wrong way—and if he tried it again, he was losing his nuts.

"Benny, I can't tell you how much your support means. I've been so worried about Mother that—" I lowered my head as if I were holding back tears. From the corner of my eye, I saw Drew's head whip around in disbelief. "But I'd expect her old pals to rally 'round. Is Mother a good friend of yours and Jolly's?"

The superior host I'd tangled with earlier walked through the bar announcing the license plates of the cars in the supermarket lot about to be towed. Drew picked that moment to go to the men's room; it was probably just a poor sense of direction that sent him out the front door.

Benny didn't seem to notice. He blasted me with a cloud of smoke, while appearing to ponder my question. "I can't say about Jolly. As fuzzy as he is now—I mean, how could you tell? But I don't know Martha at all."

"Kinda funny, considering she and Jolly were contemporaries," I suggested.

"Yeah, but remember, she was at Hargrove and Regency, and Jolly was with MGM for most of them old studio days."

That would explain why they may not have worked together, not why they were unacquainted.

A smirk split Benny's skinny face. "At least, that's what Martha figured when we laughed about it last week."

Huh?

"Oh, that's what you meant when you asked if I knew her." Benny smacked his hand so hard against his head, the freckles changed shape. "I ran into her here last week. You know what I mean? And I'm like, 'Martha, we're both eating alone. Why not, you know, get together?' And we was just saying how her path and Jolly's had never crossed."

This guy was clearly a product of the California school system. Given my own years in it, it was a wonder I could think at all.

One of Benny's tiny phones buzzed. He didn't bother to answer it, he just raised his pudgy hand to signal the waitress.

The semi-naked server pressed against his chair. "Another round, Mr. Marsh?"

"Nah, sweetheart, just gimme the check."

"Benny, so soon?" I had to keep him talking about Mother.

The waitress deposited the check on the marble table, leaning so low that she gave Benny a shot of breasts round enough to put grapefruits to shame.

"What can I say, Trace? Time is money. I just wanted to make sure you were okay," Benny said.

Couldn't he have done that by phone? Why had he called this meeting, only to cut it short?

Benny grabbed the check. What do you know? Maybe time really was money, since Benny seemed short on both. Apparently, The Phoenix didn't carry anything in those side pockets apart from cigarettes and lots of change, though not enough to cover a few drinks in a clip joint like this. Just because he carried no bills or credit cards, it didn't mean he was broke. Lots of pikers get out of paying that way. But I was betting he was strapped. He wasn't sticking me with the bill, either; Drew would tack it onto his legal charges. I put the gouging check on my credit card and left the bimbo waitress a big tip to nick Benny for more. At least someone was happy.

Benny thrust his meaty paw at me, taking a moment to

tug up the sleeve of his knit shirt to intentionally flash me a look at his Rolex. I took hold of his sweaty hand and held on to it.

"Before you go, Benny, would you tell me whatever else you and Mother discussed?"

"How come?" he asked.

His critical faculties had to kick in *now?* "Who can say what's important?"

A nasty glint mushroomed in Benny's muddy brown eyes. I knew he hadn't forgotten our lewd encounter in the closet after all. He pulled me closer till our faces were only inches apart.

"We talked about you, cupcake," Benny said.

"Me?"

"Yeah. Martha begged me to option one of your potboilers. She said your pathetic little career needed a goose, you know? But I told her The Phoenix—he's a blockbuster man."

Benny was unprepared for my reaction. I burst out laughing. "Thanks, Benny, I needed a good one."

Benny tossed my hand away and said with gale force bluster, "I meant it."

"That's what makes it so good." I convulsed with such laughter, tears sprouted from my eyes. "If you want to be insulting, Benny, you have to get it right. Mother would *never* say that." She wouldn't even think it; she viewed me as an extension of herself, and she didn't do anything small-time.

Benny's head-freckles darkened till they looked ready to combust. The more angry he became, the more he cracked me up. I gave a thought to Drew's employment, and then the awful state of mine. But life's too short to bow to petty tyrants.

"Man, you nay-sayers piss me off. When my next book, *Deadly Shadows,* hits the top of the bestseller list, you'll all be begging for a piece of it." It would hit the top, too,

I decided—if I had to drag it there myself. Screw my publisher.

Halfway out of his chair, Benny stopped; he looked like an overstuffed boomerang. His voice dropped to a whisper. "*Deadly Shadows?* That's your new book? Is it under contract to anyone?"

Why be technical? By Wednesday, it wouldn't be. With a confident shrug, I said, "The bidding's open."

Benny produced a rigid smile that exposed all his capped teeth but never touched the wary look in his cheerless eyes. "Now *that* sounds like my kind of story." He pulled a soiled business card from somewhere and wiped it against his black knit shirt. "Promise you'll gimme first crack, you know what I mean?"

No, I didn't.

He paused just long enough to give my fingertips a hasty shake. "Tracy, it's been real."

*Sur*real, maybe. "Yeah, yeah. Love ya, babe. Mean it," I said in the local vernacular.

Benny stuffed the remainder of his possessions back into his pockets. But maybe not the pockets they started out in—everything clicked and rattled when he hurried past. I watched his rushed exit. Through the front window, I saw Benny plow into Drew, who was on his way up the front steps. He regrouped and waddled off in a flash, leaving an overwhelmed Drew to stare after him with a frown.

I studied Benny's dirty buff card, perplexed. How could he say that *Deadly Shadows* was "his kind of story" when I didn't tell him anything about it?

EIGHT

"Hard Knocks University," Regency Studios, 1952: Starring Martha Collins as Jane and Veronica Howard as Clara.

Jane, on her knees, tugs at Clara's skirt.

> ### JANE
> *How can you say you haven't hurt me? You stole my good name. You ruined me.*

> ### CLARA
> *Aw, quit yer cryin'. You're smarter, ain't ya? You know how the game is played.*

BY NOW MY TRUCK should have been able to find its way home from that restaurant on its own, but once again distraction tanked my driving skills. It must have been apparent, too. Drew pulled over and waited for me each time I caught a light. It couldn't have been that he thought I'd lose my way.

He was already in the apartment while I dawdled down the hall from the elevator, thinking of ways to make Benny talk. I stopped short when I noticed that the door to our condo stood open, and I remembered the state it had been left in.

I ran through the door, expecting to find Drew clutching his chest. Instead, he clutched something else. A snarling beast had pinned him to the wall, threatening the body part men hold most dear. Randy had gone home, and so had his mother and her stand-in. Philly was gone, along with Lorenzo. But Lorenzo had left his dog.

"Wha—what's that?" Drew stammered.

"That's Lorenzo's dog. Meet Johnny O'Toole."

"O'Toole? Sure it isn't Johnny Bignose? That thing sticking out the front is large enough to have its own zip code."

"Pretty nasty stuff for a guy about to sing soprano." I slipped to the floor next to the dog and patted his sticky black fur. "It's okay, fella. See, he's a friend." I rubbed Drew's leg as I said it. To my surprise, his muscles stiffened under my touch, and my bite wasn't nearly as bad as the dog's.

The pup lost interest in the fight. He turned away from Drew and busied himself slapping sloppy wet ones on my face.

Drew didn't budge, but he beamed at us. "Tracy, that dog's in love."

"With me? Bite your tongue."

"I get the feeling yours is the one about to be bitten." Ewwww!

"Did you adopt him, too?" Drew asked.

"I told you, Drew, he's Lorenzo's dog. That's Philly's friend."

"I thought that was just an expression," he said.

Drew flashed a sheepish grin that clashed with the sad, probing look in his dark eyes. His attitude made less sense than usual. But what didn't today?

He finally noticed the room. After a series of apoplectic grunts, he turned back to me with rigid dignity, saying, "You do realize that if a disaster strikes—a natural disaster, not the one we have here—we'll never find my emergency supplies. Is the rope ladder still under the bed? Have you forgotten my evacuation plan? If we're struck by an earthquake, fire or flood—"

"We're on the third floor, Drew. If a flood hits, my evacuation plan is to ride the wave out the window. California girls rule!" Jeez, I was starting to sound like Benny.

"Should I ask what happened here?"

"Nooo!" I insisted with a groan. "Let's just end this day before it kills us. But first find one of those emergency boxes and dig out some rope. You need to take the mutt for a walk."

"Why *should* I? He's *Lorenzo's* dog," Drew protested.

That did sound like an expression. "'Cuz if he leaves it here, it will be our poop."

Drew saw the logic, but he found another solution to the problem. He took one of his belts from the hanger Philly had hooked to the top of the walnut wall unit. The mutt offered him a doggie smile when Drew formed a loop and passed it over his head. I thought the belt made a pretty short lead, but it wasn't going to be my nose that close to the operation.

As they made their way to the door, I shouted route instructions for the leisurely walk the dog deserved. The instant the door clicked shut, I rushed to the phone in my study. I punched the speed-dial for my parents' number. After suffering through five droning rings, the machine clicked on, and my dad's cheerful drawl encouraged me to leave a message.

"Where the hell are you?" I demanded of the message. Once it beeped, I shouted, "Pick up, Yolanda. *Please,* pick up."

A sulky voice with a sing-song Mexican accent came onto the line with, "Grainger res'dence."

I didn't have time for Yolanda's games—Drew could return at any moment. "Yolanda, tell me Mother came home."

"Nope. And if Miz Martha thinks I'm delayin' my vacation—"

"Enough with the vacation. Start it Wednesday exactly as you planned. I'll pay you for the extra four days. But till then, you have to let me know the instant she returns."

Yolanda went silent for a moment. "I hear bus'ness class is real nice on the flight to Acapulco."

When did I stop being in charge of my life? "Business class it is." Who needed money, anyway? Go nuts enough, and the state'll pick up life's tab; I was halfway there. "*If* we have a deal."

I heard the front door click open—so much for my route suggestions. I concluded my negotiations quicker than I'd planned.

A little breathless still, I said, "That was fast."

"Well, he's a smart boy, this Johnny." The way Drew beamed at that dog, you'd think the mutt was his only friend. "You know, it wouldn't be so bad having him around. Maybe Lorenzo would—"

"Does the name Harriet Houdini mean nothing to you?"

"Harri's still our cat. She just prefers living with your parents. Martha would never let this mound of fur—" Drew's eyes went wide. "Your mother. Where is your mother?"

Jeez, that took long enough. "Relax, Drew, I sent her home." And I thought I was having a bad day.

"Alone?" he demanded.

"Um…Philly went with her." And if he returned before I had a chance to brief him, I was screwed. Where was he, anyway?

"How?" Drew demanded. "The police impounded her car, and Philly doesn't have one."

"Valleywide Taxi did the honors today." I always like it when I can sprinkle in a bit of the truth—makes me feel so virtuous. "Drew, did you expect her to stay here? Look at this place. There isn't room for Philly now."

He muttered something about silver linings. I tried to

make him go out for pizza or Chinese food. I needed more time alone—Mother was sure to call. Drew had to be the last man on Earth to accept the idea that food tastes best when someone brings it to you. Tonight he insisted on having it delivered. Then he paced before the door till our order came. Did he think I was going to make my escape from this loony bin?

But not even Mandarian Palace's Tsing Tao Beef raised Drew's spirits. His mood was so bleak, you'd have thought it was *his* mother on the lam. As if that could happen. While Drew absently tapped his chopsticks against the bottom of a take-out container, the dog left more of his hot, moist breath on my leg. An unexpected sauna. Since my husband seemed determined to avoid speech, I used the dog's tarry fur as an excuse to leave. I took the mangy mutt to the guest bathroom for a scrub, but not before I snatched the cordless phone.

I threw my arms around the mountain of fur to lift him into the tub, but when I felt the weight of it, I knew his fur would never dry. No wonder he was always panting. I remembered the trimmer Drew had bought when he decided to grow a beard. Since the beard didn't last thirty-six hours, the trimmer had never been used. Lorenzo might kill me for shearing the pathetic beast, but the world deserved to see such soulful eyes. Not that this mutt was getting to me or anything.

He stood perfectly still while I cut through his tangled mane. The trimmer blade gave out as I shaved his aft end, so I switched to a pair of scissors. It might have been a little choppy over his butt, but he didn't complain. Relieved of that punitive blanket, the pup pranced around the bathroom, his warm brandy eyes glowing.

While I ran the bath water, I placed another call to Mother's house. Yolanda had replaced Dad's outgoing message with one of her own. "Still not here, Tracy. Bus'ness class."

Business class, my eye, if that's what she considered keeping me informed. Where could Mother be? I risked another call to Biggie's Billiards, Philly's hangout, but Biggie said Philly wasn't there. Was he out looking for her? Or just avoiding me?

The dog was no water rat, but he endured the bath stoically enough. Eau du Wet Dog filled the room. I lifted him from the filthy water and gave him a vigorous rub with a towel. Goop as gooey as tar clung to the sides of the drained tub. I reached for some disinfectant cleanser, till I remembered Philly used this bathtub. Let him deal with it.

Without the heavy length pulling it down, the pup's fur curled. My styling wasn't bad at all; he looked like an oversized Benji. He pranced to the bedroom, where Drew slouched on the bed, scowling at the TV.

Drew's face lit up at the sight of him. "Tracy, he's gorgeous! What a great job—" The words ceased when he looked at me. Instantly, something dampened his excitement and his mood changed as though another personality had taken over. No fair—I had dibs on the nut house.

Fed up with everything, I announced I was going to bed. I found a blanket on a stack in the living room and spread it on the kitchen floor for the dog. What I couldn't find was the T-shirt I usually slept in. I stole Drew's white polo and finally shed the grimy dress I'd worn all day. I noticed the stressball I'd taken from Sperry's house was still in my pocket. Drew had never noticed my hip goiter. Something told me the honeymoon was dead and buried.

But once the lights were out, Drew threw his arm over my body. Just as I was drifting off, he muttered, "Babe, do you ever think we're too different?"

Talk about putting the kibosh on sleep. Too different for what? Life? Love? He fell asleep within minutes of dropping that bomb. The mutt jumped on the bed right after.

Despite two warm bodies close by, mine still felt cold and alone.

Sometime after three, I gave up on sleep. I slipped from under Drew's arm, which hadn't moved all night. So he feared we were too different, huh? When he found I'd lied about sending Mother home, he'd be sure of it. It was crazy to think I might find her at this hour. I had no idea where else to look except that abandoned warehouse. But I had to try.

Not wanting to risk rummaging around in the piles, I put on that rust dress over yesterday's pantyhose. Yuck! I felt my way to the study and grabbed my purse, then inched back for the heels I'd also worn yesterday, even though my feet were starting to stiffen into the standing position. Then I slipped from the condo without raising a stir.

DURING THE DRIVE to the Kenney Avenue warehouse, the unabashed curiosity of the woman from the awning plant came back to me. What was it about the place that hooked her attention? If it were truly abandoned, it seemed unlikely that it would hold her interest. Though my shoes already pinched my toes, I parked a couple of blocks away and approached on foot.

At the mouth of the warehouse turn-in, I stepped onto the grassy roadside strip, hoping to go unnoticed. To my surprise, motion-sensitive floodlights lit up the night when I passed into their range. All that wattage gave me a bad feeling. But why was I worried? Mother couldn't be there. She must have checked into a hotel to make it harder for the police—and me—to find her.

I had to be sure. I pressed my ear to door. Even at that hour, there was too much ambient noise to zero in on anything inside.

I heard some sound behind me—a step and a rattle. I

started to turn when something heavy came down on my head. In my mind, I heard the opening bars of ''The Night the Lights Went Out in Georgia'' before darkness overtook my universe.

NINE

"Truth-Seeker," Regency Studios, 1953: Starring Martha Collins as Erika and Carl Langford as Jim.

A couple hover in the shadow of the Berlin Wall.

JIM
You can't go in there. You have a daughter now to think about.

ERIKA
If I don't make it out, tell my daughter I died fighting for what's true and right.

I AWOKE TO THE SOUND of someone's groan. A splash of water hit the back of my head, sending drops scurrying down my scalp like a stampede of baby spiders. By the time the water reached where my face was pressed against cold concrete, I achieved enough consciousness to realize that the person groaning was me. All the pain in the world had been stored at the back of my head. Slowly, I rolled onto my back. But the white light streaming into my eyes from straight above spiked my agonizing headache into the stratosphere. Someone pulled me into a sitting position.

Not just any old someone. The old bane of my existence. Mother.

"Tracy, my poor, precious child." She held up two fingers. "Speak to me, darling. How many fingers do you see?"

Anger alone gave me the nerve to flip her one very special finger of my own. "You tell me."

She released my arm, causing me to fall back against something hard. A lump of cold metal dug into my back, but it was beyond my ability to adjust away from its bite.

Mother sighed. "What did I do to deserve you?"

What indeed?

I took a look at where she had landed us. It was a strange little room with pink insulation stapled to the walls and ceilings, even on the knobless door. The only spots that escaped being insulated were the ceiling skylight and whatever hard surface held up my poor body. A homemade storage chest, padlocked shut, I discovered when I found the strength to sit up. I always said my mother should be in a padded cell, but for me to end up there *with* her defeated the whole fantasy.

What the accommodations lacked in atmosphere, they made up for with privation. The floor was cold and dirty. On a piece of cardboard was a slice of dry white bread and a few packets of American cheese. Even in my dazed state, images of us overtaking our jailer during the next meal delivery floated into my mind. Then I noticed the hinged flap at the bottom of the door; they probably shoved food through there.

Okay, so we wouldn't jump the Wonder Bread man. But the hinges were fairly high—maybe ten or eleven inches off the floor. They'd have to be to accommodate the galvanized bucket that Mother had discretely pushed to the farthest corner of the tiny room. Maybe we could slip under. I crawled to the door and gave it a tug, but the little flap was locked.

The last thing I remembered was arriving at that warehouse. I assumed I was still there; that building had a skylight like the one above me. But I couldn't hear any airport or street sounds. Why would anyone have built this strange, insulated room?

I listened at the door. There were sounds out there, but they were so hushed that they didn't rise to the level of whispers. I couldn't even tell what produced them. Was the whole place padded? If we were still near the airport, it had to be padded and then some. For the first time, fear overrode my pain.

Mother's face crumpled in despair without regard to the wrinkles forming between her brows. "Darling, I can't bear to see you looking like this."

I had to hide the fear, be brave for both of us. She could never handle what I was thinking.

Mother rushed on with the true cause of her dismay. "Didn't I teach you not to wear the same dress two days in a row?"

Nothing like having priorities.

She grabbed a green bottle that looked like an old Gallo Wine jug. Now we were talking. Mother pulled a lace handkerchief from a tiny pocket on her suit jacket. Her suit was also on its second day, even if it did look fresher than the Wonder Bread. She tipped the bottle, sloshing its contents on the floor. Water, wouldn't you know? She scrubbed my face with the dainty wet hanky.

"Mother, don't waste that water on me."

"What better use could I possibly make of it, darling?"

As foolhardy as it was, I found the remark touching.

Then she clarified, "Tracy, it's *tap* water, not bottled."

Won't someone tell me who my real mother is?

AFTER MY BATH, I found my purse, which our captors had been nice enough to toss in with me. As I pawed through it in search of something that would help us escape, I said, "Okay, Mother, let's hear how you ended up *here*."

I found enough bookmarks to paper the walls of that dreary little room, as well as sufficient pens to sign all the books I wouldn't be publishing.

"I don't think I'm going to do any more visitations,"

Mother said with a martyred sigh. "They're not working out well."

"No. Just because they led you to a dead guy and your own abduction?" I snorted. "Get off it, Mother. There is no such charity."

Yes! The bottle of Tylenol was still here. I put three on my tongue and took a swig from the Gallo bottle. Yuck! They hadn't rinsed it first.

"Is too," she said.

"Is not." I told her about seeing my picture in Sperry's house.

She shrugged indifferently. "So he had your picture. How many dry cleaners and restaurants have mine? Just because they put my photo on their walls, does that mean I know them?"

They left my wallet in the purse with enough credit cards to charge my way through anything—except the door that kept us there. Someone had lifted all my cash, however, though that might have been Philly; he tended to regard my wallet as his ATM.

"So you never met Sperry before you dropped in on him that morning?"

"Well…that's not…completely true."

Finally.

"It was so ghastly, finding him like that. Later I realized we had met, though not for ages. He wasn't a friend, Tracy, just someone who tried to muscle into my crowd. That's why his name never meant anything to me when Drew talked about him. You can't expect me to remember someone like that years later, can you?"

Of course not. She met so many people, I'd buy her story in a flash—if I weren't certain everything she said about Sperry was a big fat crock. Why would a casual acquaintance from decades past have written to her in such an insinuating way?

"And what about this place?" I asked.

She bit her lower lip in an embarrassed grimace. "I might have transposed the address and stumbled into something here."

I didn't buy that, either. Though she did transpose numbers occasionally. On the off-chance that part of the story was true, it would mean that no potential rescuer would have any reason to look for us here. I reached into my purse with renewed determination.

"Look. They left my keys." I jingled the key ring.

"If we can't reach your door, what good are they?" she asked.

"Don't dismiss 'em so fast." There were more keys on that ring than doors in my world. I've had a fascination with keys all my life. Not even my initiation at age two, when I stuck a key in an electrical socket and sailed backward across the room on my fanny, had put me off. Once I had discovered keys sometimes opened locks other than the ones for which they were intended, I began my collection in earnest. Three tiny brass beauties jumped out at me now.

Turning back to the padlock on the storage cabinet, I studied the shape of the keyhole. It seemed to match my trustiest small key, which came through for me again when it slipped right into the padlock. Crunch time; I paused before turning it.

"Pray for guns," I said.

"Tracy, there's something—" She stopped, weighing her words, then rushed on. "—something I haven't told you."

The tension in her voice made my shoulders contract.

"I tried to visit Sperry one other time, the night before...you know."

The night before he was shot? Jeez, she really wasn't alibied. "You were in there when—"

"No, darling. I didn't stop. I saw someone approaching his door and just drove past."

I grasped her hands in mine, pleading, "Mother, don't you see what that means? You saw the killer. Can you describe him?"

Her long scarlet nails dug into my fingers. "You don't want me to." She hesitated. "Darling, Sperry's guest...it was Drew."

TEN

"Back Street Gal," Regency Studios, 1954: Starring Martha Collins as Belle and Jake Crandall as Marshall McGraw.

In the Old West, a lawman and a dance hall girl talk in a saloon.

MARSHALL
Jimmy's pa said he was working on the ranch. How could he have robbed the stage?

BELLE
You just can't accept the truth, Marshall. Not when you hear it from a dance hall girl.

I FELL AGAINST the storage bin. "What are you saying? That Drew...? No! It was a meeting, okay? Maybe a settlement offer."

"Without Sperry's lawyer, darling? Is that kosher?" Mother sat against the opposite wall.

"Sperry's attorney was just late. Come on, you know Drew is too much the Boy Scout to—"

She kept shaking her head. "I doubled back. No one else came." Reaching across, she patted my hand and said, "Don't judge him too harshly, Tracy. He was under pressure to win that case."

I flung her hand away. "Don't judge—"

While making a minute adjustment to her hose, she said,

"I blame SCREWED for it." That was her name for Slaughter, Cohen, Rather, Word & Dragger, Drew's firm. "They don't have to work young junior partners that hard. That last hotshot they added to the firm's name must be responsible." She gave her shoulders a lazy flex. "I remember when it was just SCREW, and you have to admit that good advice beats a bad description every time."

Maternal wisdom to be treasured forever.

Leaping across the space between us, I grasped her slender arms. "Mother, what is it you think Drew did? That when he couldn't make a deal with Sperry, he—killed him? Drew is too upright to be a killer. Too uptight, too."

She gave my cheek a comforting pat. "That's the type that snaps, Tracy. Admit it—he's not as free as you and me."

Who was?

I turned away and applied myself to the key that was still poised in the padlock. I remembered how Drew had acted last night, clingy but distant. Ashamed? Guilty? What a nightmare. When the key turned in the lock, I was so lost in my troubling thoughts, I scarcely noticed. I removed the padlock and lifted the plywood lid. The bin wasn't even filled with guns, just bales of heavy-duty rope. Useless rope.

Mother crawled over and peered into it. "Now I'm sorry I refused to let you climb ropes in gym when you were little. I didn't think it was suitable for a girl to do."

I felt a smile tugging at my lips. "Now I'm glad I forged your signature."

FIFTEEN MINUTES of trying to lasso the skylight hardware—and all Mother accomplished was knocking over the Gallo water bottle.

"Why did I listen to you?" I snapped. "How would you learn to lasso?"

The heavy rope narrowly missed tumbling onto her

head. "Don't you sass me, miss," she said in a tremulous voice. "You're not too big to hit."

Yeah, yeah. She had never hit me. Many people insisted they could have guessed that.

"I'm a little out of practice, but I can do it. I told you, Tracy, I learned it during one of those Westerns I did."

"How? You never played the plucky little cowgirl— you were always the town tart."

I tapped my fist in frustration against a stud on one wall of the tiny room. It startled me when a soft sound came back. An echo in an empty warehouse or was someone there?

She gave her arms a shake. "That just demonstrates the difference between life and art, baby. The sweeter they were on the screen, the more likely those girls were to spend their breaks flat on their backs, studying the top of the prop truck through their ankles. I made the stuntmen teach me to rope."

Mother squared her jaw and widened her stance. She tossed the rope with so much vigor, she grunted.

This time, the lasso hooked.

She never ceased to amaze me.

NOW WE JUST NEEDED to agree on how to make use of it. We stood in the middle of that little room, glaring at each other.

"Wait," I said. "You expect me to do—what?"

"To carry me out of here piggyback. What did you think? Really, Tracy—this experience has shattered me."

Shattered *her?* I missed a night's sleep worrying about her, and three Tylenol barely dulled the pain that was *exploding* in my head. We didn't even know if the skylight would open—*if* we could make it up there.

"Mother, can't you see I'm wasted?"

Mother's eyes drifted to the Gallo bottle. "Darling, it really is just water."

Why do I bother? "Oh, for chrissakes!" At least I made her carry my purse.

Once we worked out the travel arrangements, we addressed the timing. Mother seemed to think our captors weren't always there.

"It might be better to wait till the next time they leave," I suggested.

"What if they come for us?"

"Right. Seize the moment, that's what I always say."

"Me, too," Mother agreed.

The commonalties some mothers and daughters share must make them feel closer; ours just weirded me out.

We climbed onto the storage bin. I had to be even rustier at rope climbing than she was with a lasso—I was maybe all of fourteen the last time I tried. The coarse rope fibers itched against my sissy palms. Focusing on the only positive I could see in failure, I decided when I slipped down the rope and burned my hands, *that* would take my mind off my headache.

Sourly, I said, "Let's do it."

I dipped my knees so Mother could wrap her arms around my shoulders. Once she was in place, I reached up the rope and pulled till my feet lifted off the storage locker.

"Ooh!" I grunted.

Nearly lost it there. Suspending the weight of my own body would have been bad enough, but two bodies? Talk about a monkey on your back. Someone once described Mother as ethereal—but let me tell you, that woman packed the weight in somewhere. But it was more than my life was worth to say that.

Instead, I muttered through clenched teeth, "I haven't had this much fun since the last time I was on bivouacs."

What can I say? Terror comes out in me as sarcasm. Terror, joy—whatever; I've got a smart mouth. But now I really was too afraid to budge. Finally, I risked removing my bottom hand. When we didn't crash to the floor, I lifted it over my death-grip hand.

"Quit your complaining, young lady. Do you know how long I was in labor with you?"

That terror-sarcasm connection was obviously a family trait. "Less than five minutes," I countered.

The story of my birth was a closely guarded secret— known only to the immediate world. Frustrated by three bouts of false labor, Mother picked a fight with Dad, sending him off in a huff. Once he left, the real thing got underway. Apparently, it didn't occur to her to call for help. She just hopped in the car and took off on her own. When the first bad contraction hit, she lost control of the wheel. I arrived on the steps of the church she crashed into.

Contrary to rumors, it wasn't St. Tracy's. There is no St. Tracy's in Beverly Hills. And wouldn't that be a silly basis for naming a child? The real story is more subtle. You might remember that Veronica Howard and Mother were great rivals at the time. But you might not know that Miss Howard's much younger third husband was having a torrid affair with a mere child named Tracy West. Clearly, a better way to choose a baby's name; I'm glad I was able to provide my mother with that opportunity.

I kept inching up the rope. Once we passed the halfway point, I would have breathed a sigh of relief were I not close to hyperventilation. My arms shook like saplings in a hurricane. But I knew that if I could hang on this long, I could make it all the way to the skylight. The wiggle I felt in the rope told me the hardware wasn't locked. I figured we were out of the woods.

When would I learn?

At the sound of a bolt being thrown—my racing heart stopped dead. Jeez, were they coming in? Would they find us like that?

But the bolt I heard proved to be the one on the flap at

the bottom of the door. Someone pulled it open and shoved in another cardboard tray. Despite the increased occupancy of that room, they hadn't included a bit more food. Cheap bastards.

I ceased my climb while the flap remained open. But I expected it to close when the food came through. No dice. A man's hand, covered in gang tattoos, extended past the flap. He flipped his fingers back twice in a gesture that said, *come on,* and seemed to imply he wanted us to give him something. *What?*

Mother appeared to know. She stretched her leg toward the floor. At the expense of my throat—her arms pulled across my windpipe! I heard the sound of the slop bucket scraping against the rough concrete as she nudged it toward the door with her toe.

To keep my mind off asphyxiation, I tried to identify the sounds coming through the flap. I heard a set of shoes tapping against the floor somewhere, but they didn't echo as loudly as I expected. There were other noises, too. One sounded similar to choral singing, only faint, and I couldn't pick out any words. It was like a group murmur or the ringing voice they might assign an alien character on a science fiction show. Aliens, right. I was getting light-headed. Probably just a whistling breeze.

About the time I flirted with my second blackout of the day, the metal bucket reached its destination. The hand took it away, then pushed it back. Another moment, and the bolt slid home.

"Mother, please," I gasped in a helium voice. "You've got to take the pressure off my throat. I'm strangling."

"You, Tracy? I just saved your life. Why is it always about you?"

Yeah, I hate it when I do that.

WE MADE IT. Who would have thought? Once we crawled through the open skylight, I had nothing left. I stretched out on the roof, trying to slow my heaving lungs. The morning sky was still pale. What time was it? I propped myself up on my elbows and stared off in the distance. Some of the businesses in the area were open, but not all. It probably wasn't any later than seven-thirty or eight. But the ladies and gentlemen of the night had already gathered for the dayshift.

I thought staying on the roof till our keepers left to be the safest course, but Mother had other ideas.

"Tracy...?"

"Yeah?"

"I have to use the bucket."

It took a moment for me to follow that one. "If you want to go back for it, Mother, you're on your own."

"I'll hold out for something more suitable. But we'd better get going or there won't be any point to it, if you get my drift."

Keeping an eye peeled for the Wonder Bread man, I hung the rope over the side of the building. We lowered ourselves to the ground. Single-file this time. No way was she going down on my back, too. Green grass grew below us—it wouldn't kill her to fall.

Showed what I knew—it practically did. No, she didn't break any bones. She just wouldn't leave till she brushed the specks of dirt from her royal Chanel suit. While she was bent over, examining her skirt, a man came strolling around the corner of the building. I didn't know who was more startled, him or me.

Me, definitely. He had the wits to pull a gun from his underarm holster. Mother saw him—and froze in his sights. I looked to the ground for something to throw. Nothing. I noticed the stressball I'd taken from Sperry's house, still bulging from my hip pocket.

I hurled it at the gun. It missed but plowed into his eye, making the guy reel back. The gun went off.

I grabbed Mother's hand. "Run!"

Behind us, the man slid the noisy warehouse door open and shouted something in Spanish. Three sets of pounding footsteps came after us. We ran down the Kenney Avenue extension and took a left at the end.

Fortunately, I'd driven every inch of that area the day before. Though it seemed bigger on foot. Running in heels and skirts might look cute in old movies, but don't try it in real life. I thought about removing my shoes, but I knew Mother wouldn't hear of it, and we'd argue the point—literally—to death.

I remembered where I stopped yesterday to check my map, when the boy hooker tapped my window. There had been a small space between one building and the next, where someone had piled trash. At the corner, I stopped to focus. The popping sound of a silenced weapon went off somewhere behind us. Before I could react, a bullet just missed me.

"Man, that sucker whizzed right past my ear!" I gasped.

In a tight voice, Mother asked, "Did you have to say *whizzed?*"

The hiding place would only work if we reached it before our pursuers saw us. I yanked Mother into traffic. Cars screeched to a halt, but we picked up seconds. We slipped into the space, pulling a large garbage can behind us to block the entrance.

The commotion we caused in traffic told our pursuers too much about our escape route, however. They stopped at the corner, looking off in every direction, and gestured with great agitation. I wished I could have focused instead on a building that was open, rather than a vacant one. It wouldn't take them long to discover the only place we could be hiding.

I left Mother to keep watch and ran the depth of the space. It ended in a brick wall. "No dice," I muttered on my return.

"What we need is an escort," Mother said. "I don't

suppose you have a phone in that suitcase you made me carry?"

Nope. I'd left it in the truck—in its uncharged state, the only place it worked. It wasn't like *she'd* shown great foresight, either—or we wouldn't be in this mess.

"Escort…?" I mused aloud. "…no hookers."

"Darling, is that in code?"

I explained to Mother the area was swarming with working folks the day before. "I saw them gearing up for the day when we were still on the roof. Now they're gone." I remembered thinking the area was ripe for a police sweep. I stared off in the distance. "Look at the intersection. There's a black-and-white stopped at the light."

Mother sounded less than thrilled. "A police car, Tracy? What are you going to tell them?"

Good point. How could I explain why we were being pursued?

Mother snapped her fingers. "I know. We'll get you arrested."

"Excuse me?"

She cast a critical eye at my dress. "Too conservative for our purposes. Well, really, for any purpose. Tracy, what were you thinking?" She knelt at my side and examined the inside seam. "A slit will do the trick."

"Wait! Do you know what I paid for this dress?"

"They sure don't make 'em like they used to," she said with a cavalier grin. With one swift move, she tore the dress up to my hip. "Now go out there, baby, and show me what you can do."

My own mother was sending me out as hooker bait. Aghast, I demanded, "Why me? You're the actress."

"Tracy, really. I'm—well, I have a few years on you."

I finally get her to make that admission—and it backfires on me. As the patrol car cruised through the intersection, I timed my approach. Too fast, and the bad guys were gonna pop one off before the cops ever saw me; too slow, and the paddy wagon would roll past before I reached the curb. The decision was made when Mother inched the protective garbage can aside and shoved me out.

"Work it, baby, work it," she muttered.

Do other mothers say stuff like that? What the hell. If I died, it might as well be with style. I swayed my hips to the runway beat that drifted through my mind. I posed at the curb with my leg peaking from my new slit.

The black-and-white rolled to a stop before me. But the cops didn't even step from the car; the chubbier officer in the passenger seat just lowered the window. Maybe there was something about my demeanor that said I was not the kind of girl who stands on the corner waiting for any guy with an itchy bill in his wallet. Then again, maybe it was my approach.

I leaned into the car. "Let's cut to the chase, boys. I'll do you both for twenty bucks."

Despite the masks cops wear, the chubby one shared a look with his younger, fitter companion behind the wheel. "Honey, you seen the paint job on this car?"

I treated the statement literally, turning my head as if to inspect it, when I really wanted to peek at our pursuers.

The two guys gathered at the next building tried looking unobtrusive, but they wouldn't walk away. I threw a glance the other way. The third man busied himself reading a sign, but he was holding firm, too.

Mother felt safe enough to come up behind me now. Can you blame me from extracting a little revenge against her?

"Yeah, that paint job's first-rate. Tell you what, I'll throw in my mother for thirty."

"Now they're bringing their mothers," the cop muttered.

But I'd pushed them too far to look away, even if they didn't know what to make of my solicitation. They stuffed us into the black vinyl back seat of the patrol car; it reeked of Big Mac Special Sauce and something that belonged in a bucket, not a car. One officer did a double-take when he glanced at Mother in the rearview mirror. But he just gave his head a shake, as if to dispel the thought.

I stifled a sigh when the patrol car pulled off. As good as it felt to be out of that frying pan, I sensed the flames were going to be too hot to handle before we knew it.

And, once again, it was up to me—alone—to save us both.

ELEVEN

"Treachery," Regency Studios, 1955: Starring Martha Collins as Kathy and Dean Parrish as Brett.

A rough longshoreman stops a wholesome girl from entering a seedy dockside hangout.

> ### BRETT
> *You crazy, naïve kid. When are you going to learn you can't trust anyone?*
>
> ### KATHY
> *Not even you, Brett?*
>
> ### BRETT
> *Especially not me.*

OUR SAVIORS, Dave and Leon, the cops who picked us up for prostitution, dropped us off close to my truck.

"Great looking truck, Tracy," Dave, the chubby one, said. "I can't agree with you there, Martha. That's one fine set of wheels."

"Maybe so, David, but surely you can see it's not easy for an older woman like me to climb into it," Mother said.

"I don't see any older women back there, do you, Leon?"

Leon agreed. There was so much love in that patrol car, I wanted to gag. When the car stopped, Dave jumped from the passenger seat and helped us out.

"Now remember, ladies, next time you try out a part, let us know ahead of time," Dave warned, "and there won't be any misunderstanding—"

"Understood, boys," Mother trilled. "Thanks awfully for being such a help."

"Yeah, thanks," I echoed acidly.

I climbed behind the wheel of my truck. Mother stood at the curb waving till the police car was out of sight. She didn't want them to see how easily she could scale the front seat.

I cranked the ignition. "Are you coming?" I growled.

Mother climbed into the truck and with a sigh, propped her feet on the dash. "You know, Tracy, I was thinking—"

"Excuse me, I'm not talking to you."

"I *knew* you were mad." She chuckled to herself. "You prefer to think I create all the problems, while you do all the fixing. You can't admit that I can get us out of fixes, too."

Yeah? So why did I carry her up a rope?

"What did you expect me to do?" she asked. "I couldn't allow myself to be associated with a prostitution charge."

But murder was okay.

"And I have a bone to pick with you, young lady. Where do you get off suggesting I could be had for thirty dollars?"

I meant they could have us *both* for thirty.

"I'll have you know that once in fifty-two, a man offered me one hundred thousand dollars—and that was a fortune in those days—for one hour alone with me."

If I had it, I'd pay someone ten times that to keep her an hour.

WHEN WE RETURNED to the condo, Philly rushed from the kitchen to greet us, drying his hands on a dish towel. In his brown tweed suit, he made the third person in this household still wearing yesterday's clothes, though it was less unusual for him.

His forehead contracted into deep, anxious grooves. "Kid, where were you? Drew was frantic this morning when he realized you'd left. What were you doing?"

With my hands on my hips, I glared at Philly as if he were the source of my frustration. "What was I doing? I was *not* getting arrested for solicitation, I'll tell you that!"

"That's too too bad," Philly said, raising the inflection of his voice enough at the end to make it into a semi-question. His eyes traveled to the ragged slit Mother had torn in my dress. "Wearing that, too. What were they thinking?"

He looked over my shoulder to where Mother stood on the narrow path that wove through my possessions. "Morning, Martha," he said with downcast eyes.

In a voice cold enough to end global warming, Mother said, "How good it is, Phillip, depends on where you spent the night."

Holy freakin' Friendship Day. What happened between them?

Mother rubbed one of her hands against the other, a la Lady MacBeth. "I need a bath, Tracy. And then I'm going to sleep for a day." With less thought than usual about her dignity, she began climbing over a pile of my possessions.

That pile looked higher than it had last night, since big hunks of drywall and strips of insulation had been added to the top. Despite the evidence that more passages had been carved through our walls, I didn't hear the sounds of repairs being made, or even any more damage.

"Philly, where's Randy?"

"He went to another job that started early. He said he'll call you."

Or maybe some village out there in search of its idiot had found him. I wasn't surprised. Contractors must have

to turn in their hammers if they don't disappear for a while
after tearing your place apart.

Looking at the bright side, I said, "At least that means
I don't have to deal with his nutty—"

Philly made a frantic gesture toward the bedroom. "Angelique stopped by, and she's still here, taking a nap."

Mother groaned. "Wake her up, will you, Tracy? Tell
her I need some rest. Angelique will understand."

Who wouldn't understand being awaked from a sound
sleep so someone else could use the bed? I'd feel outrage
on Angelique's behalf—if that bed had belonged to either
of them.

"Mother, the woman is disabled. I can't ask—"

"Don't matter anyway," Philly said. "Martha, Drew
called. Schuller has more questions for you. They're on
their way here."

Mother's muttered suggestion for Schuller sounded like
a physical impossibility.

"Philly, what made Drew think Mother was here?" I
asked.

"I…uh…told him you went to pick her up." He
shrugged. "I bought you gals a little time."

He'd sweated it out, too. I could tell from all the little
tufts that stuck out from his head; under stress, Philly always pawed through his coarse hair. I gave him a grateful
smile, but it didn't appear to lift his drooping spirits.

"Now I need that bath more than ever," Mother said,
still perched on the pile. "Schuller can wait."

If anyone needed to bathe, it was me. I longed to check
into a hotel, where I could spend a few days in one of
those fluffy white robes, living on room service and the
macadamia nuts in the minibar. The sound of doom short-
circuited all our escape plans. No, not that of Schuller's
arrival, but something far worse—the squeak of Angelique's oxygen tank.

"Marty!" She pulled Mother off the pile and into a bear hug.

"Delightful, Angelique," Mother muttered into her friend's robust chest.

Mother's simulated enthusiasm fell short of an award-winning performance, but Angelique didn't seem to notice.

Angelique grabbed a strip of pink insulation from the stack, and with a nod to me and a vigorous shake of the strip, she said, "So what do you think of these two getting together? Something, huh?" She drove the remark home with an elbow to my ribs.

When I realized the insulation was Randy's stand-in, I sent my mother a silent eyebrow appeal to clarify this situation.

Angelique rattled on, "Oh, Martha and I shared a lot of men in our time, hey, Marty?"

I could have lived without knowing that.

"Just wait, Angelique—I'll have another one for you soon," Mother muttered with a frigid glance at Philly.

Angelique appeared not to hear. "Yeah, Tracy, your mom always passed on her clothes and her men to me. The clothes never fit, but the men sure did."

That I *really* didn't need to know.

Angelique laughed so hard, I feared it would trigger a fatal coughing bout, but she recovered in time for another jaunt down Memory Lane. "She even gave me a job as her housekeeper one time. Can you imagine the two of us together all the time?"

Bet the fun never quit. Just like now.

Mother extended her hand and gave her old friend's ratty, pale hair a gentle stroke. "Great times, Angel."

Angelique lowered her head in a respectful nod. "I really want to thank you for getting this job for me, Marty."

What job had Mother obtained for *her?* It took a moment before I grasped she meant the work I gave to Randy. Angelique always talked as if she and Randy were one-in-

the-same. I'd make fun of the overgrown lout for still being so connected to his mommy—if I didn't believe, in
the privacy of her own mind, that was how my mother
thought of me.

"It's what we do, Angelique, you and me," Mother
said, proving my point. "Now how would you like it if
Tracy made you a nice whiskey sour? Then you can go
back to your nap?"

"Oh, could you, Tracy? That'd be swell, hon."

I pushed the bartender duties off on Philly with a jerk
of my head. He led the squeaky old bat to the kitchen but
dashed back a moment later.

"How am I gonna make a whiskey sour, when you
don't have the stuff?" he demanded.

"Just splash some orange juice in a big glass of
brandy," Mother said. "She'll never notice."

From the twinkle in his blue-green eyes, I gathered
Philly liked the idea so much that he planned to make a
pair of them.

"Mother, did you really turn your friend into your
housekeeper?" I asked.

She sighed. "I gave her a room and a salary, and I
provided a nurse to detox her. She was pregnant with
Randy at the time."

I hate it when I learn something that raises my low opinion of her. The ripple effect makes me question my whole
philosophy of life.

"And look at how he repaid you." I gestured to the
ruins of my home. "Was this the way he remodeled your
house?"

"No, but look at what he had to start with here."

She scaled the pile and headed down the hall toward the
guest bath. I remembered how filthy it was after the dog's
bath and tried to beat her to it, but I slipped on some
insulation. When I finally reached the bathroom, I found

her standing before the mirror, tiredly running her fingers through her soft, blonde hair.

"Yes, Tracy?" she demanded in a weary voice.

I glanced at the tub, looking for the grimy ring. But now it gleamed as brightly as the wall's shiny amber tiles. Someone had scrubbed it spotlessly clean. Sure wasn't Drew. No amount of guilt could have produced that.

What to say...? "Just wondering. Did Angelique ever take a man away from you?"

With no thought to the affect it would have on her skin, she brought her fair brows together in a furious frown. "What do you think?" She slammed the door in my face.

I went to the bedroom, where Angelique's impression remained in the downy surface of the pale blue blanket. Lorenzo's dog was stretched out nearby. His head popped up at the sight of me. He sure was a cute little cuss. But it was still a nuisance having him here. Lorenzo better pick him up soon, or I'd put the mutt out onto the street. No more pets for me. Since he was here now, I tapped my hand against my thigh to call him—in case he was lonely. I mean, I owed that to Lorenzo.

The pooch and I went to the kitchen. To my surprise, it was also as clean as a model home. The taupe countertops gleamed, the almond sink sparkled. Either I had acquired one of those serfs a certain Beverly Hills exchange provided—or my uncle-in-law was working off something big.

The odd thing was that the room was empty. I found Angelique alone in the laundry room off the kitchen, pointlessly shaking a box of soap, while sucking down a water glass full of some brownish-yellowish muck.

But Philly had vanished again.

BEFORE I HAD TIME to wonder where Philly had gone, I heard the sound of a key turning in the front door knob. Drew was home—with Schuller.

I reached the living room in time to see the door fly
open. Schuller pushed past Drew and strode into the room.
I was getting used to the debris now, but I'd expect any
first-timer to gape. Not Schuller. Though his feet never
strayed from the narrow path cut through our stuff, his eyes
zeroed in on me alone.

He looked like an elongated cantaloupe today. Every
item he wore matched the color of a perfectly ripe melon.
The polyester fabric even captured the fruit's knobby tex-
ture. Where did this guy shop?

His hands were still thrust deep in his pockets, where
he shook those ever-present coins to a furious beat. Un-
bidden, the strains of Bob Seger's ''Miami'' flooded my
mind. What a curious effect he had on me. Schuller's presence in our lives might mean a long stretch in the big
house for Mother, but he was like having my own juke
box.

Schuller marched into my personal space and spat into
my face, ''Something you forgot to tell me about your old
lady's production company?''

Shit. He discovered she didn't have one. I knew he
would eventually. How had he accomplished it so fast?

''All bets are off, cookie,'' he said. ''Now where is
she?''

''I'll get her.''

Before I did, I glanced at Drew. My heart contracted at
the sight of him. His skin had turned to oatmeal. Over-
night, twenty years of sorrow had collected in his face.

Oh, God! Schuller was right: All bets *were* off.

I dashed to the bathroom. I found Mother sitting on the
edge of the tub, still in her suit, and not looking like she'd
even combed her hair. I slipped into the room and pressed
the door closed behind me.

''Time?'' she asked.

I nodded. ''Schuller is livid. And Drew looks—bad.''

Mother rose to her full five-foot-two and tugged her

jacket down with military precision. "So—we protect him at all costs?"

"You gotta ask?"

She gave me a crisp nod, before turning to the mirror. "Tell the bastard I'll be along in a moment, Tracy. I want to fix my face."

Drew wasn't there when I returned to the living room. I heard the sound of the fridge opening in the kitchen. I didn't hear anything taken from it, or of it closing. When times are tough, I often find comfort staring into the refrigerator, too. Just before eating everything in it but the light bulb.

Schuller tried to pace but kept running out of room. "You people live like pigs," he threw over his shoulder.

That cinched it—we were leaving it like that.

His arms had been swinging freely, but he brought them home to his pockets, and "Miami" took up where it left off.

Jeez, I was getting a headache. Hadn't this clown ever heard of coin rollers?

My breath caught in my throat. Coins...? I had heard something rattle before I was knocked unconscious outside the warehouse. Now I realized it sounded like something striking against change in a pocket. Proving it was the song that floated into my mind before I blacked out.

Schuller...? I stole a glance at him, but found myself already fixed in his sights. His lips were pressed into a mean slit slashed across his face. The person who struck me must have looked out with that kind of hatred.

What do you know? I got it right when I interpreted the title of his stupid screenplay: The cop really did do it!

The miserable bastard who knocked me unconscious outside the warehouse—*was* Schuller.

TWELVE

"Thumbin' My Way," Regency Studios, 1956: Starring
Martha Collins as Janey and Henry Brown as Bill.

*A down-on-his-luck hitchhiker can't believe it when the
girl he left behind stops to pick him up.*

BILL
*I can't ask you to give me another chance, Janey, not
after letting you down.*

JANEY
*So don't ask, just get in. This journey we're taking
together isn't over yet.*

SCHULLER DECIDED he couldn't question Mother in that
messy space and took her back to the station. I hid my
shocking revelation till they left. Only then did I let my
jaw drop.

Holy crap! *Schuller* was the bad guy? What reason
would he have for killing Sperry? Had to be hired muscle
for Benny. *Donated* muscle. Benny still had the best motive for getting rid of Sperry, and Schuller would do anything to get into the biz—a marriage of mutual expedience,
the kind Hollywood likes best.

It all fit...only not exactly. Benny's motive stemmed
from Sperry's lawsuit. What was Mother's connection?
Benny must have framed her, but how? On an impulse, I
went to the study and booted up the computer. I clicked

onto the Internet to search for the link between Mother and Benny and Sperry.

Instant gridlock on the Information Superhighway. My search delivered just a fraction of the thousands of articles on each of them. Too many to determine whether any connected the three together. I stabbed the shutdown button.

God, I needed help. I sent a mental appeal to my dad in the hopes that somewhere, somehow he would know I needed him. With a sigh, I short-circuited the transmission. I might be a native Californian, but I wasn't that cosmic.

Much as I hated to upset the delicate order in my life, I couldn't bear wearing the torn dress a moment longer. Back in the living room, I overturned everything till I came across my jeans and sneakers. Were those jeans getting tight? Nah, must have shrunk in the wash.

Unable to find a T-shirt, I took Drew's green knit shirt off the stack. So the half-sleeves drooped past my elbows—it wasn't like nobody ever noticed I wasn't a fashion plate. I found an okay bra, but I couldn't locate any underpants other than an ancient cotton pair, as dingy and baggy as Drew's. They had to do. I stuffed my dress and tattered pantyhose into a black trash bag someone had left there. My life made less sense to me every day.

I drifted to the kitchen and yanked the fridge open. Now I understood why Drew just stared into it. Someone in that household needed to shop occasionally. Besides an empty orange juice carton, all we had was one packet of cheese and beer. But you could survive on that.

On a quest for anything edible, my gaze fell on the little white hook above the sink where I always hung my spare keys. One key seemed to be missing. Once, when the building manager made a repair in my condo, I palmed his keys and copied the one that opened the rooftop door. The roof had since become my private getaway. I never shared my oasis with Philly, but it didn't surprise me to learn he'd discovered it on his own.

Turning back to the fridge, I grabbed the packet of cheese and gave it to Lorenzo's dog, and I took a couple of beers. I whistled for the dog and went down the hall to the staircase. We raced up the two flights to the rooftop door; the mutt won. At the top of the stairs, I eased the door open.

Philly was there, all right, feverishly puffing on his pipe. He'd spread the green blanket I put out for the dog last night on the part of the flat, stone-covered roof that allowed him to gaze over the tan stucco parapet all the way to where green hilltops rose above a smudgy brown smog line on the far side of the Valley.

Wordlessly slipping onto the blanket, I breathed in a cloud of Philly's smoke—that my lungs immediately tried to expel. Was this some weird nonsmoking transition?

Once I could breathe, I asked, "Did you spend last night here?"

"Nah, in the backroom at Biggie's Billiards." Before I could object, he jumped in with, "Don't blame Biggie, kid. I begged him to lie to you." Philly resumed his frantic puffing.

I held out one of the beers. From the look he gave it, you'd have sworn I offered him dirt for dinner.

"Kinda early, ain't it?" he demanded.

"This from a man who started the day with a really creative whiskey sour?"

Philly acknowledged the charge with a nod. He tapped the neck of his bottle against mine. We sipped in silence.

After a while, I said, "Wanna tell me about it?"

He gave off an old man's slow, stiff shrug; not what I expected from my boyish uncle-in-law. "Part of what I said was true. Martha wanted to see some place, so we skipped lunch and took a cab to this spot near an airport. Looked like a—"

"I've seen it."

"Oh? Yeah, I guess you would have. The cab dropped

us off at the bottom of that drive. Martha went to the door, you know? Me, I waited there, figuring I'd hang with the cabby till she was done.'' Philly took a swig from the bottle. ''But these two guys jumped out from somewhere and grabbed her. And I—I—''

A car alarm went off in the street. It cycled three times till someone finally turned it off—and before Philly was ready to speak again.

''I froze, kid. I left her there.''

''Yeah? How'd that happen?''

He sucked at the pipe. ''Remember that business in New York?''

My first case? How could I forget it?

''I tried to be a team player there, didn't I? But look at what it got me,'' Philly squawked.

It had almost cost him his life. I always focused on the fun we had, but that wasn't my throat a killer's hands had wrapped around. ''How 'bout Lorenzo? How'd he come into it?''

''Cab almost clipped him.'' A sudden breeze carried off a piece of burning tobacco and dropped it on the blanket.

Not wanting to hamper the flow of information, I quietly twisted my leg into a pretzel and crushed it before we both went up in flames. ''Wasn't he in a crowd of day workers?''

''Well, they were more like *hourly* workers.'' Philly's chuckle ended abruptly. ''And he was a little ways off from them. He kinda popped out from behind a bush. When I told the cabby to step on it, he took me too seriously.''

I scraped the soot off my shoe against the roof gravel. ''So what you're saying is—the cabby was as frightened as you were.''

''Just 'cuz another guy craps in his drawers, don't mean I have to. He didn't know Martha.'' Philly gave his head a sad shake. "I'm no hero, kid. I've always known that. But maybe now I'm more of a rat than I knew."

Or just a scared guy. Even if it was my mother he threw to the wolves, I couldn't blame him. We are what we are.

The knuckles wrapped around his pipe bowl blanched. "Now I've wrecked everything between us. All our plans."

"Plans...?" I asked. That didn't sound good.

He smiled sheepishly. "Yeah, Martha and me—we're kinda an item."

I buried my face in my hands and groaned.

"Now it's never gonna happen," Philly said.

It was never going to happen anyway. "Philly, my parents' relationship isn't easily understood by outsiders." Talk about soft-peddling.

"Now don't you worry, kid. I'm not trying to edge out your pop or anything. I mean, he's your real dad." Philly put his pipe on the rooftop and shyly took my hands. "But you gotta know, Tracy, that I love you like my own."

"Me, too," I whispered.

He flung my hands away. "Only now Martha hates me."

Why did people always worry about what she thought about them? Granted, Philly had left her in the lurch. But she was using him as ego-food. If she kept tossing people away like used matches, one of them was going to burn her. A fantasy for another day—right now I had to fill the hole in Philly's self-respect.

"She's really gotten herself in some deep doo-doo this time, Philly. And Drew might be right there with her."

He jerked. "Drew? How?"

I shook my head. "I need help, Philly."

He held his hands out in the stop position.

I rushed on with, "If I promise to keep you away from danger, can't you pitch in?"

Philly gave his head a vigorous shake. "Don't try to con a con, kid."

"That's it. It's your expertise I need," I pleaded.

The faintest of lights seemed to ignite in his devilish eyes. "You're running a con? Drew'll have a fit."

Not if it was his sorry ass I saved. "Maybe just a little shell game. No danger, I promise." I *hoped*.

He hesitated, but that light glowed brighter now. "Partners again?"

"Partners."

The last time we made that agreement we shook on it. This time, he crushed me to him in a bear hug.

I BROUGHT PHILLY UP to speed while we knocked back our beers. Coors, the real breakfast of champions. By the time we tossed the bottles on the growing pile of soda cans and Chee-tos bags I was keeping there, we had a plan.

As we raced downstairs, I said, "I need to make a few phone calls to set things in motion." I jumped the last few steps, landing flatfooted at the bottom. Zeroing in on a specific target had lit a spark under me. "We'll need a third person. Can you find Lorenzo?"

Philly shrugged. "He was at Biggie's when I left."

Despite our liquid nutrition, my stomach growled. I followed Philly to the kitchen. In the freezer compartment, beneath a pair of chicken breasts, packed in ice crystals since the last millennium, was a battered white envelope in a plastic bag.

"What's that?" Philly asked.

"Drew's earthquake stash. Never heard of cold cash?"

Philly's eyes bulged when I spread the envelope to reveal a stack of U.S. currency. Too bad most of them were singles. Drew popped a few bucks into that envelope pretty regularly so we'd have emergency cash when the Big One hit, as we Californians describe the earthquake that will set us adrift in the ocean. For me, the big one hits in one form or another every day.

I pulled the lone twenty from the top of the stack. "Would you run to the 7-Eleven and get some sandwich stuff? I gotta make those calls."

After Philly left, I went to the study. The red light on the answering machine winked three times. How long had it been since I checked it?

I played the first message. "Wayne, here," a blasé voice drawled, "Logan Wayne." Not exactly James Bond; that was the stupid twit at USC who made Mother's career the focus of his life. "We *must* get together soon to discuss this *dreadful* ordeal your mother is enduring."

Yeah, that would happen. When he told me how a guy who'd lived his whole life in Southern California developed a mainline Philadelphia accent. Phony baloney.

Logan chuckled with droll amusement. "Tracy, what is this I hear about your next *book?*" More chuckles. "And here I thought you *never* listened to me."

What the hell did that mean?

I didn't hear the start of the next message, which built from a whisper. "...haven't heard from you, I have no choice but to sever our connection."

Carolyn, my editor. How dare she pull the plug. I still had a day. True, I had no intention of meeting her stupid deadline, but that was my choice. How had everything turned to crap so fast?

I heard the front door opening. Philly was back, and I still hadn't made any calls. There was still one message left on the machine. Charlotte, Drew's fussy mother, was overdue for a return call. Who needed that now? I hit the erase button and pulled the phone toward me.

I TRANSFERRED A FEW essentials from my purse to my black leather backpack. I made a pit stop in the bathroom for some makeup remover wipes that I popped into the backpack. By the time I returned to the living room, I found Philly sitting on the pile he'd propped on the sofa, with his feet crossed over the stack he'd put on the coffee table.

"Take care of everything?" I asked.

"Sure did, kid. I called Biggie's from the phone at the 7-Eleven. Lorenzo's waiting for us."

"How 'bout the sandwich stuff?"

He gave his head a shake. "Nah, I got to thinking, that's why they make fast food. So you can grab it on the run."

Sounded like that was what he did with Drew's twenty. I wanted that sandwich now. But with a smile, I watched the jaunty strut return to Philly's step as he and Lorenzo's dog marched to the door ahead of me.

"By the way, Trace," he said over his shoulder. "I took the rest of the stash from the freezer. Who knows what we'll need."

Wait till he found out how little it was worth. I shook my head; some things never change. And considering the insane plan I'd set in motion, I'd better hope that was universal.

THIRTEEN

"Another World," Regency Studios, 1957: Starring Martha Collins as Aurora and Elliott James as Ryan.

An alien in a silver suit works the controls of her spaceship. Her passenger seems surprised to find himself aboard.

RYAN
Where are you taking me?

AURORA
Prepare for takeoff, Ryan. It's time you explored my world.

I DID OKAY scaling the eight-foot chain-link fence surrounding the far perimeter of Regency Studios' sprawling backlot. But I lost my footing at the top. An eight-foot drop wouldn't have been fun, but the ground was soft; I would have survived. Unfortunately, I landed at the top of a steep slope and kept tumbling. Over a boulder and scores of rocks, into several clusters of chaparral. Sliding on my side, tumbling head-over-heels. By the time I managed to point my brain North, I finally came to a stop—having planted my fanny flat on a spiny succulent at the base of the hill.

"This would have been way more fun twenty years ago," I muttered to myself.

I took stock—jeans ripped, arms scratched, hair torn out

by the roots. How do other detectives hold it together? Drew's knit top had pushed up during my tumble. Now I carried more dirt in my tattered underpants than a dump truck.

As I lumbered across the lot to the Austrian village where *Mortal Friends* was shooting, my stride kept evolving to match my surroundings. On the Old West street, I was Gary Cooper at High Noon. Once in the small-town America neighborhood, I became A Rebel Without a Cause. In the Austrian village, I was Richard Chamberlain in any one of those Ludlum mini-series, struggling to prevent an apocalyptic World War Three. The stuff contained in my genes was downright spooky. It was a wonder I turned out as normal as I did.

The force of all of those pissed-off personalities propelled me toward the largest of the trailers provided for the movie's stars. Just as I reached for the door, an earnest young studio executive, who looked like she should be running the high school chess club, stepped into my path.

"No one sees Mr. Griffin without my clearance." Her pale face quivered with importance behind her no-nonsense steel eyeglasses.

The backlot characters within me played paper-rock-scissors for the privilege of telling her off. "Honey, you think you can take me? Have at it." I planted my feet in a wide stance and gestured for her to come and get it. Right, James Dean won.

Twenty second glare war—and she blinked. I pushed past her and yanked the door open. A man stood in the doorway.

"Elly-Belly, you son-of-a-bitch," I shouted. "I called you, I told you I was coming. How dare you tell the front gate guard not to let me in."

Elijah Griffin, the man *People* not only designated as the world's sexiest man but the nicest, collapsed on the trailer floor giggling like a girl.

FIVE MINUTES LATER, he was still snorting laughter through his straight, photogenic nose. "Payback, T. For every time your mother left us a pass and you made me scale the fence anyway."

"That was training, bud. I was trying to turn a geeky duckling into a hunky swan."

A lock of the swan's caramel-colored hair fell over his bronzed forehead. His gaze moved from the tear in my jeans, to Drew's sagging green shirt, to my dirty face. "It looks like it's not a moment too soon to return the favor," he concluded.

He gestured toward the sitting area of the lavishly appointed trailer, which contained a pair of mushroom-colored leather sofas on either side of a teakwood coffee table. Alongside was a tiny built-in kitchen and dining table. Considering the size of the trailer, there was probably a makeup room and a bedroom and bath beyond it. I went to the refrigerator tucked under the stone-colored kitchen counter and helped myself to a can of Diet Coke.

While I popped the top, I said, "You better call the front gate and clear my ride to come through. He has another stop to make before we leave."

"Already did it, right around the time I figured you'd be sailing over the back fence. Your uncle says he likes your truck so much, he's keeping it."

I feared that when I left Philly behind the wheel. After the guard turned us away, I knew one of us would have to take another way in. Philly might be young in spirit, but he was in no shape to scale the eight-foot fence. Hell, it almost killed me. I'd had him drop me off at the most accessible spot and told him to wait at the front gate.

I flopped onto one of the leather couches and let my head fall back against the polished teak paneling behind it, so abundant in that dump that it might have been an ocean liner. "By now Philly's probably engaged in one of our infamous slow-speed freeway chases. If he had a driver's license to lose, I'd worry.''

Elijah just laughed at my pesky concerns.

A beep sounded from the desktop computer that filled the dining table adjacent to the kitchenette. Elijah shook the mouse to break up the *X-Files* screensaver. A chessboard appeared on the screen. His eyes narrowed in thought before swiftly entering a move that made his face beam with smug satisfaction.

Sipping my soda, I watched him with amusement. A streak of the boy I had known was still evident, but I had to give Mother sole credit for foreseeing the man Elijah Griffin would become.

I met the kid known on the playground as Elly-Belly in the third grade. Bored with an arithmetic class, I faked a seizure for an excuse to visit the nurse. No one took it seriously, but teachers always seemed glad to get rid of me. While passing a janitorial closet, I heard a whimper. I threw the door open, hoping to find a puppy that would then be said to have followed me home. Instead, hanging from a hook by the elastic of his BVD's, was the future recipient of a Golden Globe and the current beneficiary of a world-class wedgie.

I helped him down and, just like my mythical puppy, he trailed home behind me. I tried to give the little nerd some backbone, but it was Mother who actually filled him with confidence. She convinced him to trade the glasses for contacts and to try allergy shots to stop his perpetual sniffling. After that, only his horse-like oversized teeth destroyed his appearance. Who knew that when he grew into them, he'd have a toothpaste-ad smile that would capture the world?

I wouldn't have pegged him as an actor; he didn't run true to the shallow types who vexed my existence. Granted, he'd always begged to run lines with Mother. But I took that to be a more inventive form of sucking-up than an Eddie Haskell "You're looking lovely today, Mrs. Grainger" approach. This was the kid who won science fairs, the first to own a computer. No one was more surprised than I, when I tried out for the senior play, that the computer geek who tagged along took the lead, while I went unnoticed among the walk-ons.

Elijah sat across from me on the other sofa. "Okay, T— spill it."

I had planned to do just that, but during my fall down Regency Mountain, it occurred to me that it might not be fair to play the legal system's version of *Celebrity Jeopardy!*

"I don't know, Elly. I could be making you an accessory to something pretty gnarly," I warned.

"If you don't, I'll hang you by a wedgie." The memory glowed warmly in his sherry-colored eyes. "I owe everything I have to your mom. There's nothing I wouldn't do for her."

"Because she taught you to be an actor?"

Irritation muscled the warmth from his eyes. "I was already an actor, as our senior play demonstrated. She taught me to be a *star*."

Freaky thought. The world wasn't big enough for two like her. I shrugged and gave him the shorthand version. "So you see," I concluded, "there's some connection between Mother and Vince Sperry and Benny Butler Marsh."

"If there is, I'll find it," Elijah promised.

I reached into my jeans pocket for a slip of paper—only I pulled out a fistful of dirt. Elly giggled again. I considered throwing the dirt onto the floor, but he didn't clean the place. Instead, I rose and dumped it into the brushed-aluminum sink and ran a little water to rinse it down the drain.

I stuffed my hand back into that gritty pocket and found

the paper at the bottom. "That's a warehouse in Van Nuys. Can you find out who owns it?"

The slip of paper disappeared into his fist. "If our county's nineteenth century computer is operational, that's a no-brainer. What else?"

I explained that Benny Butler Marsh seemed too flush after producing the budget-stomping '06, especially since it was tied up in litigation. "I need to know where the money is coming from."

He pursed his lips and offered me a long, unblinking stare. Was I asking too much? After a moment, he gave his head a definitive shake and went to the computer. On a blank screen he quickly produced a page of type and printed it out. Back at the sitting area, he handed it to me.

"You need to find a way to get some time alone with Benny's computer. I can't think how you'll do it, but I know you too well to doubt it." He shrugged. "Call in a bomb scare."

I wrinkled my nose. Anyone could do that.

"I'll leave that to you," Elly said. "Just get into Benny's computer files. You find anything suspicious, use the instructions on this sheet to send the file to me. I'll figure out what it means."

I rolled the sheet up and stuck it into my dirty pocket. There was a knock on the metal door just before the junior executive I'd tangled with earlier pulled it open.

"Five minutes, Elijah." For him, she produced an unexpected pair of dimples in her pale cheeks.

"No problem, Amber."

Amber? What a joke on her parents. They wanted a country singer and wound up with an officious MBA. Is anyone ever happy with the parent-child relationship? Lord, I hoped not.

After Amber left, I started to rise, but Elly waved me back into my seat. "Didn't any of this business rub off on you? You should know when they say five minutes, they mean ten or more. Hurry up and wait, that's the name of the game. There's something else I have to know."

That wary expression returned to his eyes. Elly leaned forward, pressing his strong forearms to his lean thighs. I took a swig of Diet Coke.

"The hot rumor racing through Hollywood today is that Benny Butler Marsh has an option on your next book? You're telling me everything, right? You're not tied into Martha's mess?"

Diet Coke erupted from my nose.

Elly didn't seem to notice I spewed Coke over his teak coffee table. "Tracy, I know Benny represents big bucks, but—"

Gasping for air, I coughed out, "Every cent in Fort Knox wouldn't be enough money to make me work with Benny, Tiny Elvis. Not in this lifetime."

With the faultless timing the critics adored, he rose. I took a peek at my watch; exactly nine minutes had passed since Amber popped in. Without giving the appearance of tossing me out of his plush retreat, my old pal guided me toward the door. He *had* learned something from the master.

But he paused outside the trailer, so much tension knotting his brow he'd need collagen injections a year sooner than he'd probably planned.

"Mr. Griffin!" the makeup woman called.

"Coming," Elly shouted back. But he didn't budge.

A few members of the crew stopped at a camera crane parked a few feet from where we stood. One of them was smoking, and a whiff drifted my way. As before, my nose twitched at the acrid odor. Frankly, it was starting to seem like a stupid idea now, this business of sucking hot air through dead weeds. Maybe I had finally freed myself of the feral beast. Though I would sell Elly to Amber for a cheesecake.

Before I could enter into those negotiations, Elly took

my arm and pulled me away from the crew members. His voice dropped to a whisper. "This rumored deal between Benny and you must have come from him. I don't like it, Trace. Isn't there anything else I can do for you and Martha?"

Committing a few felonies on our behalf seemed enough. There wasn't any deal with Benny, and no amount of talk would make one. Hell, there wasn't even any book now. Then it hit me—not something Elly could do for Mother, but what he could do for me. I was tired of my publisher shoving me—it was time to push back.

My fingers curled into fists. "How hard is it to hack into a big company's emails and internal memos?"

Elly grinned as he had when we hid stink bombs in the backpacks of the boys who had hung him in the janitor's closet. "Hell, girl, I thought you'd at least ask for something *hard*."

Now maybe things would finally turn my way.

As I MADE MY WAY across the lot to Teddi Olin's office, I recalled all the times I'd tagged along with Mother when she went there for her costume fittings. Her favorite costume designer's shop was located in a small peach-stucco building that once served as some star's dressing room. Then, as now, it was the most welcoming office on the lot. An old brick path filled with rich, green moss curved through beds of colorful wild flowers to a carved mocha-colored door that stood ajar.

Philly must have been watching at the door. The instant I stepped onto the brick path, he threw the door open, twirling in the doorway in his borrowed duds. "Pretty spiffy, huh, kid?"

He wore the ivory linen suit that had been Dad's costume in *The Devil's Workshop*. Not a bad fit, either. Only by looking closely did I see the gussets that made the jacket roomier. But it was already so wrinkled that it looked as if Teddi had taken it straight from storage without having it pressed. At least it matched its occupant.

I stepped into the cottage and saw Teddi approaching behind Philly. With her white hair and wicker cane, it would be easy to dismiss her as just another industry elder. Only the burgundy and heather-green chamois scarf wrapped gypsy-style around her middle was *such* a good match for her cranberry leather boots and her piercing green eyes. Mother always said Teddi had the best sense of style in the biz; I couldn't see that anything had changed.

"Philly, I told you not to sit," Teddi snapped, as she had to generations of actors she made look their best.

"I didn't," he said, wounded. It was a gift he had.

Lorenzo stepped from another room, dressed in full chauffeur livery. He offered me a regal nod of his head.

I gave him a little salute. *"Hola, Lorenzo."* I wanted to thank him for helping us. *"Muchas gracias."*

Lorenzo wished me good day in Spanish, and said, with a curious little dance of straight black eyebrows behind rich horn-rimmed glasses, either that the gratitude was his or it was hot in Scotland. Something like that.

Lorenzo's dog came from elsewhere in the cottage and leaped onto the blue-and-white striped sofa Teddi had placed before the front window. She tapped her cane against the hardwood floor, and mutt slinked to the floor.

Years ago, there was so much activity in Teddi's workroom, it practically jumped off its foundation. While there were still framed copies of her Academy Award winning designs on the walls of the sitting room, I didn't see signs of many ongoing projects today. Hollywood had moved on to younger designers. But she still had enough clout to enlist the services of a makeup artist and hair stylist.

The hairdresser gave me pause. Her own mousy brown hair hung unevenly over the hospital greens she'd taken from the *Miracle City* set. But the woman was a genius.

She'd actually combed Philly's unruly mop so it approximated Dad's sweeping white mane—at least from the vantage point of outer space. I didn't think anyone could make Philly look that good.

"Philly, you have the change of clothes?" I asked.

"Already packed in the truck. You're the only holdup. Go get pretty, kid."

Stomping off with Teddi and her crew, I muttered that I already was. But nobody seemed to care.

LESS THAN A half-hour later, I emerged from the inner sanctum. Teddi had outfitted me in the mod look of the late sixties—tangerine and hot-pink mini-dress, orange pillbox, and matching pink-vinyl go-go boots. Fortunately, my haircut was already similar to sixties hair. It didn't take much tweaking to make me look so much like my mother once did that I swore off mirrors for life. Once was enough; I never wanted to see it again.

To my surprise, Philly's face sagged. "Aw, Teddi. I thought you'd make her look like Martha did in *Tijuana Temptress.*"

"At her age? Come on, Philly, Martha couldn't have been more than nineteen or so then."

"Excuse me?" I said.

"Eighteen, I think," he continued, as if I hadn't spoken. "I was…sixteen or so when I sat in that theatre looking up at her. The girl stole my heart."

He was thirteen, maybe. "Yeah, you and about a hundred million other little boys," I said with sour grace.

They continued their pattern of ignoring me. "I'm sorry, Philly, but I had to keep it age appropriate."

I shouted, "Age appropriate? Mother was *forty* when this dress was in style. I can remember her wearing something like this when I was a toddler, and I wasn't born till—"

"Gee whiz, Trace. So your book deal fell through,"

Philly said. "That's no reason to sound bitter about getting old."

I glared at him. "As soon as I can find the sofa that served as your bed, Lorenzo's dog is getting it."

My threat so worried the old fart, he shouted his intention to drive the truck and danced from the cottage, with Lorenzo and Lorenzo's dog on his heels.

Through the white plantation shutters at the window, Teddi watched Philly roughhousing with Lorenzo. "You will keep him from jumping in mud puddles, won't you?"

With a sigh, I said, "When are people going to get it? I'm not Philly's mother."

Teddi's eyebrows contracted in disapproval. "That suit Alec wore was on its way to a museum, young lady. If Philly destroys it, your hide will be displayed instead."

So now I was young again. I gave her a sharp salute.

I wanted to leave, but the way Teddi stared at the pale maple floor told me she still had something on her mind.

"I take it you're hoping to jog…someone's memory with these…re-creations," she said.

I nodded. I bet she knew *whose* memory, too; there weren't a lot of secrets in this town. Just a few really important ones.

"Has it occurred to you, Tracy, that Martha has gone to great lengths to keep those memories hidden? It appears that she's willing to risk imprisonment rather than reveal what she knows."

My unspoken fears burst out. "They wouldn't convict her, would they?" Everyone knows that L.A. is a city where anyone can get away with murder.

Teddi shrugged. "Maybe, maybe not. Either way, your mother would be poison in this town." She gestured toward the studio's black steel executive tower in the distance. "The bean counters aren't known for their loyalty. Tracy, what could matter so much to Martha that she'd risk a lifetime of work to keep it hidden? Are you sure it *should* be unearthed?"

FOURTEEN

"Time Traveler," Regency Studios, 1958: Starring Martha Collins as Jill and Sidney Gilliard as Rupert.

A man in contemporary dress stops a woman in turn-of-the-century clothing as she climbs into a time capsule.

RUPURT
What if you can't make it back? Jill, the problems are here—in our time.

JILL
But the truth is back in theirs.

PHILLY DROVE LORENZO, his dog, and me over the hill. Fortunately, he drove so recklessly that it kept me from obsessing over Teddi's wintry warning. But occasionally, at stoplights or when there was nobody to cut off, Teddi's words drifted back to me. Were some secrets better buried? I wouldn't know that till I dug this one up.

After the thrill ride, Philly brought the truck to a surprisingly gentle stop across the street from the Beverly Vista Home for the Airy-Minded. Well, maybe they called it something else. But that was what the facility, located on a quiet side street not far from downtown Beverly Hills, truly was. Reluctant to relinquish his place behind the wheel, Philly took about a week to park, giving me time to case the joint.

Keeping Jolly in this palace must have set Benny back

more than fighting Sperry's lawsuit had. I'd seen five-star hotels that looked like dumps in comparison. It was a sprawling, California-Spanish structure, four stories high in some parts, three in others, with elegant cream stucco and neat rust-colored trim. Wrought-iron grills covered some of the windows, a decorative compliment that served a useful purpose in this place. Lush violet rhododendrons still in bloom and a rainbow of impatiens lined a lawn as vibrantly green as a field of emeralds. The only identification was a tasteful brass plate next to the door. Anyone who didn't know what it was would never guess.

"Willya get a load o' that dump? When I lose my marbles, put me there," Philly said.

I had news for him: If he squandered his marbles, he could get in line behind Angelique to shake the soap in my laundry room. If anyone lived in this comfort, it was going to be me. And let's face it—despite my relative youth, these days, dementia was a shorter leap for me.

We had parked a little way up the street, so no one would wonder why Martha Collins rode in a big black truck, something even she questioned. I thought about arranging for a limousine, but I wanted to drive something I was accustomed to handling, in case we needed to make a quick getaway. Not that I'd be driving my own truck much anymore, now that Philly had developed a taste for it.

Naturally, Lorenzo had taken the front passenger seat. That left me to share the back seat with the dog. Well, all the space not taken up by the plastic-wrapped replacement clothes and the box that held the last of my published books. Why couldn't Lorenzo hold his own dog?

I tapped the front seats. "Okay, boys, let's kick some Marsh butt."

Ol' Lorenzo must have understood more English than he let on. I saw a twitch alongside his tight-lipped mouth. He leaped from the truck, and assuming the courtly manner of a chauffeur, helped me from the back seat. He didn't seem to give a thought to his poor dog. I was the one who reminded Philly to lower the windows so the mutt could breathe while he waited in the truck.

As PHILLY AND LORENZO sailed across the wide street, I paused and took a deep breath. When I let it out, I had to *be* Martha Collins, all the way through. Anything less would show. I took a few steps, easing into her distinctive rhythm. By the time I hit the far curb, I was so into her that it would have scared me—had her character not made me too self-involved to care. Man, my gene pool was a time bomb. What if *I* never came back?

Philly and Lorenzo waited for me at the door. I'd already prepped them on the routine. The door was kept locked at all times, and visitors announced themselves by ringing the bell or using the big, copper-green gargoyle knocker.

I learned how Beverly Vista operated when a friend's grandmother had stayed there. She hadn't been suffering from Alzheimer's but had checked in to recover in comfort from a broken hip. To be fair, Beverly Vista did provide standard nursing home care, and even housed, if I remembered right, a small, critical-care hospital. As if to punctuate my point, an elderly woman, hobbled on a walker from the rear of the complex along a small side path, stopping long enough to stifle a laugh at my costume. There was nothing wrong with either her smarts or her taste. But the care and coddling of affluent, aging airheads had proven to be Beverly Vista's claim to fame.

Lorenzo did the honors with the knocker; Philly and I hovered royally behind him. Before the echo of the knocker's resonating clang drifted away, the door was opened by a dowdy older woman whose eyes widened when she looked at me. Philly's and Lorenzo's looks were timeless, but mine must have seemed pretty funny to contemporary eyes. I felt like going into a *Laugh-In* routine just to push her over the edge.

Instead, in a delicious imitation of Martha Collins at her most imperious, I said, ''Darling, we're here to see poor Jolly Marsh. Would you be a dear and prepare him for a visit?'' Without waiting for a response, I brushed past the woman, precisely as Mother has run over every objection that's ever popped up on her path. Damn, I was good.

Once in the vestibule, I realized the doorkeeper was younger than I thought. Probably fifty or so; it was just the lack of coloring in her greying hair that aged her. The combination of the frumpy, black pleated skirt and low-heeled, sensible pumps also added years to her appearance, not to mention making her legs look like bowling pins. But she was a good choice for that place. She must have reminded the inhabitants more of the secretaries or house-keepers they had in the past than a nurse. Or a jailer.

From elsewhere in the complex, I heard the muffled whine of an electric drill. Though the sound was faint, it set my teeth on edge. I couldn't get away from construc-tion, even here. But these people didn't experience the realities of renovation as I did. The directors of Beverly Vista were paid handsomely to keep all the nasty trappings of reality hidden from those people who were mostly too gone to recognize it anyway.

In a cut-crystal English accent the Queen would have envied, the bug-eyed greeter asked us to call her Didi. She frowned when I didn't offer my name. Mother expects people to know—without being told. Most of the time, they do recognize her. But I was an anachronistic Martha Collins whom Didi couldn't quite place, given the doubtful look in her faded blue eyes. Fortunately, no one's guests were subjected to much scrutiny at Beverly Vista.

Didi led us across the pale marble floor to a small office. On the bare surface of a small, antique mahogany desk she placed a blue satin guest book, in which guests were not only expected to write their names, but that of the patient they were visiting and their arriving and departing times. Having signed a green tweed one when my friend and I came to see her grandmother, I was prepared. So was Philly. He wandered back across the foyer to where a bronze figurine of an eagle was captured, mid-flight, on an oak stand.

Aping Dad's charming drawl, Philly said, "Didi, honey, what can you tell me about this piece?"

Didi joined Philly across the vestibule, making like a docent with the uninspired works of art scattered throughout the building's opening. As instructed by Philly—in what language, I didn't know—Lorenzo stood behind, blocking me from Didi's view. Trying to ignore the distant tapping of a hammer, I went right to work.

Scanning through the visitors' names, I spotted some of my folks' cronies among them, but nobody I knew well. My Dad had come to see some of his chums, though never Jolly, lending credence to the idea that my parents didn't know him. But Jolly didn't lack attention—Benny was such a good son, he dropped by every week, even if he never stayed long. As near as I could tell, in the moments allowed me, neither Mother nor Vince Sperry had recently entered the place, to see Jolly or anyone else.

At the sound of returning footsteps, I flipped back to the current page and scratched Mother's name on the next line. Since I probably hadn't faked her signature since high school, I was glad to see that I still had it. Forgery, just like riding a bike.

PHILLY HAD COME THROUGH, too. Not only had he distracted Didi, he'd convinced her that we were *such* good friends of Jolly's, she agreed to let us wait in his room till he awoke from his nap.

Jolly's room was bigger than I expected, and well placed at the rear of the complex, with a great view of the lush garden. A brass queen-sized bed claimed one side of the long room, while the other half contained a seating area filled with the dark heavy woods and brass-studded, deep-red leather furniture associated with men's clubs.

A human form huddled under a cocoa blanket in the center of the bed. In his prime, Jolly Marsh had been a bear of a man. I remembered seeing him once at a premier I went to with one of my girlfriends and her parents. A tanned, fit giant with a shaved head, he stole the show with his booming, boisterous manner. It wasn't even *his* movie premiering that night, but all the cameras were trained on Jolly when he crushed some helpless little starlet to his barrel chest and did the tongue tango with her. It didn't surprise me in the least that his son grew up to star in life as the amazing, colossal Pigboy.

Still, the ravages of time can be cruel to witness, no matter what the target. With Philly and Lorenzo behind me, I crept toward the bed, unsure of how hard I could be on this old man. I need not have wasted my sympathy—at thirty-four, I'd already lost more muscle mass than Jolly Marsh. The robust specimen in the crisp robin's egg-blue pajamas looked like he pumped iron in the prison yard, rather than slept the day away in a frou-frou old folks' home.

Jolly's head was no longer shaved, but it sported what looked like a sparse, white Afro. He seemed more at peace now than during that night so firmly fixed in my memory. The eggshell linen pillowcase had slipped off, and while Jolly slept, he chewed gently on the pillow below. As sweet as a baby—if any woman gave birth to giant bruisers. It looked as if he gnawed that pillow regularly; his teeth had almost cut through to the down fill.

While we watched, Jolly's eyelids fluttered open. Rheumy, sleep-dazed hazel eyes drifted in my direction. I was prepared for our presence to upset this child-man, strangers as we were. But the startled eyes that snapped to attention just looked furious. I still expected to hear a frail, elderly voice—not the one that boomed out at me.

"Martha! You stupid bitch. What the fuck are you doing here?"

I REELED AWAY from Jolly's bedside. The proof of Mother's repeated lies flabbergasted me. I struggled to stay in her miserable character, not that Jolly would have noticed.

"Martha, have you lost what little sense you had?"

Talk about the pot calling the kettle *noir*.

"You know we agreed never to see each other," Jolly went on. "Have you forgotten already?"

Already? Was Jolly speaking from the present time or the distant past?

Heavy work boots tapped and stuttered against the floor outside the door we'd left ajar, distracting me, especially when the workman stopped to tap a nail. I struggled to retain my grasp on Mother's persona.

"Jolly, darling, I *had* to see you," I insisted in Mother's voice.

Jolly looked over my shoulder. "Aw, Christ! You brought Alec, too. It was all his fault, you know that. I wanted to wash my hands of it, but, no—he had another idea. Who's that other clown?"

What was Dad's fault? "He's my driver."

"Get rid of him," Jolly snapped.

Philly led Lorenzo off to the sitting area. I slipped into a bedside chair in red leather and studs. My plan had seemed such a long shot. Since this man lived in the past, I thought immersing him in our version of it would loosen his recollections. I didn't realize it would mean wrestling with someone who really had been a titan in his time, rather than his son's frail imitation. How was I going to make this domineering man spill his guts?

"Did something happen?" Jolly asked in a hoarse whisper, so low it could not have been heard even one state east of Kansas. Where was the volume control on that voice? "Do they know about...Windswept?"

Windswept? There was that word again. The one Sperry had typed in his threatening letter to Mother. Why did it always tickle something in the recesses of my mind?

I ran out of patience. My desperate need to know pushed Martha out, and Tracy flooded in. I leaped to my feet. It took all I had not to grab the crisp blue lapels of his prissy jammies and give him a sound shaking.

I lost Jolly instantly. Confusion clouded the old man's eyes, causing his chin to quiver like a small boy about to burst into tears. Jolly's synapses might be fried like onion rings, but his emotions guided him these days, yielding a surer navigation than anyone would expect. Despite what he saw through his eyes, a truer sense told him I wasn't Martha Collins.

I fell back into the stiff leather chair, expecting the giant-sized toddler to howl at the top of those powerful lungs. Instead, slowly, the clouds drifted from his eyes. I thought I saw a malicious glint come into them. I figured I'd given him too much credit till I heard that malice reflected in the sound of his nasty laugh.

Rising to falsetto level, Jolly's voice said, "Two-two-three on the lane swept by the wind."

Stunned beyond words, I groped through my own mind for understanding. Jolly seemed to have an accurate read on my confusion. He threw his head back in laughter, banging it into the brass headboard—something that didn't seem to faze him, the hard-headed bastard. He kept repeating that phrase over and over in a tone a little girl might use.

It took a while for understanding to seep through my own hard head—the old goat was poking fun at *me*.

FIFTEEN

"Dream Thief," Regency Studios, 1959: Starring Martha Collins as Paige and Alec Grainger as Rudy.

RUDY
You stole another woman's life, her dreams, and you act as if you have a right to them.

PAIGE
Stealing makes them mine. Unless she wises up and steals 'em back.

JOLLY'S REMARKS so shocked me that I could barely function. At the door, I adjusted my steps to avoid the workman I heard. Only he was gone now, and I careened into an elderly burn victim. At least I took the white hair hanging below his shoulders to indicate age. I couldn't have guessed from his fire-ravaged, pink-and-puckered skin. I stood staring at the poor guy—not held by his appearance—simply incapable of thought. But he must have thought I was gaping at his scars, not that I saw any expression in his black, unblinking eyes.

Finally, Philly took over. "Excuse her," he said to the guy and dragged me away.

In the back seat of my truck I clutched Lorenzo's dog for comfort. The dog focused his soulful eyes on me and grunted from the back of his throat.

I hugged him tighter. "Did you hear that? He's talking

to me. Man, there's one sympathetic monkey in this dog suit.''

While navigating the hairpin turns of Laurel Canyon, Philly twisted around behind the wheel to look at me. "Snap out of it, kid. It ain't over yet, and you'll need your wits next time."

"Not if I die on the canyon floor. Will you watch where you're driving?" Even Lorenzo seemed to be clutching the dashboard with tight, white knuckles.

Philly chuckled. "Aw, you know this truck ain't gonna survive with you and me driving it."

I knew it now.

But I did need to sharpen my thinking if we were going to pull this off. Easier said than done. I couldn't shake the belief that Jolly had been mocking *me*. I kept hearing that silly refrain in my mind: "Two-two-three on the lane swept by the wind." Only now the voice signing it was my own toddler's voice.

The jingle sounded like something a parent might invent to teach a child her address. Yet that child couldn't have been me. I'd stayed in many places when my parents shot films on locations. And during their break-ups, Dad always made a room for me where he lived. But none of those spots were *home*. Home was Mother's house on Joshua Drive. She'd bought that house before the dawn of time, or maybe in her early thirties—whichever came first. She always said when people ramble as much as we did, they need to know where they belong. So how could another address be so deeply embedded in my mind? Or was it even an address at all?

I also couldn't shake the conviction that Jolly accurately read my true identify. Would the traits I displayed as a toddler still be so strongly in evidence that a man with his limited skills could make the connection? While I had no recollection of him, I sensed Jolly had known me well.

I might have stayed lost in that fog if Philly hadn't decided to use a crowded intersection to test the meaning of a red light. To the accompaniment of wailing horns, he flew through a car gauntlet and turned into the lot of a coffee shop, screeching to a halt just before we crashed through its front window.

"Admit it, kid," Philly said with a grin. "All those states that denied me drivers' licenses had their heads up their butts."

Well, someone did.

With that, we grabbed the other garments Teddi had provided and dashed into the coffee shop's restrooms to change. When we met outside again, I wore a short-skirted tomato-red suit. Philly had assumed Hollywood business attire—crisp, dry-cleaned jeans and an eggshell turtleneck beneath a black leather blazer. He'd even drawn his hair back into a teeny one-inch ponytail. How perfect was that? As a con-man, he'd forgotten more about protective coloring than I ever knew.

Once Lorenzo emerged in his next look, he hid on the floor of the back seat beneath a blanket. I grabbed the driver's seat this time, remembering to put my backpack on my lap so I wouldn't forget it. Philly acted as if he couldn't care less, but I noticed that, while he nibbled at the stem of his unlit pipe, he kept sending longing glances at the steering wheel.

I stopped at the Hargrove Pictures guard shack. I hadn't arranged for a pass there, so I was going to have to talk my way through—and that hadn't gone well the last time I'd tried.

I leaned out the window to draw the guard's attention away from the lump behind my seat. "Tracy Eaton for Benny Butler Marsh. You'll have to call for clearance, but he'll see—"

The guard looked up from his clipboard. "No, Ms. Ea-

ton, you're here. Mr. Marsh said it was just a matter of
time till you turned up.''

He did, huh? Was that good news or bad? I hate it when
I don't know.

BENNY'S OPERATION was also housed in a freestanding
building on the lot, but his was new. A squat modern box
of cinderblocks and glass bricks surrounded by unclipped
beds of ivy.

I took a quick jog around the building. I was pretty sure
Drew told me that Benny's office had a private rear door.
Should I have been wrong about that, we'd have to move
on to Plan B—and that would take some doing, since we
didn't have one. I counted on a guy like Benny always to
need a way out, and he didn't fail me. Once I confirmed
the door's existence, I raced around to the front where
Philly waited. Taking a moment to hike the backpack into
position, we approached the etched glass door and
knocked. Nobody answered, but the brushed aluminum
knob turned in my hand.

We strolled into an unoccupied reception area with a
big granite desk surrounded by some trendy black leather
chairs. Off the reception area were a half-dozen doors, all
open, not counting the one closed door dead ahead. The
desks I saw in those offices were cleared of work and
unoccupied. I brushed my fingers across the pricey reception desk. Dusty. The Phoenix ran a small shop.

Wrapping my knuckles against the granite slab, I yelled,
''Anybody home?''

Benny called from behind the closed door. ''On the
phone. Be out in a sec. My secretary called in sick.''

Sure. Only I bet she described it as ''filing for unem-
ployment.''

A few moments later, Benny popped from that closed
office. He stopped when he saw me, never even glancing
at the short skirt I'd chosen just for him.

''Well, well—look what cat dragged herself in. Like, I

figured you'd be turning up soon." He jerked his head at Philly. "Who's this? Your kneecap breaker?"

Huh? "This is my agent, Philly Chase."

Come to think of it, that had a nice ring. The joker in New York who was supposed to be guiding my career hadn't even called me when my series was flushed. Maybe agenting was the respectable occupation I sought for Philly.

Whoa! Was that an erroneous assumption—and I wasn't talking about Philly.

Benny belched out a laugh. "The joke's on you, my man. Don't think your cut's gonna be fat—you're sucking blood from a stone." A ball of spit collected in Benny's cheek that he almost let fly, till he noticed it would be his own white Berber he spit on.

Before I had a chance to question Benny's odd welcome, Lorenzo entered on cue. Dressed in full clown regalia—white face, orange wig, big red nose—he burst into the office waving a gun. A prop gun Teddi had given us, though it suddenly looked a whole lot more authentic. I produced a realistic enough scream, and Philly muttered something convincing, while Benny kept shouting that he didn't keep cash in the office.

Without uttering a word, Lorenzo patted down both men with his free hand and relieved Benny of his tiny cell phones. From the pocket of his baggy clown pants he pulled a roll of bright blue duct tape and thrust it at me. He gestured for me to use it to restrain the two men. It wasn't much of a gesture, but having devised it myself, it wasn't hard to interpret, either.

If only everything worked so well. I'd grabbed that tape from a box of supplies Randy left in my condo. Naturally, it was junk. The adhesive was so gooey, I couldn't peel back the end of the tape. Anger flashed in Lorenzo's eyes, but it was no match for the venom I saw in Benny's. If Benny got his hands on Lorenzo, the poor slob was dead meat. Finally, Philly grabbed the tape and tore it with his teeth to get it started.

I sat the two men on the floor, back to back, and taped their hands and feet, then slapped a strip over their mouths. Philly's tape was as loose as I could make it, but I really wound Benny up good. When I appeared to have completed the operation to the clown's satisfaction, he grabbed me around my waist and put the prop gun to my temple. Let me tell you, the barrel felt a lot more serious now than it had in the truck. Lorenzo dragged me into Benny's office and slammed the door behind us.

Once the door was closed, Lorenzo released me. As rushed as I was, I couldn't help but notice that Benny's private office was a grander version of the reception room, with a granite desk that dwarfed the secretarial one and sporting so much black leather that it looked like an S-and-M bar. He'd added a glass case behind the desk to house his lone People's Choice Award.

Even before I rounded that huge desk, the hum I heard indicated Benny's computer was on. But what I saw on the screen after clearing the Phoenix screensaver gave me pause. Windows. My second favorite computer platform—after everything else. Macs rock.

While I went to work on the computer, Lorenzo peeled off the clown clothes and stuffed them into my backpack. He wore his shabby street clothes underneath, and they looked strange with the white face. He found the makeup-remover pads I'd brought and wiped his face clean. Once finished, he slipped his horn-rimmed glasses on and stood looking over my shoulder.

I gave Benny's accounting files a quick study. Marshland Productions was losing the farm, as I expected. But I didn't see anything that explained Benny's extra cash. Still, I pulled out the instructions Elly had given me and sent a copy of the ledger by modem to Elly's computer.

I opened files at random. For a self-involved toad,

Benny proved to be a prodigious letter writer, though fittingly, he never ran the spell-checker, and his spelling was worse than his grammar. I had spot-checked every file when I heard a sound that raised the hair on my neck—voices coming from the outer office—a place where no one should have been able to speak.

Despite the design of the chi-chi building, the interior walls were thin. I realized that when Benny shouted to us. Now it alerted me that we might need a Plan B after all.

"There, got the strip off," Benny's voice said, quite distinctly now. "Thinks he can gag me, does he?"

"You're free?" Philly asked, too loudly; a warning to me. I'd only stuck the tape to one side of Philly's mouth.

"Halfway there," Benny announced. "Good thing I never trim my nails. They make great blades, you know?"

Crap! "Get going, Lorenzo. *Vamos*," I said.

"*Ve?*" he asked in the critical tone my Spanish teachers always used.

We were about to get sent up the river, and he was correcting my Spanish. "Fine. *Ve*. Get outta here." I looked around the office for something he could take to give the appearance of a robbery. Reaching into the armoire, I grabbed the People's Choice Award. "Here, take this—it's not like he deserved it."

Beyond the wall, Benny cried, "Almost got my hands free!"

"Almost got your hands free. Think of that," Philly shouted.

"Go, Lorenzo," I muttered through clenched teeth.

I turned back to the computer. There *had* to be something there. But what could I find in one second that I hadn't found before? My eyes landed on the recycling bin. In sheer desperation, I opened it. Most of the contents were discarded letters, but the name of the last file in the list bore a resemblance to a file I'd already checked, with the sole modification of today's date. What the hell. I opened it.

I gasped when I saw what Benny had *almost* deleted. "All right! Baby, come to mama!" As fast as my fingers could fly, I sent the file off to Elly's computer.

Lorenzo tugged at my arm. Taking a moment to set the screensaver again, I turned to him. "Okay, now—let's *vamos*." Conjugate my verbs, would he?

We slipped out the back door as Benny shouted, "My hands are free! Just the feet now!"

Lorenzo and I sprinted across the lot. Once we were far enough away, I sent him on a circuitous route back to where we'd parked the truck, while I leaned against a tree, deciding how I would make my reappearance.

I spotted a woman approaching an old-fashioned washtub outside a soundstage. She carried one of those carafes restaurants use to serve house wine, only hers was filled with some yucky brownish-green substance.

"Wait," I shouted before she poured it into the sink. "What's that?"

"Fake puke," she said, as if it were the most natural thing in the world. She wore a blue work shirt, the kind car mechanics wear, with the name "Wendy" stitched in an red oval over the pocket. She'd either picked up a bargain from a uniform catalog or paid a mint for it in some Melrose Avenue boutique—I couldn't tell which. "But the director wants it greener."

This was the way it was supposed to work. My timing had been off since Mother made that ominous phone call announcing she was suspected of murdering Sperry. Now I was cooking again.

I gave her an eager smile. "May I have it?"

Wendy leaned back and seemed to be assessing if I was dangerous. "O-kay," she said, stretching the word out as people do when they don't want to come right out and say you're nuts. "Put the bottle in the sink when you're... finished with it."

I split before she could change her mind, racing toward Benny's office. The idea of putting some of that stuff on my face didn't thrill me, but it would sell the story. I breathed through my mouth when I patted a little around my lips and smeared with the back of my hand. But it actually gave off a pleasant oatmeal smell. Kinda like the cookies your mom might have baked—unless you had a mom like mine. When I reached Benny's ivy patch, I performed my own form of projectile vomiting—from a jar—before running back to the washtub to dump the evidence.

When I finally staggered through Marshland Productions' front door, two security officers were there taking Benny's statement.

Benny measured his hand a full foot over his own head. "Huge, I tell ya. The guy was big."

Yeah, Lorenzo must have been a whopping two inches taller than me.

Philly had been leaning against the secretarial desk but jerked to his feet when he spotted me. "Tracy! Are you okay?"

"That's the girl," Benny said, pointing. "The one the guy dragged off."

As the security officers crowded around, I slowly sank into a black leather chair. "He let me go at the far fence." I lowered my eyes. "I made it back here as fast as I could, but I'm afraid I was sick behind the building."

The older security man indicated with a toss of his head for the other one to check out my story. When the second man returned, his face twisted in disgust. Too bad Wendy would never know how convincing the color really was.

The guards took our names and let us go. Keeping the act going, I leaned on Philly as we walked out the door. Just outside, we heard a scream.

"He took my People's Choice!" Benny shouted loudly enough to shatter all the glass blocks in his building.

AT THE TRUCK, we found Lorenzo waiting for us in the back seat with one arm draped around the dog, while casually drumming his fingers against the door. Apart from a few white streaks along his jaw—and the award between his feet—he gave no sign that he had just committed a crime. Either he pulled off felonies every day, or he knew a better way out of them than I did.

After fighting our way through heavy midday traffic, we crossed back over the hill and again ended up in Elijah's trailer. Philly and Lorenzo sat on one of the mushroom sofas, nursing beers, while the remains of the lunch Elly had served to us were spread on the coffee table. The set caterer had even rustled up a few burgers for the pup.

Elly and I huddled before his computer. "He has two sets of books, right?" I asked. "Why was the one with the extra income in the recycling bin?"

Elly shrugged. "Probably keeps it on a floppy somewhere, but he prefers the speed of working with it on his hard drive. Lots of people don't follow through with deleting files." He inched his chair closer and pointed at the screen. "I've cross-referenced all his projects, Tracy, eliminated the usual sources of income. And look at what we have left—periodic bumps of twenty-five thousand bucks, followed by a couple dozen hits of fifty thousand each. If that keeps up throughout the year, it will be…" he trailed off while calculating.

Leave it to the con-man to reach it first. "About five million a year. Tax-free," Philly concluded.

Elly nodded. "Not a lot for a guy who spends it like Benny. But enough to keep the boat afloat."

"Where's he getting it?" Philly gave his head a slow scratch. Probably trying to figure how *he* could scam some.

I shrugged. "I couldn't find anything else incriminating in the computer."

Philly kept staring at the screen. "So we'll keep looking." He might have said that a bit too eagerly.

"Me, too," Elly said. "The county's computer is down, and I haven't been able to trace that warehouse yet." He shook his handsome head. "That dinosaur computer is so unreliable. Why are we paying taxes? How would the economy function if the rest of us only worked half the time?"

I kept the thought to myself—but he *did* only work half the time. I asked him to include the Windswept jingle in his search, assuming it was an actual address.

Elly went on, "I had better luck with the Martha-Sperry-Marsh connection. It's not *Benny* Marsh she has a association with, but *Jolly.*"

No shit—given our encounter at Beverly Vista. "What's the connection?" I reached across and took a leftover French fry from Philly's plate, absently nibbling on it.

"Martha, Sperry and Jolly owned a production company together," Elly said.

I choked so hard, I nearly sucked potato into my lungs. Schuller's comments when he picked Mother up came back to me. He wasn't pissed because he discovered she didn't own a production company—but because he learned the names of her partners.

"My mother really *is* a producer?" I muttered in disbelief.

Elly shrugged. "Well, once upon a time. Those three formed a company called On Our Own Productions, but they only made one picture, and it flopped. Barely earned back its costs. Pretty awful reviews, too. I don't think that was one of the pictures she used to show us."

He paid attention to the films she forced us to watch?

"What was it called?"

"*Deadly Shadows.* Great title, huh?"

SIXTEEN

"Lost in the Shadows," Regency Studios, 1960: Starring
Martha Collins as Linda and Jane Darnell as Mother.

*A cold, repressed mother turns her back on her shattered
daughter.*

MOTHER
*You demanded the truth—and I gave it to you. Now
you're complaining.*

LINDA
*You might have mentioned it would change my whole
life.*

BACK AT THE TRUCK, I slipped behind the wheel and buried my face in my arms. My companions endured the delay
for a good minute.

Finally, Philly asked, "Trace, we gotta get home. Don't
you want to know whether or not Schuller has arrested
Martha?"

Sure, that's what mattered most to me at that moment.
I raised my head. "I'm gonna hurl—for real this time."

Philly gave my shoulder a reassuring tap. "Yeah, it's
hard at first, but once you get used to pulling scams, it can
be fun."

I hoped the look I gave him delivered a full measure of
scorn. I can bullshit with the best of them, including him.

"I'm talking about the horrible discovery I just made. I

wrote a book with the same title as the only movie Mother ever produced, a film I never heard of till five minutes ago.''

"Don't sweat it, kid. Ideas are in the air.''

I gave my head a sorry shake. Since Mother got her hooks into Philly, he could no longer think for himself. "Ideas are in the air'' is Hollywoodesse for "I stole your screenplay.'' That's how everyone explains it when two similar movies are released at the same time. Everyone claims to believe it, and no one does. But in the collective air is not where I find the plots for my books.

"I have to figure out what happened,'' I muttered, more to myself. "And *then* I'll kill myself.''

On the way home we dropped Lorenzo off at Biggie's Billiards, and I stopped at the supermarket for some supplies. Then I looked for a place to get some wheels for Philly. We needed more freedom to move. Besides, I wanted my truck to last until the end of this caper. The Beverly Hills office of Budget Rent-A-Car offers luxury models like Ferraris and Rolls Royces, so visiting celebs don't have to rent the tin cans the rest of us drive on trips. All the way home, Philly made his case for a red Lamborghini from Budget. Instead, we went to a place that rents used cars. But I felt like such a piker when I asked for their cheapest model that I popped for a black Mustang convertible. The scruffy old coot looked pretty spiffy behind that set of wheels.

Neither Drew nor Mother were at the condo. I checked the answering machine to see if Drew had called in. Only one wink this time. I hit the play button.

My mother-in-law, Charlotte, whined, "Tracy dear, why haven't you returned my call? That strange man who answered your phone said something about your book, but really—''

I stabbed the erase button. My book was the last thing I wanted to think about now.

I remembered the message that pompous idiot, Logan Wayne, had left the day before. He coupled together some mention of my next book with the joke that I never listened to him. Though I would rather eat ground glass than talk to Logan, I went to my desk phone and punched up his number.

After the third ring, he drawled his signature greeting. "Wayne, here. Logan Wayne." What was wrong with *hello?*

Before I could get to my reason for calling, Logan cut me off. "Dear girl, I so wish you'd called earlier, but I'm getting ready for a premier tonight. *Twilight Forest*, you know."

"Yeah, Logan, you're Mr. First-Nighter." It was only two in the afternoon. How long did it take to turn himself into an obnoxious bore? "I only need a second. Tell me about *Deadly Shadows*."

"Yours or Martha's?"

Bile rose to my throat.

"I already told you, Tracy. It must have been…oh, a year or so ago. I assumed you agreed with me that it was an absolutely ma-a-ar-valous story, when I'd heard from the rumor mill that you'd adapted it to your latest novel."

Adapted? I didn't adapt—I created. I pressed my hand against my fake oak desktop to steady myself.

"Now, dear girl, I simply must fly. Can I afford to be late?" He tittered, "I think not."

You're telling me.

"But here's a idea, Tracy. First thing tomorrow, I'll FedEx my copy of the tape to you. Just don't tell Martha." He chuckled at his naughtiness. "It's a bootleg copy, and I know it's not her favorite performance."

This bozo didn't know the difference between a fart and whistle. She loved all her performances. If I didn't remember her talking about *Deadly Shadows*, it was only because I stopped listening when I was in the cradle.

But I couldn't wait. "Logan, could you send it today by messenger? I'll pay, of course." Hadn't I already paid for my own messenger's transportation? "No, I'll send my uncle for it."

"Grand! Love to meet him. Martha's brother or Alec's?"

"Actually, he's Drew's uncle."

"Oh."

Once I disconnected from Logan, I wrote out his address and sent Philly on his way.

Then, alone in my messy condo, I waited for the axe to fall.

IT FELL.

Though Philly had left to return Logan's tape long ago, I remained perched on the end of the bed, staring at a blank TV screen where the awful truth had played. There was no question in my mind now, Logan's wordy rendition of one of Mother's lesser-known movies had influenced my own creative process. I always tuned him out consciously, but my unconscious mind sucked it up like a treacherous sponge. Man, I tell you, if you've gotta live in the real world *all* the time, life's not worth the bother.

But there were also differences between Mother's *Deadly Shadows* and mine. Whereas I assigned the ensuing madness to Tessa's student, the heroine of Mother's movie suffered it herself. And my book offered the reader closure; Tessa proved that the man whom no one believed in actually did exist, saving her student's life and her reputation. The ending was indeterminate in Mother's movie—we never knew whether the heroine survived the ordeal.

The film's production values were also horribly jerky. Unexplained plot threads wove through, only to be abandoned without explanation. At times the actors didn't seem to be playing the same characters as in other parts of the story. And the writing—some lines were so corny that I didn't know how they could deliver them with straight faces. While I found others haunting enough to make me wish I had written them myself.

So? I'd stolen everything else—why not the lines? Any way I cut it—unintentional or not—I was a plagiarist. Even worse, I had copied from that worm, Vince Sperry. The credits listed him as the screenwriter, with Jolly the director and Mother the star. If this ever got out, Schuller would think *I'd* killed Sperry.

Seeing the movie did confirm something, though. That photograph of me in Sperry's house—it must have been taken on the *Deadly Shadows* set. The dark-haired man in the photo with those intense eyes was Edward Rivers, Mother's co-star and the stalker in the movie. I would have expected that to be a good part, but ol' Eddie couldn't have had much clout. They shot half of his scenes from the back with his face in shadows. Talk about some strange camera angles. An extra could have played all but a few scenes.

Another thought occurred to me—and finally, one that brought a smile to my face. Since Jolly directed the film, I guessed the smarmy little boy in the photo must have been Benny; I should have recognized his skinny rat face. I loved that the photographer had caught me hitting him over the head with a doll. No wonder it had felt so comfortable bopping him with an umbrella the night he groped me in his closet. I'd practiced that move earlier.

Did Benny remember when we were kids? He must have—he wasn't a baby then as I had been. Why did he pretend he didn't know Mother? How much *did* Benny know? And what about Sperry? He retired right after that film debuted. In his letter, he thanked Mother for her "generosity." What was it about the bonds forged by that one miserable picture that it demanded generosity?

Who would have thought one deck could contain so many jokers? My thoughts drifted back to Edward Rivers. I'd never heard of him. How could an unknown take bill-ing just below Mother—yet still warrant so little camera time?

Though my last computer search proved fruitless, I'd do anything to avoid thinking about the bleak future that stretched before me. Even if I managed to change my editor's mind, my book couldn't be published now. I trudged back to the study and searched for Rivers' name. Lacking the years of celebrity that Mother and the Marsh boys enjoyed, this search produced fewer results and nothing at all current. Where was this guy today?

Starting with the earliest dates, I skimmed over his background in old fan magazine articles. Described as an Irish nobleman, accounts said Rivers, seventh Earl of Rahway, had brought a great "treasure" here from his estate in Northern Ireland and took Hollywood by storm with his "dashing good looks." Sounded like the background bilge the studios used to churn out for their stars. He didn't display any Irish accent in the picture, though he played an American tough; anyway—he hardly spoke.

I couldn't quibble with the good looks part. Those mesmerizing eyes of his reinvented the cliché, "Making love to the camera." But unless he was a truly great actor, something told me there was a splash of cruelty in Rivers' make-up. The stalker's few good scenes showed him enjoying the game he played on the movie's heroine a tad too much.

Were looks alone enough to explain what seemed to be a stunning career in the making? He started at the top, capturing the leads of two pictures before *Deadly Shadows*. Why none after?

I clicked on another of the sites that came up in my search of Rivers' name, one dated during the filming of the picture. When I read what appeared on the screen, I understood all the technical problems that had doomed the movie. I'd been kidding when I suggested an extra could

have played the stalker in many of those shadowy scenes.
But I was right—an extra *had* played them.

During the filming of *Deadly Shadows*—Edward Rivers
had died.

STUNNED BY the possibilities, I read every account I could
find of his death. Three weeks into shooting, the company
broke for the weekend. The trio of producers met at someone's country home that Friday night to iron out some
details for the next week, while the rest of the cast and
crew scattered. Rivers took his boat out for an evening
cruise, as he was often known to do. Somewhere between
the California coast and Catalina, his boat blew up, lighting the night sky with such a ball of flame that people
reported seeing it from San Diego to Santa Barbara.

No sign of his much-touted "treasure" ever emerged,
though people had combed the beaches for days in search
of valuable debris. Rivers must have spent money faster
than he made it; he died intestate and in debt.

Only one significant fact emerged from my reading the
accounts of the explosion: Rivers' body was never found.
The boat was reduced to sawdust. One report quoted a
Coast Guard officer as saying no one could have lived
through such an explosion.

Maybe not. But he could have gotten off the boat before
it blew. Would anyone wait thirty years to stage a comeback?

SEVENTEEN

"New Game in Town," Regency Studios, 1961: Starring Martha Collins as Sunny and Alan Garvey as Uncle Elmer.

A woman shakes her fists in frustration, while an older man looks on with amused tolerance.

> SUNNY
>
> How could everything go so wrong? I thought I had all the answers.

> UNCLE ELMER
>
> You did, my dear. Life simply threw you a new set of questions.

I PACED A HOLE through the small part of the fawn-colored carpet in my bedroom that was devoid of Randy's legacy in our lives. Now I understood why the movie, *Deadly Shadows,* was so uneven. Their star died during production, forcing the production trio to punt. Even if nothing had gone wrong, that bunch probably didn't have it in them to hit a home run.

The more I thought about the Edward Rivers factor in our present situation, the more I liked it. With nothing left of the boat for analysis, the authorities could only guess at what caused the explosion. But a fuel-pump problem had plagued the boat for some time; Rivers had planned to have the boat serviced after the production wrapped. Was it so farfetched to think the faulty fuel pump might have ignited a fire that led to the explosion? What if Rivers had been burned in that fire? Wouldn't a vain man rather be thought dead than suffer the world's pity?

But why would he have waited so long to surface? Maybe the coverage of Sperry's suit against Marshland Productions brought it back. If everyone else was coming out on top, why shouldn't he?

I looked at the clock on Drew's maple nightstand. Almost five. What had happened to Mother? Could I risk broaching the subject of Rivers with her? Or should I run it past Drew? It was possible Drew already knew. Perhaps he went to Sperry's house that night to settle the lawsuit, as I suggested, and something happened to silence him. He wasn't a murderer, for chrissakes.

But if he didn't spill his guts to me soon, he was in danger of becoming a victim.

Speak of the devil. I heard the sound of a key slipping into the front door lock, and I raced to the living room just as Drew dragged himself through the entry.

He glared at me. "Ever consider becoming an orphan?"

"More than you know. How did it go with Schuller?"

"Wonderful. Your mother refused to answer any of his questions, even the ones *her lawyer* advised her to answer."

And that surprised him? He had to know she'd be the client from hell. "So…what? Schuller arrested her?"

Drew viciously flung his tan leather briefcase onto one of the piles. But he shook his head—no arrest. "I dropped her off at home."

He took a step forward, but I blocked his path. "Alone? Yolanda's leaving for her vacation on the redeye tonight." Did I really have to tell him how easily Mother could slip the harness?

"Angelique Barlow had some kind of attack, and Martha had to check her into the hospital."

"Angelique? What happened? What hospital did she go to?"

Drew's shrug seemed to require too much effort. He no longer cared about any of this.

I turned away, biting my lip. I was kidding myself. Drew's depression wasn't the result of being hamstrung by legal ethics. This funk was personal. Something was eating through his soul.

I glanced out the front window in time to see Philly's attempt to park the Mustang along the curb. The space was too small, but by continuing to tap the bumpers of the cars on both sides, he squeezed in. The jolts so unnerved Lorenzo's dog, lying in the back seat, he anxiously jumped to his paws.

"Why don't we ask Philly to spend the night at her place?" I suggested. "Just so there's someone to watch over her. He's been running an errand for me, but I see he's back now."

The old, anal Drew momentarily surfaced. "You're not letting him drive your truck? You know he doesn't know how to drive."

Though my heart leaped at the return of my picky, law-abiding spouse, this didn't seem the time to explain that there's a difference between being an officially recognized driver and knowing how to drive. Though when you take Philly's parking technique into account, Drew might be right.

Instead, I said in all honesty, "He's not driving the truck." He probably didn't want to know how I deceived the car rental company, either.

"How will he get to Beverly Hills?" Drew asked.

"He'll manage," I said.

Back in the doldrums, Drew just nodded.

I seized the chance to escape from his depressing funk and raced downstairs to ask Philly to keep Mother company at her house. There was a sacrifice. I returned with the dog in tow and found Drew on the bed, staring aimlessly at a tabloid talk show on TV, a book open in his hands. He probably didn't notice that he held the book upside-down.

We passed the evening like strangers, bound together in some awful definition of hell. Drew declined any dinner—couldn't tear himself away from *Jerry Springer.* Though I'd gotten dog food when I shopped, I fed Lorenzo's dog the steak I bought for Drew. I swear, if I didn't have the mutt to keep me company and a pint of Cherry Garcia ice cream to soothe my soul, I wouldn't have made it.

By eight o'clock, I couldn't stand it anymore. I marched into the bedroom, determined to have it out with Drew. Only he'd fallen asleep already, facing away from my side of the bed. He hadn't even said good-night. I swallowed a sob. Why was he doing this? How could he sacrifice us to his guilt?

I felt so demoralized, I just peeled my clothes and dropped them where I stood. I crawled into bed and drifted off into a troubled sleep. The dream house appeared as it often did. But for the first time, a room with odd little reminders of *Deadly Shadows* scattered about spun in circles. Mother's version of *Deadly Shadows,* not mine. The dream-time I spent in that house had always been comforting; tonight, it made me queasy.

I awoke around ten that night with an idea. From a casual remark Mother had made, I knew where to look for answers. Quietly, I put on yesterday's jeans and Drew's dirty green knit shirt, along with my tattered pair of undies. It was wrong to try to stop being a slob—this suited me. I might never shower again.

I grabbed my purse and made my way to Drew's bureau, where he left the contents of his pockets when he went to bed. I groped in the darkness till I felt the one object that might open the door to the answers I needed. Then I dashed away before I woke up the only person who could stop me.

FOR WHAT FELT LIKE the thousandth time today, my truck and I made the journey over the hill, stopping first at a gas station to quench its parched tank, and at the ATM, since my wallet needed a little quenching, too. I made one last pit stop at a Starbucks for yet another kind of fuel. Let's face it, sometimes the only difference between us and the animals—is a Caffé Americano. Then I grabbed the closest freeway entrance and flew over the Sepulveda Pass to Drew's Century City law firm.

SCREWED occupies three floors in a steel and glass high-rise. During the journey, I considered my approach. Invading that firm could be tricky at any hour, even one so close to the witching hour. With the competition for partnerships so fierce at SCREWED, there might be more associates and junior partners logging billable hours at midnight than there were at noon.

Gaining access to the fortified suite would be no problem. The object I clipped from among Drew's pocket stuff was his electronic key card. Law firms have become so security conscious, they post electronic sentries at every door these days. Why, I couldn't say, considering how easy it was getting hold of one of those cards.

Fortunately, too, I knew the drill. When a flu outbreak ravaged the staff last winter, I helped Drew before a critical trial. It also meant that once I got before a terminal, as long as the complex computer system hadn't changed much, I was on firm ground. It's always a mistake to try to keep out someone like me.

I popped the truck into Drew's parking space in the underground garage. The garage elevators only went as far as the lobby, where I'd meet my first test. But it was excitement, not fear, that made my heart tingle when the elevator doors closed. Nothing thrills me like being somewhere I don't belong. Life, for me, is one big game of hide-and-seek.

I stepped from the elevator into the vast marble lobby. On the way to the tower elevator bank, I waved Drew's badge over my head in the direction of a dozing guard watching TV at his station in the corner. He scarcely tore his eyes from *South Park*. Not even a sporting challenge.

The lowest of SCREWED's three floors housed mostly support staff. I figured I'd have the best chance of slipping in there unnoticed. When the elevator doors opened, I crawled past the empty tweed-covered secretarial carrels to the stairs. I scaled two flights of concrete steps and eased the door open at the top.

Rats! Voices.

"You're not gonna stay much longer, are you, Gail?" a man asked in a voice shaky enough to betray his anxiety. Bet they both sucked up to the same supervising partner, and he wasn't coming out ahead.

"I think I'll surprise Russell by having that brief on his desk in the morning. Run along, Fred," a woman answered with nasty superiority.

Jeez, didn't these losers have lives? I heard the sound of shoes scuffing heavily along the carpeted hall to the elevators, where, after a moment, the doors opened and closed. I expected the woman to walk off in the opposite direction. But she didn't budge. One minute, two. Had I left my bed—only to spend the night in a stairwell? Three minutes, four. Finally, as if she had been ticking off the time, Gail sighed and made her way to the elevators, where she, too, headed out.

They had lives—lives of pointless gamesmanship. I had to get Drew out of that zoo. Unless it meant the place he moved to would be a cell.

I listened for another minute after she left. Office buildings were deliciously creepy places at night—the steel groaned something awful, and I saw more monster-shaped shadows than when I watched a *Halloween* marathon. Once I was sure none of those shapes were the kind that moved, I crept down the hall toward Drew's office.

The firm's hierarchy dictated the office assignment. Senior partners drew the large corner offices, while junior partners settled for the smaller window offices between the corners, with their billings determining the views they commanded. Drew's office faced the ocean and was only two down from the corner he craved. But these days, that distance could be measured in miles.

Along the way, a smart detour occurred to me. Ice cream makes a better than average dinner, in my opinion, but it doesn't stick. This dump was full of little conference rooms, each of which held a selection of snacks. I flashed the key card at the one just ahead. Small bottles of soda and water were neatly lined up on an oak sideboard inside the door, but the ice bucket was empty, dammit. Shoulda called ahead. I took a Diet Seven-Up, a small bag of Doritos and a couple of packages of Oreos. Next time you wonder why your legal bill is so high, check out the munchies ledger.

With my arms laden with provisions, I slipped from the conference room to Drew's office. I had to shift my burdens around to free up a hand to wave the badge. While waiting for Drew's door to click open, I heard the sound of humming and the pounding of feet from somewhere in the suite. I froze, till the steps disappeared behind a swinging door, probably the men's room. The instant Drew's door clicked open, I dashed in. I pressed it closed with my back, leaning against it till a grin overtook my face. Sex should be this good.

After dumping my goodies on Drew's neat oak desk, I took a swig of Seven-Up. I finished off a pack of Oreos right away, but decided to save the other package and the chips for later. A two-course dinner.

I sank into his leather executive chair, trying not to notice that it gave off Drew's personal soapy smell, and focused on the files stacked on the desk. That's where Drew kept his recent cases. Many of them involved Marshland Productions, just as I'd hoped. I put aside the ones that dealt with the Sperry-Marsh plagiarism trial and hunted for files that covered Benny's conservatorship of Jolly. Somewhere in that file had to be a list of Jolly's properties; I felt sure I'd find the Van Nuys warehouse among them. But I went through everything, and the warehouse wasn't listed.

What now? While booting up the computer, I twisted a couple of Oreos open and scraped the cream filling off with my teeth. Yum. Once the computer was ready, I ran an internal search for Vince Sperry. Not surprisingly, given the litigation, the file list was extensive. I tore open the bag of Doritos and chomped on a few, while I ticked off every file notation listed in the computer against the folders on the desk. I smeared a little of the orange Dorito coating on one folder, but I wiped it off on the tail of Drew's knit shirt. Most of the numbers corresponded, but not all. I ran another search for a more detailed account of the entries that didn't correspond to the plagiarism case.

Bingo. The cases that appeared all pertained to On Our Own Productions, Inc., the production company Mother, Jolly and Sperry had formed together.

I knew it! If my head hadn't hurt so badly after getting slugged outside that warehouse, I would have picked up on it then. While locked in that hellhole, Mother had babbled on about Drew's firm, referring to it as *SCREWED* as she always did. But she also said she remembered when it had just been called *SCREW,* and she blamed the last partner added to the name for changing the character of the place. In all the time Drew worked there, she never mentioned she'd been a client of the firm—but who else would remember what it had been called?

I tried to decipher the date inherent in the coding system.

I'd been presuming the files for On Our Own Productions were all thirty years out of date, and that would mean they'd be rotting in a warehouse somewhere. But I began to think the notation assigned to On Our Own Productions wasn't for an inactive file, after all.

There was a file storage room on this floor for active clients not involved in current cases. I knew that room well—Drew kept inventing reasons to send me there while I worked for him; maybe he was better suited to the gamesmanship in this place than I thought. I chugged the last of my soda and finished off most of the snacks. Except for a lone Dorito that I placed dead center on Drew's black leather desk mat. Let him wonder.

I popped my head out the door. When I didn't hear the hummer, I scooted down the hall. But in the shadowy office, all the corridors confused me. I stopped, lost.

The shake, rattle and roll of a big set of keys grew in volume from somewhere in the suite. Sounded like the guard making his rounds. Louder, louder—he was closer than I thought! On tiptoes, I crept to a secretarial cube, where I slipped under the desk well. Peering through the opening, I watched the indifferent guard from the lobby bopping down the hall, swinging his huge key ring and bouncing to the beat of a Walkman tuned so loudly, it echoed in the empty suite. When I finally sprung Drew from that dump, maybe I should let the partners know how lax their security was. Nah, never know when I might want to sneak in again. Just for old times' sake.

While I waited for the guard to pass, I oriented myself, finally spotting the perpendicular corridor I'd missed. Then I crept down the hall and pressed the key card to the sensor outside the file room. But once inside—I came to a dead stop.

There are definitely way too many lawyers in this country. If you doubt that, check out the day jobs of half the authors writing mystery books—lawyers, all of them. Or just consider the rows and rows of files I found before me. Floor-to-ceiling, on and on for thirty feet or more, broken only in the center for a narrow passage. I nearly packed it in. But after checking out some of those files, I had to admit anal people like Drew have their uses, too. Despite the thousands of files shelved there, they were arranged in perfect numerical order. Not the way I would have gone, but it worked.

The file for On Our Own Productions was thicker than I expected. And even though the company hadn't produced a picture in more than thirty years, it was an active corporation. It looked as if Mother and Jolly bought out Sperry around the time of *Deadly Shadow*'s release. In the years since, someone had funded On Our Own Productions enough to pay its taxes—and provided Vince Sperry with an annual consultancy fee, one that had risen over the years from twenty thousand to his last payment of nearly forty. Bet I knew whose pocket that money came from. That old coot had been robbing my inheritance!

Stunned by the details, the file slipped from my hands. Though all the sheets were clasped to the folder, while I grabbed for it, pages flipped in every direction. I had been scanning the more recent sections of the file, but once I strengthened my hold on it, I found myself staring at one of the earliest entries. SCREW had negotiated the purchase of a warehouse for On Our Own Productions and oversaw its conversion to a soundstage.

That warehouse was located on Kenney Avenue in Van Nuys.

What was Mother doing to her life? To *mine?* I wanted to scream. I nearly did—only the hummer chose that moment to invade my hiding place. Without warning, the door at the other end of the long room opened, and someone flew in, whistling off key and noisily tossing the floating file racks out of his way.

Time to make my getaway. Quickly, but quietly, I

pushed the file back onto the grey metal shelf. I inched backward toward the door; the knob turned soundlessly in my hand. Success!

How dare Philly suggest I didn't have the nerves for fourteenth story work. I eased the door closed behind me, turned away—and ran smack into my irate husband.

Busted again. Man, I was losing my touch.

"Drew, how'd you get in here?" I whispered, waving his key card.

"*That's* the first thing you ask? The guard let me in." Drew lunged for the card as if it were a lighted match in the hands of a toddler. "Give me that, Tracy. Haven't you done enough damage?"

I yanked it away. "Me? That's funny coming from you. In my hands, mister, this is your 'Get Out of Jail Free' card."

We'd moved on to shouting, though I noticed the hummer didn't bother to pop his head from the file room. Don't tell me all my sneaking around was in vain. No, it was still fun.

Drew stomped his foot so hard, I think the building swayed. "Why would I need to get out of jail? *You're* the one in jeopardy, baby. You might as well admit it—you went to see Sperry that night."

My anger dissolved in a fog of confusion. "Where did you get that idea? I never met the man." Anger burned through the fog; I found my shouting voice again. "*You* lost it with Sperry."

Drew choked. "That's the craziest—" He stopped and frowned. "I'm confused. Martha led me to understand that you— Where did you get the idea that I—"

"Where did either of us get the crazy idea that the other one killed him?" I puckered my lips and blew so hard, my force of my breath knocked my bangs off my forehead. "Where indeed?"

EIGHTEEN

"Forty-niner Folly," Regency Studios, 1962: Starring Martha Collins as Sal and Alec Grainger as Henry.

The California goldrush. In a rustic cabin, a miner studies a map at a rickety table, while a frustrated woman pauses at the door.

> ### HENRY
> *You can't leave now, Sal. I'm close to the vein. I'm right this time, I know it.*
>
> ### SAL
> *You hit the mother lode when you met me. Now, even if you strike gold, you'll still be broke.*

Slamming the door, Sal exits.

WE TOOK DREW'S CAR to an all-night coffee shop. Still furious—at exactly what, I couldn't say—he fumed all the way.

"Why did I expect any more from you and your family? You're crazy, every one of you." Before I could object, he snapped, "Don't deny it, Tracy—you're exactly like them."

Now he was just insulting.

He jerked the Volvo to a stop at the curb. "You Graingers have so many loose screws, you rattle like a bunch of castanets."

At least we were musical. His family just rattled.

A sign in the window of the Great American Coffee Shoppe read, "No shoes, no shirt—no service." I always wonder: Does that mean a shoeless, shirtless server will make you get it yourself? We slipped into a navy vinyl booth at the window.

A stocky waitress stopped at our table and tossed down a couple of menus decorated with stars and stripes. Her Roller Derby body wasn't an ideal match for the flirty little red costume she wore. The designers of theme restaurants oughta wake up sometime and smell the Starbucks.

I peered at Drew over the top of my menu. "I still can't believe Mother made us suspect each other of whacking that man."

"And I can't believe you thought me capable of murder."

So *that's* why he was mad. "She was right about that. You are the type that snaps."

"I never snap!" he snapped.

The waitress's dull hazel eyes widened, and she took a step back. "I'll give you a minute to decide."

"No, don't go. I'm starved." I slapped the menu down. "I'll have a grilled cheese sandwich and fries. And tell the cook to leave the fries in the oil so long they cry for mercy."

Drew gave his head a sorry shake. "Tracy, you really should eat better." He asked for a broiled chicken breast on a dry wheat roll.

"So I live five minutes more—wishing I'd eaten more fries? Nobody gets outta this life alive. You pick your poison."

Drew locked eyes with our waitress as she backed away from our table, before blurting, "Change my order. I'll have the comfort food, too."

You can never have too much comfort—that's my motto.

Drew clasped his hands before him on the table and took a deep breath. "Here's how I propose we handle this—"

"Hold it." I made a counter-clockwise motion with my finger to indicate a turning back of time. "We're not finished with the postmortem yet. I can't believe you thought I bumped off Sperry. You should know I can always find a better way out of anything. How did she convince you?"

He shrugged sheepishly. "She let me think you went there to talk Sperry into settling. So I'd make senior partner."

"I have more confidence in your legal skills than you do, bud. She told me you went to have it out with him."

"I was at the office all evening, surrounded by the whole trial team." He waved a finger in my face. "But Martha said you weren't home when Sperry was stabbed, and after telling her you would be. That's why she didn't have an alibi. She said she went to see you, but you stood her up."

The whole time he talked, I kept shaking my head.

"No, huh?" he asked.

"Home all night—as you'd know if you'd called. Holy freakin' April Fool's Day, Drew! Could you have made it any easier for her?"

"What's with all the freakin' holidays?" Drew demanded.

I growled, "I'm feeling festive, okay?"

The waitress extended two thick white cups on saucers. Her hands shook so badly that half the coffee spilled into the saucers. She skidaddled fast.

I nodded my head to where the waitress disappeared into the kitchen. "She thinks we're a couple of tough characters."

"Instead, we're just related to one." Drew cleared his throat. "Tracy, let's face it, your mother lied to both of us."

"No. Alert the media."

Drew went on as if I hadn't spoken. "Obviously, Martha set us up to hide her own guilt."

A big guy in a ketchup-smeared apron served our sandwiches. Given his vague smile, I sensed our reputations were growing.

My teeth sunk into my sandwich. Greasy and gooey, the way I like 'em—though oddly stingy on the comfort. Maybe since I always associate grilled cheese sandwiches with my mother. She can't cook much; truly, the woman burns water. I must have been eight before I realized other families don't have some stranger living in the room off the kitchen who performs that service. But Mother does grill a mean cheese.

Sometimes, when I was little and had a bad day, that's what she made to cheer me up. It didn't happen often. When she wasn't working, she was off somewhere playing celebrity; our schedules rarely overlapped. But the infrequency of those times made me treasure them more. We would sink our teeth in greasy sandwiches. And I'd share everything that happened with the one person who always understood.

A pair of fat tears rained on my plate from...somewhere. I scrunched my eyes, in case they were the source.

"She didn't set us up," I reasoned slowly. "She just contrived a way to keep us both in there fighting for her, while making sure we'd never compare notes."

Drew slapped his hands on the table. "To what end? That's how people end up in jail."

"She wanted to keep us too busy to wonder about the person she might be protecting. That's the only answer."

"That's insane, Trace. Who would she care enough for to risk her life protecting? You, certainly, but you didn't do it. Maybe me, but I didn't, I swear. Who else is there?"

Drew seemed to get the idea that I didn't want to answer that question. Maybe because I pressed my face against the table, groaning. Fear screamed a name in my mind, but I couldn't bear to bring it through my lips.

"Isn't there *anyone* else you can think of?" I turned my head to stare up at him. "Come on, Drew. What do you have to say?"

His eyes drifted off, before widening in disbelief. "Holy freakin' doomsday!"

Couldn't have put that better myself.

DREW'S VOLVO must have been in shock—it had never received the jolt of gas he supplied all the way to the airport.

After stewing together at the coffee shop, Drew had shouted, "Yolanda! We have to catch her before she leaves for Acapulco."

He had slapped a twenty on the table and grabbed my hand. I didn't even have a chance to take my sandwich.

"Drew, Yolanda's plane leaves…" I struggled to read my watch on the run. "…*now*. We'll never make it. Call her after she arrives at her sister's."

Drew kept moving till we reached his car. He wouldn't even drop me off at his garage to retrieve my truck. Once behind the wheel, he wove from lane to lane at such high speeds, I thought we'd take flight from a freeway overpass long before we reached the airport. Sure, that's how *I* drive, but I know what I'm doing. These maneuvers were not in Drew's job description.

With grim determination, Drew said, "In the interest of time, I'd suggest you spill your guts."

As unprecedented as it was, I considered it. But I had a deal-breaker. "Only if you impose a moratorium on your own rigid judgments."

"I'm not—" Even in the darkened car, when we glanced at each other, I could see he knew he couldn't pull that one off. "Agreed."

He came up behind a driver whose only offense was

cruising at sixty-five in the slow lane, and he leaned on the horn. While he took on my driving personality, I assumed his ethical code. I did something I never thought I would—I told the complete truth. What an ordeal. Is it any wonder I lie now and then?

Drew reverted to type. "You *stole* evidence from Sperry's house?"

"It's not my fault Schuller's sloppy." I gripped the armrest as he took the Century Boulevard exit on two wheels. "What about your promise?"

"Hah! How do you like it, Tracy, when people break their promises to you?"

When I do it, it's different. My new motto: *Be careful what you wish for.*

THE AIRPORT WAS nearly deserted at that hour. Even the pseudo-missionaries, who have collected enough money at the base of the escalators to solve the homeless problem a hundred times over, had gone home for the night. There wasn't a line at the security check, naturally, but Drew has such a magnetic personality, he had to strip to his undies to get through.

Once he did, we ran all the way to Yolanda's gate. But it was empty.

I bit back the *I told you so* and gave Drew's back a conciliatory rub. Man, I hated this metamorphosis I was undergoing.

Then, from behind me, I heard in an irritating whine that always made my teeth hurt, "If you two came here to see me off, you're too late. I already left."

YOLANDA VALDEZ IS the anti-Martha Collins. Stout to Mother's frail, dark to her light, irritating to her charming—but they both had elevated pointless stubbornness to a fine art, and neither considered any issue too petty not to defend to the death of those around them.

"It's your fault, Tracy. It's 'cuz you only agreed to bus'ness class at the last minute that I had to take standby. Because o' you, I got bumped.''

"Yeah, agreeing to pay a fortune so other people have better vacations—I hate it when I do that.''

Drew jumped between us before I bopped Yolanda. "Tracy, maybe we should buy Yolanda a drink.''

"Sure, Drew, get the maid drunk,'' Yolanda smugly reasoned. "Then when someone steals her money, she won't be able to afford her trip, and you won't have to pay for her ticket. Are you *loco?* I gotta spend the night in the airport.''

I hissed into Drew's ear. "You know, I really couldn't have killed Sperry, but her...?''

He shot me a cautionary glance and turned back to Yolanda. He looked down to where he'd left her sitting, but now she was on her feet. Even so, with her short, stout body and her dark auburn hair, she looked like a fireplug. A really mean one.

"Well? Where's that drink?'' Yolanda asked.

Drew glanced at me. "You deserve a medal.''

"Haven't I said that?''

Drew encouraged her to sit again, and he knelt on one knee at her side. "Yolanda, *if* there's any space available on the next flight, how would first class appeal to you?''

"Keep talkin'—''

"Tell us who came to the house the night Sperry died.''

Yolanda prided herself on never blinking—that was how she survived with Mother. But when she brought her deep brown eyes to me, I saw they looked troubled.

I cried, "Oh, God—it's true! My father was there!''

"Nice going, Trace,'' Drew snapped in response to my leading the witness.

Yolanda gave us a sad nod.

Drew tried a different tact. "I don't believe it. Alec was in Del Mar.''

Yolanda looked at Drew so crossly, you'd have thought she was putting a curse on him. "After all these years, you think I don't hear them fighting enough? Mr. Alec, he come back from Del Mar and he say 'I'm sick of that leech sucking you dry. This time, I'm gonna put an end to it.'"

NINETEEN

"Endless Tunnel," Regency Studios, 1963: Starring Martha Collins as Nora and Lane Chandler as Brad.

Two passengers panic as a runaway train approaches a tunnel.

NORA
They'll be able to stop the train when we reach the other side, won't they?

BRAD
What makes you think we'll get there?

WE WENT TO Beverly Hills to confront Mother. During the drive, I said, "Dad's words sound damning, but you know my father is the gentlest man who ever lived."

In the darkened car, Drew gave a tight nod. "I'll grant you, Alec is a quiet man, but he blows on occasion."

"And then it's over. Come on, Drew, when this man finds a spider in the house, he releases it into the wild."

"A spider wasn't hurting Martha—Sperry was."

The 405 Freeway slowed to a long, winding, red-tailed centipede. Doesn't anyone sleep anymore? I shared my theory that Eddie Rivers was still alive and was behind all the havoc.

With a sigh, Drew shook his head. "Tracy, that's crazy. Faking his own death, compounding resentments for thirty years. Things like that don't happen in the real world."

"My parents and their friends don't live in the real world."

He sighed in frustration while pumping the brake. "Accept it: Rivers died thirty years ago. The authorities determined that at the time."

"They were wrong," I insisted mulishly.

Drew took the Wilshire exit and sped toward Mother's house. "Yeah? Where's he been all this time? I know! I bet he's been holed up on his vast estate in Ireland. And why is he bothering them? Oh, right—for money. No, doesn't he own a great fortune?"

Somebody needed to take the bonehead classes at sarcasm school. "Treasure," I said through clenched teeth. "The articles all referred to it as a *treasure*."

"Give it up, Trace. The sooner you accept what you're dealing with, the sooner you can help your dad."

Nobody ever won by surrendering.

DREW PARKED AT the curb in front of Mother's house, a big, sprawling mansion on a wide street in the Beverly Hills flats, as the non-hilly areas are called. The style defies classification. A magazine once described it as, "Tara meets the Taj Mahal." The lacy iron balcony railings on the second floor provided an especially gaudy touch. It's been known to give architects raging migraines.

The house looked extra creepy tonight; it was totally dark. Neither the small copper-green lights scattered across the wide lawn nor the porch light burned, and they were on timers.

"They're asleep," I said.

"But someone is here." Drew pointed at the black Mustang convertible parked in the driveway behind Mother's Mercedes. "Whose car is that?"

I fished in my purse for my keys. "You don't want to know."

"Nooo!" he groaned. "You bought a car for Philly."

"Relax, Drew. I did not." From the darkness, I heard a relieved sigh. "It's rented."

"Oh, much better."

I rang the bell a few times. When no one came, I unlocked the door. While Drew went around turning on lights downstairs, I flew up the stairs. But at Mother's closed bedroom door I hesitated. What if she wasn't alone? What if Philly hadn't slept in the guest room? Was *that* an image I wanted to be scarred with for life? Taking a deep breath, I threw the door open.

There weren't two bodies in that bed—there weren't any bodies. Though someone had slept on one side; I could see the rumpled sheets where the covers had been tossed aside.

I rushed down the hall to the guest room. I opened the door and threw on the light. Empty, too. They'd both abandoned their rooms, but Philly had left his pipe and tobacco on the dresser.

I ran down the stairs so fast I nearly tripped. "Drew? Drew, where are you?"

"In the kitchen," he called.

I pushed through the Japanese dining room's swinging door, to the big designer kitchen with its beechwood cabinets and commercial appliances. It was as neat as Yolanda must have left it, apart from a small copper pot on the six-burner stove and a couple of navy ceramic mugs of cocoa on the pine table. I wrapped my hands around one of the mugs. Cold.

Drew pounded the granite countertop. "They're on the lam."

"How did they get there? They left their cars here."

"How does she get anywhere? Maybe they flew on her broomstick." Drew's voice sounded shaky.

I told him about finding Philly's pipe paraphernalia. "He wouldn't have left without that stuff. Not voluntarily."

"What a nightmare. Where do we begin?" Drew ran a hand through his wavy hair; for once it didn't fall so perfectly into place. "Well, we can't do anything more here tonight. Let's go home and get some sleep. We'll tackle it again once it's light."

"You're forgetting Harriet Houdini," I reminded him.

After a childhood in which I was given every privilege, but denied all pets—once Drew and I set up our household, I went to the pound for a kitten. I showered so much affection on that little minx. My only mistake was giving in to Mother's request to take care of the cat at her house when we went away one weekend. After two days, the damned cat refused to come home.

With a sigh, Drew said, "I'll round up her carrier and some food. You find Harri."

Just like him to claim the easy job. There was a reason why the kitten we first called "Fluffy" came to be known by the name of a famed prestidigitator. No one could hide like Harriet Houdini. I secretly believed it was our tiny, boring home that Harri rejected, not us.

Drew went out the kitchen door and headed across the yard to the detached garage at the rear. I started at the front of the house and made a systematic sweep of every spot a six-pound cat could squeeze into. There were no shortage of them, believe me. By the time I reached the den, I was royally pissed.

I paused with a sigh before setting to work on the desk. For a woman rarely seen to work at them, Mother has gone through more desks over the years than the architectural styles reflected by her home. The current version stretched across the room in front of the French doors that led to the pool and was so big, even a CEO's ego would have found room to roam there. The surface was a huge slab of greenish glass held up by two large, teak pedestals. Filling the pedestals were a variety of drawers of every shape and size, none of which fit any known business function.

I took a moment to grab Mother's address book and stuffed it into my purse. Then I started with the larger of the drawers and kept moving to progressively smaller ones. Most were emptied of any contents, not to mention a cat. I figured I'd skip the ones that were too small, but that cat was tiny and had some amazing gifts. I tried a little square drawer. It seemed to catch. From the additional weight of a small feline?

From the back of the house, Drew called in a happy voice, "Look who I found in the pool house."

He sailed into the room with a little silver-and-white tabby traitor nuzzling his neck. I geared up for a crack—only by tugging at the drawer, I'd cleared the jam. What I discovered there made my head spin.

"Trace…?"

The drawer was stuffed with letters, dozens of them, all anonymous. All threatening.

"It's been going on for a long time. Why didn't she tell us?" I muttered.

"What has? What are you talking about?"

The letters appeared computer-generated and printed out on a laser printer. I read a couple silently to myself. "Give it back—or you'll pay," one letter said. "I know how to hit you where it hurts—give me what's mine," read another.

I kept flipping through them till I hit one that took my breath away. I shook that sheet before Drew's face. "I told you. It isn't Dad—it's Rivers. He's *not* dead. Who else would have written this?"

Drew snatched the letter with his one free hand and read aloud, "Last chance: Give me my treasure—or I'll take your life."

TWENTY

"Oasis in the City," Regency Studios, 1964: Starring Martha Collins as Teri and Alan McNeill as Drake.

On a smoldering city rooftop, a couple savor some stolen time.

TERI
It's not going to last, is it? This peace we've found here.

DRAKE
Knowing our time is short—that's what makes it special.

ON THE WAY BACK to the SCREWED garage so I could claim my truck, Drew groused, "Who uses words like *treasure?* What is it, jewelry or something? Why doesn't she give it up?"

"I'd guess she doesn't have it. She wouldn't risk her life to hoard material wealth. She *can't* produce it."

The Master of Understatement, Drew said, "Not good."

He dropped me off at my truck but insisted on transferring the cat's carrying case to my passenger seat. "Come on, Trace. You two need some bonding time. Harri thinks you don't like her?"

"*She* thinks it?"

The cat that was an angel in Drew's car went into vocal

overdrive in mine. How could such a tiny body produce such loud, irritating squawks?

Despite the escalating noise, I tried to think. I wouldn't admit it to Drew, but I was just as skeptical about this Irish nobleman crap. By the early sixties, the big studios had lost much of their power, and with it went the machinery that created colorful backgrounds for stars. A more combative media was also growing that would have exploded the myths the press meekly accepted in decades past. That someone felt a need to manufacture a cleaned-up history for Rivers told me there was something awful in his past. What kind of "treasure" could it have produced? And why would he think Mother had it?

But maybe I was completely wrong about Rivers. I took him to be an aggressive man. Would a guy like that assume the passive approach and write to Mother?

Despite my intention to ignore it, Harri's voice was a flesh-eating worm that bore into my brain and turned it to mush.

"Give it a rest!" I exploded. Round eyes in a silver tabby face glared at me through the cat-case screen—before letting out a cry so loud, I nearly lost control of the truck. I gave the small fry a nasty smile. "Wait till you meet your new roommate."

The nastiness turned on me when I remembered who was burdened by this brood. No pets, I had vowed; now I was juggling a pair.

I STRUGGLED TO BEAT Drew home for reasons I didn't bother to explore. Sometimes one-upmanship is all I have. I made it to the garage first, but while I lugged the cat case to the elevator, he must have zipped up the stairs. I found him standing on the living room path, viewing the chaos with the same dazed look as always. Get over it, already.

"Where did you pick up the feathers?" I pointed to a

pair of white fluffy feathers that stood out against the black towel Drew happened to be standing on.

He shrugged. "Maybe our pillows found their way in here."

Our bedroom pillows were foam. While it wouldn't surprise me to learn our down comforter exploded under the weight piled on the sofa, I couldn't see how the feathers would have drifted there.

Lorenzo's dog flew from the bedroom. He pressed his big nose to the cat-case screen. Harri let out an outraged shriek and swatted it. It took a half-hour to introduce those two, during which time I sustained three scratches—only to discover they seemed to think chasing each other through the ruins of our possessions was more fun than pigs have in shit.

"As we speak, the neighbors have to be circulating a petition to throw us out," I warned, shouting over the dog's gleeful bark.

"Who cares? A cardboard box under a freeway overpass would be quieter than this." Drew looked longingly at the bedroom. "Let's try to sleep. The noise will settle down."

I hesitated. "The bars are still open in Mexico." I pulled Mother's address book from my purse. "I have to find Dad. Who else can tell us about Rivers?"

"You don't need my help, do you?"

With a regretful sigh, I said, "Your Spanish *is* better."

He closed his eyes and nodded. We went to the study, where I divided the book's loose-leaf pages. I gave Drew my desk phone, thinking that would be more comfortable for him. Instead, he complained about a chair cushion that only fit my behind. I sat on the floor and used the fax phone.

I tried to buck-up my growing despair. Over their years together, my mother had collected the numbers for a sizable amount of bars and race tracks across Mexico. But how many more existed? After an hour of telephoning, we learned only two things: My father was still well-known to his fans south of the border—and we should have done this a day earlier. He'd already left several of those places.

A day late and a dollar short, seemed to be my motto, suddenly. Wonderland's Alice never fell into a place this crazy.

My last call proved to be the most discouraging. After tracing a route that hop-scotched all over Mexico, I tried a Baja number again that had been busy the first time. Jorge Rios, the owner of a stop in Dad's standard Mexican pub crawl, happened to be one of a few I actually knew.

"Your timing really stinks, Tracy," Jorge said in his nearly unaccented voice. "Alec passed through here earlier today."

"Was he headed home?" I asked eagerly.

"Don't know, *chica.* He just said he was on the move." I asked to leave a message, but Jorge cut me off. "You know how Alec is. I could see him next month, or it might be next year. Don't worry, Tracy. Your dad will surface when he's ready."

When *he's* ready? What about me? My frustration finally erupted. The instant Jorge clicked off, I began rapping the phone frantically against the wooden floor.

"No, no, no!" I shouted in time to the dents forming in the parquet.

Drew ended his call and rushed to my side. "It's all right, baby." He gently wiped something off my face. "Don't cry."

"I'm not crying, dammit! You know I never cry." I burst into wailing sobs. "I can't stand it anymore. Why are they doing this to me?"

"They're not actually doing it to—"

"I don't care! What's happening to me? I can always shape the world so it works for me—except when Mother enters the picture. You can't imagine what it's like going through life playing Ethel to her Lucy."

Drew pursed his lips. "No, just Ricky to yours."

"*That's* the way it's supposed to work," I snapped.

Drew rocked me in his arms, cooing softly and stroking my hair. "Let's turn in, babe. We're through for the night."

Not quite. Not the way I felt. I couldn't smoke, I hadn't had a chance to eat—I needed something. I twisted my fingers into the fabric of his pewter shirt and pulled him into a kiss. Drew caught on fast.

Breathless, Drew broke away and dashed to the living room. He returned dragging a thick, queen-sized sleeping bag, a legacy from our one attempt at camping. I tumbled onto the sleeping bag and pulled Drew on top of me. I kicked the door closed. Almost immediately, noisy canine sniffs came from under the door, followed by the sound of a cat hurling herself at the doorknob. I tuned out all the noise. I was on a mission.

While drilling Drew's teeth with my tongue, I wrestled with the buckle on his khaki pants. He started to help me, but I took his hands and planted them were they belonged—on me. *Get with the program,* was what I was trying to convey. This wasn't one of those love-making sessions when you can practically read soulful poetry in the process. It was the night sky on the fourth of July, two runaway trains on a collision course. Anything that didn't end in a ball of flames wouldn't do.

With a low, rumbling groan, Drew seemed to get where I was headed. He sank his teeth into my lip till I tasted blood. I tugged at his waistband and heard the button pop and fly across the room.

After ripping off his shirt, I dug my nails into Drew's broad back and ground my hips against his, driving him, flailing him like you would a racehorse. Yes! This wasn't love, not at this moment, I admitted to myself. It wasn't even lust. This was my reclamation of myself.

Faster and faster. Needing nothing, demanding everything, I grasped for what I wanted. On and on, till—finally, I ignited.

Yes! Yes! YES! Tracy Eaton was back.

LATER, STILL STRETCHED out on the sleeping bag, I propped myself up on my elbow and traced patterns around the boo-boos I had carved into Drew's back. Who knew I was such a lusty little thing? Drew rolled over and spotted the surprise I'd plastered on my butt.

He tapped the red-and-black temporary tattoo I'd applied, reading from it, "Bad to the bones!" He chuckled. "Very cute. But shouldn't that be singular? Isn't the expression, *Bad to the bone?*"

It was! What a rip-off tattoo. Miss Marple had it way easier.

Drew just took my fingers in his hand and pressed them to his lips. An A for effort anyway.

"Did you mean it, Drew? What you said yesterday," I asked tentatively.

"What did I say?" he asked in a drowsy voice.

"About us being too different." *Please,* God. I'd give up anything else. "That was when you thought I offed Sperry, right?"

"Right." Drew chuckled, but the laugh ended quickly. "Though we are, you know. Different, I mean. Sometimes I think it's as if there's a rushing river between us, with a current too fast to ford. You can never see how things are on my side, and I've never been to yours."

No. "We seemed to come together pretty good here." I tapped the sleeping bag.

"Babe, we always came together good here." Drew laughed with contentment. "But there's more to life than cyclone sex."

Other girls' mothers warned them men only wanted one thing; mine promised it. They'd all lied.

I fell on my back and stared at the ceiling.

Drew idly wrote little messages on my tummy, causing my skin to tingle. "Do you ever wonder about your parents' relationship?"

Talk about instant turn-off. "As little as possible. Yuck!"

"I don't mean sex, I mean…well, what holds them together. Do you think Martha was messing around with the Earl of Rahway?" He coated the last few words in sarcasm.

"Your guess is as good as mine." And mine was very good.

"Why does she do it?" Drew asked.

I flexed my shoulders in a sort of a shrug. "I've never known whether there's a hole inside of her that she tries to fill—or if she's such an adoration junkie that she can't get enough from the same ol' guy."

"It's usually men who say, 'It didn't mean anything.' And they're lying. For a short time, it means everything to them. That's true for her, too." Drew sighed at the ceiling.

I nodded. I'd seen her steer our family vessel onto the rocks too many times to believe her dalliances were meaningless. But neither were any enduring. I also knew that.

"What about Alec? Sometimes I have a hard time respecting him for letting his wife do that to him. Other times, I find myself thinking that he's stronger than the rest of us. At the end of the day, he knows he's her rock and always will be."

I just wanted him to be *mine*.

Drew lifted his head toward the window. "It's almost dawn. What now?"

"Lacking Eddie Rivers' address and the telephone numbers for the remainder of Mexico's flophouses, I think I have to go back to that warehouse. Then to see Benny, and maybe Jolly again. I don't know what else to do."

"Did you really carry your mother out of that warehouse on your *back,* climbing a rope?"

"I'm still stiff all over from it."

He laughed. Not like Drew. He should have told me I had some 'splaining to do.

"Would you have done that for *my* mother?" he asked.

"Of course," I said, smiling sweetly. His mother would have been easier—I'd have drop-kicked her out of there.

"Well, I can't let you go back to the warehouse, it's too dangerous," Drew said, rising.

Now that was my Drew. Naturally, I had no intention of listening.

"Not alone, that's for sure," he added. "I'm coming, too."

Whoa! "Drew, don't you have to work today?"

He looked aghast. "Tracy, do you really think I'd abandon you and your mother at a time like this? Don't you know me better than that?"

Maybe not. I didn't make it across that river too often, either. Drew dragged me to my feet.

"Now get moving, you sexy tattooed wench, before I forget what we have to do and try it again—at my pace this time."

But the view seemed pretty good from those opposing banks. I wasn't hiding much from him.

He gave me a slap on the ass. "Onward!"

TWENTY-ONE

"Missing Pieces, Extra Pieces," Regency Studios, 1965: Starring Martha Collins as Nancy and Alec Grainger as Ted.

A couple read through old issues of a newspaper.

> ### TED
> *This is hopeless. I haven't found a thing. How about you?*
>
> ### NANCY
> *Sometimes I find pieces, but they seem to fit a different puzzle.*

WE HEADED BACK to the warehouse in my truck. Though it was well before the start of the workday, police barricades blocked some of the streets in the area. But not Kenney Avenue, nor the addition that led to the warehouse.

I had a bad feeling about those barricades. The neighborhood was absolutely deserted. Without any conscious thought, I made a hard right into the parking lot of the awning factory where the Asian woman had told me how to find the warehouse.

I drove around the back of the building and parked next to a silver Taurus. I'd hoped to find a fire escape or something we could use to climb to the roof, but I never expected such a perfect accommodation. Someone had propped a long aluminum ladder against the building and extended it all the way to the top.

We stepped from the truck. The crackle of static from somewhere above broke the silence. I raced for the ladder. After only a slight hesitation, I heard the soft sound of Drew's shoes tapping against the rungs below me.

At the top, I gazed across the roof. A man crouched at the opposite parapet, looking through a pair of binoculars with such intensity that he didn't react to my approach. The crackling walkie-talkie rested on the roof next to him, and he wore a navy windbreaker with white lettering that spelled out: F-B-I.

There was something familiar about the line of the fibbie's shoulders. Once it hit me, I swung my feet over the side and waited for Drew to join me.

"Look who we have here, Drew," I shouted.

The agent spun around, dropping the binoculars to his side.

"This is Lorenzo, the guy I told you about."

"The migrant laborer?" Drew asked. "Really great that he found a day's work—with the FBI."

Lorenzo didn't look nearly so impoverished now in his pricey Nikes and Levi's. I should have suspected the truth when I first saw his well-framed glasses.

"That's Special Agent Perez!" he snapped in perfect English. "Tracy, shouldn't you be out somewhere adding to your purloined award collection?"

Drew shot me a dangerous look. In my complete and truthful accounting, I might have neglected one or two details.

Lorenzo went on, "You'd have thought twice about that if you realized you were palming it off on a Federal agent."

"No, I wouldn't," I insisted.

He looked at me with renewed surprise.

"You must find my honesty refreshing, huh?" I said.

"Honesty!" His eyes returned to the binoculars, but his lips twitched with amusement.

I sidled up next to him, confirming that he was watching the warehouse. The Bureau must have been interested in it for some time. Philly had said, when his taxi almost hit Lorenzo, that he'd been hiding behind a bush at the curb.

"What do you want, Tracy?" Lorenzo asked.

I dropped the levity. "Mother and Philly are missing."

"They've been abducted," Drew said. "Look, Agent Perez, if you want us to leave—"

So much for Drew's transformation to free spirit.

Static from the walkie-talkie cut Drew off. A voice crackled through the speaker, "Checkpoint one. He's on his way."

"Too late," Lorenzo said. "It's going down."

As we watched from the rooftop, a black Suburban with darkened windows took the cut-off to the warehouse. Once it made the turn, a pair of men in FBI windbreakers popped out from behind bushes and closed the street with sawhorse barricades. At the warehouse, the side door slid open and the Suburban drove inside.

"Move in!" Lorenzo barked into his walkie-talkie. He jumped up. "You two stay here. I mean it—this is dangerous."

Hey, the guys from that warehouse shot at me. I knew precisely how dangerous it was.

Lorenzo dropped his binoculars and took off across the roof. "If they're in there, I'll signal you. Watch for it," he shouted.

Though Drew hogged the binoculars, I still saw countless FBI agents storm the building. When the silver Taurus we'd seen in the lot below tore up the street, two agents rushed from the bushes and moved the barricade for it. It screeched to a halt at the warehouse. Lorenzo stepped from the Taurus and marched inside. But no one had come out.

"I can't stand this." I dashed across the roof.

"Tracy, come back," Drew called.

I moved down the ladder so fast, I lost my footing and only caught it again a few rungs from the ground. I jumped from there, already running when I hit the pavement. At the barricade, the two gatekeepers emerged to stop me, but I ran around them.

When I reached the warehouse, two federal agents came out, dragging the guys who had shot at Mother and me.

"Watch who you shoot at!" I shouted.

Drew must have been running so fast that he couldn't stop. He crashed into me, knocking us both to the ground.

Lorenzo picked that moment to stride from the warehouse, and he stopped short at the sight of us. "I should have known." He shook his head. "Tracy, you and Drew will have to move aside," he said with stern insistence. "They're bringing out Mr. Big."

A caravan of vans headed up the driveway. Two FBI agents emerged, pulling a thrashing and shouting—Benny Butler Marsh.

I grabbed Lorenzo's arm. "Lorenzo, what—"

"It's an elaborate coyote operation, Tracy. Marsh and his crew take money from illegals to bring them over the border. Then they sell them to rich, white fat-cats as servants."

Right. The number everyone in Beverly Hills was talking about. As well as the source for Benny's unexplained cash. But how did Mother figure into this? Sperry? The treasure?

Benny caught sight of Drew. "Hey, man—great, you're here. Tell these bozos who I am." To the agents stuffing him into a van, Benny shouted, "This here's my lawyer. It's gonna cost—"

"Correction, Benny, I'm Jolly's attorney, not yours. And something tells me I have another conflict." Drew winked at me.

Anxiety elevated Benny's pitch. "We'll work out the

details later, you know? Jolly won't care. Drew, you owe me.''

Drew didn't budge. I threw my arms around him and pressed my face to his chest. I'd never felt so proud of him.

Benny and his cohorts were driven away, but not before dozens of stunned-looking illegal aliens were loaded into the other vans. Bound for deportation; I hoped they considered themselves lucky.

When the flood of people stopped and there was still no sign of Philly and Mother, I went to Lorenzo. ''Lorenzo, *please*. They have to be here.''

''I didn't see them, Tracy,'' he said, and added with some bitterness, ''Wrong color complexions. But go take a look.''

Drew and I ran into the warehouse. I don't know what I expected. All I'd seen was the inside of the room where we'd been kept. I stopped now before the sight of a home-made jail. There were hundreds of tiny cells, row after row of them. They must have been selling those servants clear across the country.

More focused than I was, Drew ran ahead shouting for them. I started moving again, stopping at every room. We searched every inch of that awful place. But Mother and Philly weren't there.

THE LETDOWN SAPPED us both. We returned to the truck, but we just sat in the cab, with me slumped behind the wheel and Drew sagging against the passenger door. Even in that deflated state, the questions wouldn't let go of me. Was Benny tied into the whole mess—Sperry's murder, Mother's and Philly's abduction? Or was his only connection that he used for his slave scam a warehouse Mother and Jolly owned?

Drew subscribed to the latter theory. ''Martha probably got wind of how Benny made use of her property and went to the warehouse to see for herself. His henchman just overreacted.''

''Yeah? So why did she lie about it when I found her there? Why is everything coming together *now*?''

With a sigh, Drew just shook his head.

I pounded the steering wheel. ''One thing I have figured out. It must have been *Benny* who hit me on the head when I came to the warehouse.'' His pockets rattled like Schuller's; I noticed that when he ran out of the Bistro Fleur de Vigne. ''He should be taken out and shot.''

Drew rolled his eyes. ''Glad you're not losing your sense of proportion.''

Despite my gloom, I leaned across the buff leather console for a kiss. ''In my next life, no way will I marry a smart-ass.''

Drew's brown eyes glowed warmly. ''It has its moments.''

We held each other, drawing comfort. But reality, that infernal trap, pressed in on us. With a sigh, we came apart.

While I started the truck, Drew asked, ''Now that Benny's out of the picture, who does that leave? And don't suggest Eddie Rivers. The man was fish food thirty years ago.''

I made a U-turn and left the awning factory lot. ''I don't think so, Drew. To me this all smacks of ancient revenge.''

Drew gripped the door handle while he tentatively suggested, ''Alec still has one or two things to explain.''

I glared at him. ''Don't even go there.'' I stewed in silence while we cruised through empty streets. ''The truth is still locked in Jolly's head. We gotta go back to Beverly Vista.''

''No dress-up this time?'' Drew snickered.

I couldn't believe I'd told him all that. Man, I was gonna have to watch this new tendency to blab.

''Tracy, I interviewed him a number of times. Sometimes he was pretty lucid, but overall, babe, his brain is fried.''

"I don't care if it's sautéed with garlic, that old man is gonna tell me how to find my mother. And what in hell they're all hiding."

WE COULDN'T DRIVE the truck right to the Beverly Vista doorway this time. Police tape kept us nearly a block away.

"This looks bad," Drew said. "You stay here. I'm Jolly's lawyer, let me see if I can talk my way in."

He slipped from the truck. I waited for a couple of minutes, as promised. But patience requires more endurance than I can muster; it's that hanging around that gets to me. I leaned across the seat and flipped open the glove compartment. There had to be something there that I could claim I had to deliver to Drew.

With my head at seat level, I heard a scary sound. Coins, rattling loudly, in time with footsteps. Schuller! With Benny under arrest, who else could it be? The opening strains of "Witchy Woman" drifted into my mind—though with Mother occupying my thoughts, that one might have been voluntary.

Once the sound of the jangling grew quiet, I peered through the windshield at the coin rattler's back. It *was* him. Who else would wear that chartreuse suit? What was he doing there? This was Beverly Hills, not L.A.

When he stopped at the yellow police tape and glanced around, I hit the deck again. My head was still pressed to the passenger seat when the door flew open and Drew jumped in.

"Drive," he said tightly. "Tracy, drive, dammit!"

I gunned it, and we tore out of there. "What's going on, Drew?"

"Jolly Marsh was murdered last night, smothered by his own pillow."

"Nooo," I groaned. "Now we'll never learn—"

"It gets worse. They found Martha's name in the guest book. They're swearing out a warrant for her arrest."

TWENTY-TWO

"If You Could See What I See," Independence Pictures, 1966: Starring Martha Collins as Jenny and Carl Ford as John.

A free-spirited woman twirls before a stern, repressed man.

JENNY
My life is so much freer than yours, so unfettered.

JOHN
You're not free—you're living outside the law, and they're gaining on you.

I FELT AS IF hell's escape hatch had just slammed shut. In a blind panic, I drove in the direction of our condo. "How long do you think Mother has before they come for her?"

Drew shrugged. "A few hours maybe. There seems to be a jurisdictional war brewing between L.A. and Beverly Hills. They'll have to let the D.A. decide who gets first crack."

Mother always loved it when men fought over her, but I think she drew the line at cities. And jails.

A sudden recollection popped into my head, and just as unexpectedly, my foot hit the brake.

"Holy freakin' Day of the Dead! The burn guy!" I shouted.

A gold Tercel nearly landed in the bed of the pickup.

"Tracy, what—" Drew sent a wave of apology to the Tercel driver, a guy with such thick lenses, they made his pupils look the size of giant gumballs. He flipped us the bird, but with a cheerful grin. Now the blind were criticizing my driving.

Still stalled mid-street, I said, "After we saw Jolly, I bumped into an elderly burn victim."

"Honey, you're gonna bump into far worse out here if you—"

"Don't you see, Drew? It was *him*—Eddie Rivers. *That's* who smothered Jolly."

Drew waved his hand at the road to encourage me to start moving. But he finally seemed willing to believe me. "Did it look like him?"

My foot found the accelerator but couldn't manage to give it much gas; the truck bucked like a bronco. "Who knows? You're asking me to add thirty years—and to subtract tremendous scarring—on a face I scarcely remember from the movie. They both had dark, intense eyes, I know that."

Without warning, to either him or me, I suddenly started into a U-turn. Horns wailed all around us.

"Stop!" Drew grabbed the steering wheel. "That's enough. Pull over, I'm driving this tank."

Just as well, it was getting to be too much for me. I nearly totaled a few cars in the process, but I made it to the curb. Drew stepped from the passenger seat, slamming the door behind him. He came around to the driver's side and motioned for me to climb over the console.

"You don't mind my driving your truck?" he asked belatedly.

I shrugged. "You, Philly—what's the difference."

"You let Philly—"

"When you were a kid, you colored *in* the lines, huh?" I made a T with my hands. "Truce, remember? Drew, we have to go back to Beverly Vista. What if he escapes?"

"If the man you saw is Rivers, and if he killed Jolly, he's long gone now. Besides, if you go back there, you're taking a chance that someone will realize *you* were there, not Martha."

I fell back against my seat. "Whenever I think things can't get any worse, they do."

Drew threw the truck into gear and pulled into traffic. "Hold on, babe. The fat lady ain't sung yet."

BACK AT HOME, after the animals' nonstop fun, there were no longer distinct piles of anything but a solid three-foot covering of our stuff over every surface. We flopped onto different parts of it.

Drew rolled onto his side. "Any more ideas?"

"Only one," I admitted. "But I have to call Elly first."

"Elijah Griffin? What does he—"

Knuckles rapped against the door.

Drew looked like he was about to call out to the visitor. I held up my hands to silence him and crept toward the door to peek through the peephole. When I saw who it was, unconsciously, I found myself whistling "I Shot the Sheriff" under my breath. I raced back to the living room.

"It's Schuller!" I whispered.

Drew started for the door. I threw my body into his.

"Are you nuts? When he realizes we can't produce Mother, he'll take us into custody as material witnesses. Drew, we need to be free to move."

"Come on, open up!" Schuller shouted through the door.

I led him to the bedroom. "We have to find another way out."

"Tracy, this is a third-floor condo. We don't have a back door."

Schuller pounded against the door with the palm of his hand. "I know you're in there. I saw your truck."

My brilliant husband insisted on leaving the truck at the

curb in case we needed to leave fast. He could make up for that blunder now.

"What about your evacuation plan?" I asked.

"I thought you were going to surf out," Drew said nastily.

"Not flood, fire!" I snapped too loudly. I lowered my voice. "You stuffed a costly rope ladder under our bed." I knelt next to the bed and yanked at the ladder. "I know, I laughed when you ordered it, but I now admit I was wrong."

"You want to climb over the balcony railing?" Drew's eyebrows shot so high, they nearly hit his hairline.

"Is the Pope gun-shy?"

"I'm counting to ten, then I'm coming in!" Schuller shouted.

Drew carried the rope ladder out to the balcony, where he proceeded to hook it in place—but all unconsciously. With his conscious mind, he fought me all the way. "If we leave this ladder hanging below an open balcony door, it'll be an invitation to thieves. Do the words *home security* mean nothing to you?"

"Do the words *Bruno's love slave* mean nothing to you? There's a cop about to shoot through our door."

With only a moment's deliberation, he swung over the side and started down.

"Wait!" I said. "The pets."

Drew's dark eyes smoldered. "Fortunately, we're just free-wheeling yuppies without any encumbrances."

I glared at him for several seconds; he caved. While he climbed back into room and picked up the dog, I raced to the kitchen, where I filled a couple of mixing bowls on the counter with water and a mountain of kibble.

"…four, five…" resonated through the door.

When I returned to the bedroom, Drew was already standing over the side of the balcony, gripping the dog.

He shot me a sour look as he struggled with the squirming pup. "I can't believe I let you—"

"Hey, I carried my mother on my back. *Up* a rope."

We made it to the ground. I wasn't sure we would the way Drew shook that ladder. When I paused at the bottom to comfort the poor mutt, Drew grabbed the keys and climbed into the driver's side of the truck. The pooch and I followed him.

"Where to, Tracy?" Drew asked, starting the truck.

"Don't know yet." My cell phone's lighter adapter was still plugged in. I dialed Elly-Belly's number, but it rang a long time before someone picked up. The voice that finally answered sounded groggy with sleep.

"Elly, is that you? Why are you sleeping at this hour?"

"We shot all night. I didn't get to bed till five."

I glanced at my watch. He'd had two hours of sleep. What more did he want? "I really wouldn't bother you if I could help it, but things are so critical now."

"I understand, T. Let me get my notes." *People* was right, he really was the nicest guy in the world. He came back on the line a minute later. "Now you wanted me to trace the ownership of that Kenney Avenue warehouse."

"Oh…no—that's not important now."

"No? Then you must want to know what happened with those emails you asked me to hack into. Believe me, Tracy, you have a case against your publisher for—"

"As important as that will be later, Elly, I really can't deal with it now."

"I see." His voice was starting to sound wide awake. "Well, it can't be the ownership of the property on Windswept Lane that you want."

That was exactly what I wanted. "Why not?"

"Because the person who owns that fucking house—is you!"

The nicest guy in the world hung up on me.

TWENTY-THREE

"Daddy's Girl," Piccolo Productions, 1967: Starring Martha Collins as Laura and Alec Grainger as Sam.

LAURA
When you left me, you walked out on a daughter you never knew was on the way.

SAM
I'm back now, for you and her. I swear, I'll never let either of you down again.

"YOU OWN IT?" Drew asked, turning north on Topanga.

"The Tracy Lorraine Grainger Trust, to be precise." I had called Elijah back and demanded clarification of his bombshell. Now I traced the route there on the map spread across my lap.

"Martha's never mentioned the trust. She must have wanted to surprise you with it someday," Drew concluded.

A better guess would be she set it up as some kind of tax dodge. Mother often dangled a new house before me, but this property was never mentioned.

I located Windswept Lane on the map. "It looks like it's just outside of Chatsworth. Box Canyon maybe."

"Do you know that area?" he asked.

I said I didn't. Though it probably wasn't any more than fifteen miles from our place to the northwest corner of the Valley, I'd never had occasion to go there. For the first

time that struck me as strange. The hills around Chatsworth had long been popular as a filming location for western and mountainous settings. How odd that my parents
never seemed to shoot anything there. But Mother had always insisted that the country gave her hives. Naturally,
that excluded her from the Hollywood elite who chose that
area for their country homes many years ago.

When we finally hit northern Topanga Boulevard, I saw
the western wilderness that had appeared in so many films
had been replaced by houses and high-tech industry. This
part of the Valley was now as packed as my neck of the
woods. Houses of every shape and size rose around us,
from the most modest to some that were so garish, they
startled even my eyes—and they'd been schooled in Beverly Hills, a place not known for its restraint. There was a
nice, rustic, unplanned feel to the place, though.

One natural aspect of that western terrain remained. And
it stunned me into silence. Rising up from behind the rows
of homes, which appeared to be flung along the ground
like Monopoly houses, was a small, but magnificent range
of jagged, sandstone mountains. Not as commanding as
the Rockies, but perfect in its small, natural splendor.

"Ooh, look at that."

Drew looked to where I pointed. "You mean you've
never seen the Simi Hills before."

"Only in photos." And dreams. As I stared at the
breathtaking hills, my heart began to accelerate. "Oops, I
think we missed our turnoff."

With a sigh, Drew made a U-turn at the next corner.

"Maybe you should take over the map, and I'll drive,"
I suggested.

"Sure, I'm going to trust you, as dazed as you look,
behind the wheel on mountain roads. Snap out of it,
Tracy."

I tried, but I did feel dazed. Let's face it, my hold on
reality isn't that strong in the best of times. Normally, I

consider that a blessing. But now that I needed to, I couldn't tell the difference between what was brand new to me—and what I'd imagined most of my life.

I buried my face in the map and tried to concentrate. But the distractions overwhelmed me, and not all of them came from inside of me. A warm breeze blew in from the desert. Not quite a Santa Ana wind, but strong enough to clear the smog away, making the air so clear that the colors burst with intensity.

At one point, we passed a natural preserve with gnarled old trees surrounding an unspoiled lake filled with a flock of wild geese. On the other side of the road, those magnificent boulders came down to meet us. Crusty, craggy peaks, punctuated between the rocks by desert brush in cool purples and muted greens.

Some people consider the Los Angeles sprawl to be a homogenized, featureless terrain. Others think it's all like something out of Raymond Chandler. Neither image is right. While there may not be as much of a central core as some cities, there are thousands of parts to this place, each with its own character.

Canyon communities tend to be more individualistic than most, and more casual. The rich and the poor live in cozy proximity. It's not uncommon to see the hand-laid stones of pricey private roads co-existing with the turnoffs some people use to dump old cars that will rust at the bottom of the ravine.

"Turn right here, then the first left." I brought the map closer to my eyes. "These lines are so fine, I can't tell if they're roads or flaws in the paper."

"This isn't a road like any I've seen, but I'm a city boy."

Drew slowed to a crawl, but the truck still kicked up gravel from the narrow dirt road when it went into a sharp decline. Before we'd driven a hundred yards, the road rose in a steeper grade.

"Left here?" Drew asked at the junction of a rutted private road. There was no street sign.

I shrugged. "We've come this far. What do we have to lose?" Just everything I held true.

The unmarked road was longer than I expected, and in worse shape. Drew clutched the wheel with a death grip, though the dips still caused the truck to veer to the sides, where the road dropped off entirely. It climbed to a huge rocky knoll that stood alone, offering views in every direction.

The views held no appeal for me, however. My eyes were transfixed by the structure that claimed the center of the knoll. It was a big house, built in a greater variety of styles than found in a first-year architecture textbook. Mostly Spanish, though the stained glass panels to either side of the door looked more like knockoff Frank Lloyd Wright designs. And there was a round room, plopped on one side of the second story, with turret trim that looked as if it had been swiped from a castle.

Drew cut the engine and stepped from the truck. I tried to follow. But I stalled on the running board and just leaned onto the top of the passenger door.

Drew turned back to me. "Tracy, aren't you coming?"

I sputtered, "It's—the dream house!"

"This dump? I thought you designed that in your sleep."

Join the club. But this was it, all right, though it looked more pristine in my dreams. There were big, gapping cracks in the stucco and enough dirt clung to the windows to obscure the glass. The ground that stretched out before the house had never been a conventional lawn, it was more of a desert garden. Recent rains allowed giant chaparral to flourish there; enough dried sections stuck to the succulents now to form a tumbleweed wall. Despite the state of disrepair, my heart soared at the sight of it.

Drew looked from the house to me, his expression shifting from a questioning one to something more suspicious. But he helped me off the running board and let the dog out of the back seat. He held my hand while we walked across the path of cracked Mexican tiles to the door.

Drew tried the tarnished brass knob, but it didn't budge.

"Move back." I eased him off the tattered woven mat at the door, where you could almost make out the word *Welcome* in purple beneath caked mud. I lifted one corner of the filthy thing. There was a rusty key below it on the step.

Drew frowned. "How did you know to look there? That's where you leave keys, too."

"Where did you think I learned it?"

The key didn't want to go into the lock. I spit on it and rubbed at the rust with my finger. It fit a little better on the next try. It was so tough to turn, I had to let Drew do it. But that rusty little sucker opened the door.

When Drew and I wandered in, he began to choke. I had to breathe through my mouth. What felt like decades of dust had accumulated here, filling the air with enough grime to thicken it.

While the dog ran ahead of us, eager as a kid at Disneyland, we drifted down a corridor whose thick plaster walls looked sepia tinged. Except for the few places where newer-looking smoke detectors and sprinklers protruded from the ceiling. We peered into rooms off to both sides. The floor-plan looked as creative as the exterior, with spaces flowing into other spaces with no known pattern. The furnishings also represented a variety of styles. What I could see of them; they were also caked with dust. Nothing had been covered—someone had just walked away from this place and left it exactly as it was. Someone?

At the rear of the house was a large, sprawling living room that ended in a wall of windows. The top was still raised on the baby grand piano at one corner. And several used bar glasses remained on a glass-and-brass coffee table; whatever liquid they'd held had evaporated, leaving behind a sticky, brownish residue.

I walked to the window wall and stared out at a pool so Art Deco it belonged in a Maxfield Parrish painting. The pool's plaster had separated from its tiles, however, and one side pulled up out of the ground. Probably the handiwork of the Northridge earthquake. It must have been drained at that time, but a couple of feet of rain water had accumulated since, allowing the unfettered flourishing of the most yucky green dreck.

"What kind of idiot builds a pool in this terrain?" Drew asked. "It takes more money than brains to sink a hole in this rocky ground."

I couldn't tell for sure, but when I glanced through the space between the pool and the tiles, it looked like something else had been built next to or beneath it.

The giggle that rolled from my mouth sounded hysterical. "That's my goal—to have more money than brains. Without a lobotomy, that is."

"How's that going?" Drew asked.

"Already aced it—and I'm broke."

He chuckled. "Why don't we start at the top, in that tower room, and work down? We'll search until something turns up."

Easier said than done; the route to the turreted room wasn't obvious. We had noticed two sets of stairs led to the second floor but assumed that to be for convenience. After several frustrating attempts, we discovered not all the rooms on that floor connected to each other. Only one staircase to the second floor—the one we hadn't taken—allowed access to the tower room.

Eventually, we found the curved staircase that led to the tower. It was a totally round room—even the teakwood doorway and the wood-trimmed windows curved—though someone had built a straight, floor-to-ceiling oak bookcase that squared off one part of the sphere. A Scandinavian teakwood desk floated in one part of the circle, while a small teal-and-amber tweed sofa and a black leather Eames chair formed a seating area.

There was no artwork on the dingy walls—apart from a movie poster for *Deadly Shadows* thumb-tacked to the wall. Mother's frightened gaze screamed out at us from the poster, along with the dark, dangerous eyes of the Earl of Rahway, glaring from under the brim of one of those hats men used to wear in *film noir.*

I leaned one shoulder against the oak bookcase and looked at Eddie Rivers, willing him to tell us something, anything. But he just smirked in that nasty way of his.

A slow boil built in me, burning off the numbing daze that had held me in its grip. Why had I dreamed of this place for thirty years? Why had it been left like this?

As grand as it was, there weren't any books in the bookcase. I wiped a shelf clean with my hand. Below the dust, the shelves were so smooth that it didn't look as if anything had ever been placed on them. The only object in that whole huge case was a heavy gold lighter someone had tossed there.

"Look at this lighter, Drew. It's one of those old-fashioned ones. I always liked them."

What I called old-fashioned was a rectangular lighter with a top that flipped back on hinges and a wheel that ground against a flint to make a spark. I yanked at the top till I pulled it open. The wheel was equally tough to turn, but when it did, it still lit. The tight cover must have kept the lighter fluid from evaporating.

I closed the lid and flipped the lighter over in my hand. On the opposite side, the word *Alec* was engraved in a flowing script. I threw it back on the shelf.

"Does this place mean anything to you?" Drew asked.

More than he knew. This room had visited my dreams as recently as last night. I thought the room I saw in my sleep had been spinning, but it was *round.* That also meant

I'd been here, I had no doubts about that now. Before I could begin to unravel the web of truth and lies, dreams and reality—for either myself or Drew—I heard footsteps on the landing outside the room.

I whirled around—and saw the answer to my prayers. My dad stood in the doorway.

Dressed in khaki pants and a cocoa sweatshirt, he leaned casually against the door frame. He's a small man, as so many leading men are—people are always surprised by that when they meet him in person. They're all giants on the silver screen, though I'd always considered my dad one in life, too.

With the build of a young man still and the longish hair he'd always worn—he looked to me in that moment as he had when I was a child, even if his dark hair was now nearly all white. Despite everything that had happened, despite what I still didn't understand, I sighed with relief. Daddy was here; I was safe.

His handsome face was more tan than usual, making that crooked grin of his stand out above his even, white teeth and below his dashing snowy moustache. Warmth flooded eyes the color of a tropical sea when he brought them to mine—till a spark lit in them faster than it had in his lighter.

"Tracy, what do you mean calling all over Mexico for me?" he demanded.

Any question where I get my temper? "What do you mean not telling me where you were going?"

Dad folded his arms tightly across his chest. "I left a message with my new cell phone number on your machine." But anger in Dad was always short-lived. He pulled a tiny phone from his back pocket and showed it to Drew. "I picked this up in Puerto Vallarta. Handy gadgets, eh?"

Drew kept a straight face. "So I've heard."

Dad always said he'd be the last phony on earth saddled with a cell phone. Obviously, the prediction came true.

While my father was as easily distracted as I am, he didn't stay distracted. "Are you telling me you didn't get my message?"

"Ooh! That might have been one that...somehow...got erased."

"Tracy!"

"Well, I thought it was another call from Drew's mo—" I stopped and looked to see if Drew caught that.

Drew's eyebrows contracted in disapproval. "You'll call her?"

"Sure." When it was chickens that flew back to Capistrano.

"At least we got that settled," Dad said with a sigh. He perched on the back of the sofa. "I've been driving all night, and I'm beat." He held out a hand to me. "What's the matter, honey? No hug for your old man?"

I came around behind him and wrapped my arms over his chest. My face pressed against his scratchy cheek. It wasn't obvious, with his pale beard, that he hadn't stopped to shave today. Dad took my hands in his. Those were the hands that had always been there to catch me when I stumbled. I swallowed hard, but the reflex seemed to stick in my throat. He had driven all night to reach me. My father, my hero—my *super*hero. And now I was the one who had to wave Kryptonite at him.

"Dad?"

"Yes, baby?"

"How did you know to look for us—*here*?"

TWENTY-FOUR

"Liars and Thieves," Avery Productions, 1968: Starring Martha Collins as Sheila and Randy Shirer as Doug.

A man stops a frightened woman from running away from him.

SHEILA
A man like you—you can't be allowed to win, or none of us will survive.

DOUG
When you gonna get it, baby? Liars and thieves—we're the guys running the world.

THERE IN THE TOWER ROOM I stood before Dad with my hands on my hips. "Look, Dad, we know about On Our Own Productions, about that bloodsucker, Vince Sperry, and *Deadly Shadows*. What we want to know now is—what happened to blow it all up?"

"Then you know more than I do, sweetheart. You tell me." Dad flashed a congenial smile. Only a single line tightness along his jaw gave the performance away.

The sound of the dog's claws clicking up the stairs announced his arrival. The mutt found the room easier than we did.

Dad threw a lot of energy into ruffling the pup's mane. "And who's this little fella?"

"That's Lorenzo's dog," I said.

"Gee, honey, I'm not familiar with that breed."

Drew came up the stairs carrying a couple of neatly folded sheets. I'd asked him to search for something we could spread out on the dusty furniture so we could sit. No one was leaving that house till I learned why it had been abandoned.

"Guess what I found?" Drew asked.

"Sheets."

"Better. There's a crazy room downstairs with nothing but pillows on the floor and a big fountain in the center."

Dad used one of the sheets, not to cover, but to dust the Eames chair. With a nod, he said, "Martha's meditation room. She and her friends used to smoke dope there."

Drew gave me a goofy grin, half-titillated, half-terrified, as he always did when confronted with the fact that mine are not your average parents. He still looked dazed while spreading a sheet over the sofa.

I strolled to the bookcase to amuse myself with the lighter.

"Tracy, stop playing with that!" Dad snapped.

A blast from the past exploded in my brain. I starred at Dad in disbelief, stunned by the memory that flashed in my mind.

He flushed with shame. "Sorry, baby. I hate parents who take out their moods on their kids."

"But you did it one other time," I said in a breathless hush.

Distracted, he said, "Not too often, I hope."

My voice found a hard edge. "You used those exact words to me here, in this room, more than thirty years ago." I delved further into the shadowy recollection. "Then Mother said something like, 'Just put it on a higher shelf, Alec, and take her hand. Dear God, can't we leave this place already?'"

While only half dusted, Dad sank into the leather chair.

I slipped the lighter into my pocket. "Dad, Mother's in deep shit, and it ain't going away."

Tension rippled along his stiffened jaw.

Time to play hardball. "I don't want to scare you, but you should know Eddie Rivers didn't die in that boat explosion."

Dad's eyes shot away from mine. "No? Then how did he die?"

I leaned against the bookcase. "He didn't—he's still alive. He's extracting revenge on all of you."

Something else moved through that rigid jaw now. Amusement; he was struggling not to laugh. A triumphant glint appeared in his eyes. "Afraid not, Tracy. Rivers is dead, all right."

"He can't be!" I insisted

"I should know, honey—I buried him."

I didn't want to believe it—I *wouldn't*. "Yeah? So where's the grave?"

Suppressed laughter shook his cheeks like an underground explosion. "You're leaning on it."

I jerked away from the bookcase as if it had caught fire.

I SAT ON THE FLOOR, letting a modernistic area rug in a variety of pastels grind dirt into my behind, while I stared up at the bookcase. "So that's the final resting place of the Earl of Rahway," I ventured.

"Rahway!" Dad snapped. He scowled at the poster. "Don't they teach you kids anything today? Why do we pay taxes?"

"I went to private school," Drew muttered in self-defense.

"Did they teach you anything there, son? You telling me you never heard the word *Rahway?*"

Drew exchanged a helpless look with me. "I know it's a prison in New Jersey, but—"

Dad stabbed a finger at Drew. "Bingo!"

"Dad, are you saying Rivers served time in Rahway Prison?"

"Just a little joke from a guy who liked having one up on everybody. The bastard killed a man." He stuffed his hands deep into his pants pockets. A blood vessel in his temple throbbed.

"A murder-one conviction?" Drew asked. "He couldn't have served much time."

Dad shrugged. "Someone dropped a dime on him, but the case was weak. He pled to man two."

I stifled a groan. Ever since Dad played the tough title character in *Dirty Dan, Street Cop*, we never knew when he would suddenly talk the talk.

At the desk, Drew absently beat a pencil against the surface. "I don't get it. A reporter for a high school paper could have exposed his phony peerage. Why did people accept it?"

"What you aren't getting, son, is the basis of the biz," Dad explained patiently. "People *want* to believe in make-believe."

I glared at the poster. "That explains regular people. What about producers? Did they know? They couldn't have, if they hired him."

"It was pretty common knowledge among insiders. I never knew how he pulled it off. The rest of us had to hide our dirty little secrets, I'll tell you that," Dad snapped bitterly. With a sigh of surrender, he fell back into the Eames chair. "You still want to know what happened that night?"

A little flutter in my chest made me want to stop him. But I heard myself saying, "More than ever."

In fits and starts, he filled in the background. Mother hadn't handled the relaxation of the studio system well. She formed her own production company with two friends to provide some security. But typically, she looked for someone to blame for her unrest—and chose the only anchor left in her life, my father. Their marriage broke up just as On Our Own Productions was formed.

Dad propped his sneakers on the dusty ottoman. "But they found producing harder than they thought. And your mother picked bad partners. Jolly Marsh was a brute. If you ask me, the Alzheimer's happened because there's too much he doesn't *want* to remember. I can't say I'm sorry that old bull is dead. And Vinny Sperry—he was just a hack writer."

On the floor, I shook my head. "No, Dad. Some of the scenes in *Deadly Shadows* are beautifully written."

"Sure, your mother wrote those." He jabbed a thumb at the poster. "After that clown bought it, Martha worked 'round the clock for days till they had a new script. Hell, the story idea was hers anyway, she just let Vinny take credit."

When Drew perched on the sofa arm, he shot me a nasty smirk. All I could do was sink within myself. My genes had struck again.

"What happened that night, Alec?" Drew asked gently.

Dad looked steadily at Drew. "You might want to bail at this point, Andrew. Officer of the court and all."

"It's too late for that, Alec." Given the appalled expression that flashed in his eyes, Drew seemed to be wondering how he'd come to burn so many bridges. "But maybe you should give me a dollar. As a retainer."

Dad stuck his hands into his pockets. "Didn't get a chance to stop at the ATM, though I might have a few pesos left."

With a groan, Drew accepted a small coin. "I always assumed it would be *Tracy's* career that went down the toilet."

I silenced him with a frown.

"I wasn't here...at the beginning." Dad stared aimlessly at the ceiling, but his fingers, linked together in his lap, twisted into knots. "They were together, Martha and

Rivers. He had all the women in Hollywood. But he treated 'em like dirt.''

I noticed Drew had inched forward on the sofa arm, drawn by the story. On the floor, I found myself wanting to bolt. I couldn't budge.

A hard swallow rippled through Dad's throat before he continued gruffly, ''That night, they argued about something, and he slugged your mother. Not the first time, I'd wager.''

I couldn't believe Mother had ever allowed a relationship in which she hadn't held the upper hand. Maybe now I knew why.

Dad rose and paced in agitation. ''She must have screamed. Jolly ran up here, and he and Rivers tangled. Rivers tumbled down that staircase out there and broke his neck.'' Dad's hands fisted, and he stopped at the top of the stairs and looked down. His wide, unblinking eyes seemed to be seeing the body where it had fallen years before.

Drew went to the landing and led Dad back to the sofa. ''So it was an accident. They could have explained it to the police.''

Dad offered him a smile of tolerant superiority. ''Not in our world, son. Not in those days.''

I brought my knees to my chest and clutched them for comfort. ''How did you get into it?''

''Martha called me. I was with someone else, nice lady—still feel bad about how I treated her,'' he said with downcast eyes.

For him, there was no choice. Mother needed her rock.

Dad leaped up and marched to the poster, gesturing wildly. ''Jolly wanted to throw the body in an alley somewhere. He acted like it had nothing to do with him. But I played a cop once; I knew a little about police science. I figured our safest bet was to make it seem as if he died in another way, far from here.''

I scrambled to my feet and followed Dad. "You rigged the explosion." From years of hanging with the crew, he probably knew more than any other actor about special effects. "Why didn't you place the body on the boat if you were going to blow it up?"

When Lorenzo's dog came to his side, Dad absently bent and stroked his curly black fur. "I didn't know how well the explosion would work. What if they found the body intact?"

He went on to explain that by sheer happenstance, Mother had contracted for someone to build a bookcase downstairs. The construction was to start the following week, but the supplies had already been delivered.

"So you built...?" Drew approached it, spreading his arms across that huge oak expanse. He looked flabbergasted; Drew doesn't know which end of the hammer strikes the nail. "You do beautiful work, Alec."

Dad shrugged. "I've always been handy. There was already a small closet stretched across that part of the curve. It gave me the idea."

I went to the bookcase and ran my hand over one of the smooth shelves. "It is beautiful, Dad. Too bad you have to pull it apart now."

MY SUGGESTION didn't go over well.

Dad tried to move me away from the bookcase. "I'm telling you, Tracy, there's no hidden treasure, just a suitcase with Rivers' clothes. They were only here at your mom's country place for the weekend. We packed up his stuff and threw it in there."

I refused to budge. "You better hope you're wrong. Rivers' booty is the only thing that's going to free Mother and Philly."

With exaggerated patience, Dad placed his hand gently on my head. "Look, honey, that business with the *treasure* was just another joke, like *Rahway*. It's bad enough that I had to put him in there. I'm not taking him out."

Either the frail light streaming through the filthy windows was changing, or Drew was starting to look green. He stood at the window, as stiff as an undertaker. "Tracy, the chances of there being a clue back there are slim to none. Let's let Rivers rest."

I stomped my foot and said fiercely to both of them, "Slim to none might be the only chance they have—and we're taking it!"

DAD FOUND THE TOOLS he'd used to build the bookcase right where he left them in the detached garage at the far rear of the knoll. But he couldn't bear to destroy his workmanship, insisting they take it apart carefully, so they could put it back together just as well. Though no one planned to use this bookcase, I went along with it. Where else did we have to stow ol' Eddie?

That left me free to explore the house. My dreams scarcely did justice to this place. I remembered only pieces of this magnificent monstrosity. But even those were unusual enough that I should have known it could only have been built to Mother's design. Even in my sleep, I wasn't in her league.

I wandered downstairs to the living room. Most of its large glass panels were fixed, but one held a sliding door. It hadn't been locked, either. All that trouble with the key at the front door, and the rear entrance was left unlocked. I slipped the sliding panel open and went outside to look over that absurdly opulent pool.

Such a shame about the earthquake damage. The ground seemed to have shifted along the other side of the yard as well and some erosion had occurred. Two long, heavy planks had been placed over that area to prevent further damage to the soil. I remembered the new sprinklers in the hall; Mother seemed to have the required maintenance performed, but nothing more.

I looked at the end of the pool that had pulled out of the ground. I was right, there was something beyond it. By rights I should have been looking at dirt through the exposed steel, but what I saw was a block wall under the ground.

When the dog poked his nose out the door, I returned to the house and found the kitchen. It was as big as a small restaurant kitchen, with walnut cabinets in a sleek sixties design and the brushed aluminum commercial appliances that were back in style now. This room wouldn't need much to update it.

Update it? What was I thinking? This wasn't *really* my house. Even if I couldn't imagine a better lair for a mystery writer than one with a body behind the bookcase. If this were my house, I'd shelve my mysteries there.

With the glum acknowledgment that I had no real right to this house, I dragged myself around the other side of the large center island. I found a trap door there with recessed hinges and a fold-away handle cut into the brick-patterned vinyl flooring. I tried the handle; it pulled open a few inches, but caught at that point. Normally, I'll keep at things forever, but feeling as if my dream house had been wrenched away from me, I just dropped the door.

Why was I thinking about houses anyway? Only two days ago, life had been rosy. Now not only had I lost my publisher, Drew was sure to get canned—and my mother and Drew's Uncle Philly were dead meat unless we found a treasure behind that bookcase, one that would satisfy their abductor. At this rate, I wasn't certain I could make it through another day. But how much worse could things get?

You'd think I'd learn never to ask things like that.

TWENTY-FIVE

"Deadly Shadows," On Our Own Productions, 1969: Starring Martha Collins as Francesca and Edward Rivers as Chick.

FRANCESCA
Why won't you leave me alone? You've ruined my life. Isn't that enough? I could kill you, Chick.

CHICK
Wouldn't do you no good, sweetheart. I'd haunt you from the grave.

I WENT BACK TO the tower room, where they hadn't made much progress. Dad was being so picky about not damaging the bookcase, they still hadn't pulled the thing away from the wall.

But Drew was using the time to make progress on a project of his own. I heard him saying, "...so that's my theory, Alec. Martha's covering for someone, and given Yolanda's memory of the night you came back to the house—"

I stomped my foot and shouted, "Andrew! You wanna die? We dismissed that theory as absurd."

"*You* dismissed it, Trace. Your only alternate theory resides behind this bookcase."

"But my dad wasn't here when Jolly was killed. Are you saying there are two murderers?"

Old anal Drew started making neat, squared-off gestures

with his hands. "Let's leave Jolly for now. This business with Sperry has to be addressed, and no matter how much you hate it—"

Drew did have to die. I started for him.

Dad stepped between us. "Kids, stop. Don't argue over me." He pressed his head against the end of one shelf. "I did say what Yolanda overheard. You don't know what it's been like, having the shadow of that time between us." He gestured at the poster. "And that prick—he keeps reaching out from the grave, extracting his revenge. Excuse my French, sweetheart."

Who would excuse mine?

"I left the house and started over to Sperry's place," Dad said. "But you know me, I don't fight. I just continued on to Mexico."

I believed him, but would anyone else? Hope sank like a stone in my gut. Wouldn't you know? All my life I'd wished to be an orphan—now that I was on the verge of achieving it, I wanted my mommy and daddy to stop it.

"Anyway, it's the principle of the thing. It's not like the money Vinny demanded was much of a drain to us, even after Benny Marsh refused to make Jolly's contributions." Dad chuckled. "Penny wise and pound foolish, that Benny. Always was. Leave it to Vinny to find another way to wring some dough outta him."

Drew's jaw dropped. "So that's what the plagiarism suit was about."

Dad turned back to his work, seeming to consider the matter closed. "Besides, you clean up Martha's messes too quickly, and she expects you to be even faster next time."

"I'm *never* cleaning up another one," I vowed fervently.

"You know that's not the way it works, honey," Dad said. "Those of us who love your mother can't refuse her anything."

I watched suspicion grow in Drew's golden eyes. He had to be wondering if, despite Dad's aversion to violence, he'd agreed when Mother asked him to clean up this mess, once and for all. The rock in my gut doubled its weight.

My brain side-stepped the whole problem. "What's that trap door in the kitchen floor?" Denial—a tool for survival.

Dad said around the nail he held in his lips, "Bomb shelter."

"A bomb shelter? Who did she think was going to bomb her?"

Dad took the hammer from where he'd shoved it in his pocket and gently eased out a stubborn nail. "You gotta understand, honey. It was the Cold War. Everybody was building them."

"Everybody? I've lived here all my life, and I've never seen one before."

He stuffed the hammer and nails back into his pocket. "Just don't start now, okay? Your mother filled it with enough food to feed twenty armies. Thirty-year-old cans must be exploding all over the place."

"Having more money than brains seems to run in your family," Drew said, more bluntly than usual.

Dad pretended not to hear. "Okay, I think we're ready to move this baby now." Dad pulled the upper portion of the bookcase away from the wall. "Peek in there, Tracy. What do you see?"

"Looks like…a shower curtain."

"You put him in a shower curtain?" Drew asked.

"Andrew, my boy, you ever carry a body up a flight of stairs?"

Drew's mumbled response put an end to that exchange.

"Dad, that glimpse isn't going to cut it. Dammit, I'm not a ghoul, but I have to explore what's back there."

With a martyred sigh, Dad gestured for Drew to take hold of his end of the bookcase.

"Don't scratch the floor!" I cautioned at the last second. In this room, it was a glorious peg-and-groove pine.

Through grunts when he lifted the heavy case, Drew said, "What do you care? It's not your house."

Not my house, not my dog—I had a totally borrowed life.

But they did take pains to lift the bookcase off the floor and carried it a few feet back, where they let it stand. As I crept behind it, my clinical detachment abandoned me. What if Eddie looked all weird and icky? The shower curtain had grown stiff enough to stand on its own. But it was pretty—with geometric patterns in rose and tangerine. With one bold move, I grasped the rigid plastic curtain and snatched it away.

My eyes stared straight ahead—at nothing. I looked down. The body had decomposed, and the skeleton had fallen into a pile of bones on the floor. Not icky at all. But my butt tattoo was right—this caper really was bad to the bones.

From somewhere in the room, the dog growled. Dad and Drew joined me behind the bookcase.

Behind the bones, also built across one part of the circle, were the two, white louvered doors of a closet. With a silly giggle, I said, "This can't be the first skeleton in Mother's closet."

The stern father mask, which Dad so rarely wore, came out in a hurry. "That's all we'll be hearing about that, young lady."

"Right." Holy freakin' Halloween. It was my first skeleton, gimme a break.

Rivers' satchel rested next to the bones. It was a tanned cowhide suitcase, but it was bigger and looked more stuffed than I would have expected for a weekend. Had Eddie been moving his things out? Was that why they argued?

Drew gripped the handle. "Let's do it."

He carried it around the bookcase and flipped it open on the Eames chair's ottoman. Fetid odors trapped for decades escaped into the room. Much worse than the bones. I waved the air before my nose.

Drew turned away. "This is hopeless. If there were anything valuable among Eddie's stuff, wouldn't Jolly Marsh have taken it?"

With his hands clasped behind him, Dad stared into the suitcase. "He was drunk as a skunk by then."

I pointed at the jumble of garments pressed into the suitcase. "Look at how he stuffed things. He wanted out of there fast."

I started pulling things out of the suitcase, one vile, rotting garment at a time. Though some fell apart in my hands, I felt through all of them, especially the pockets and hems. Without a word, Dad and Drew joined me.

When we'd spread about half the contents around the room, I spotted a few small, thick, spiral notebooks bound in a rubber band.

"Rivers' journals," Dad said in answer to my pointing. "He was always scribbling in them."

When I picked them up, the dried rubber band came apart in my hand. I flipped the faded dark-green cover on the uppermost journal and began reading.

"Leave those nasty books alone, Tracy," Dad insisted. "You don't need to learn the things a man like that would write."

My father obviously retreated into denial as easily as I did. How innocent did he think my life in this family allowed me to remain? I kept reading.

Drew picked up the last few pieces of clothing and hurled them across the room. He patted down the inside of the suitcase. With a sigh, he sat next to it. "This is hopeless. If he had something valuable, it was on that boat when it blew up."

"No, it's here," I muttered. "We already found it."

Both men looked at me. "And is it really priceless?" Dad asked.

"It's utterly worthless." I sank to the floor next to Drew.

I GAVE ONE OF Eddie's journals to each of them. "Some of the entries are what you'd put in a journal. See, here he recorded his memories of interludes with some women he called his cupcake, his angel, his tootsie, and his sugar."

Settling back on the sofa next to Drew, Dad nodded. "Rivers found calling women by endearments easier than remembering their names."

I held out one of the journals. "But there's a whole lot more in here than mere diary entries."

After Dad read a little of his, he shook his head. "This is incredible. That scumbag, Rivers, recorded dirt on everyone who mattered in Hollywood."

"Get this," Drew squealed. "Jolly Marsh knocked up his maid—*she's* Benny's mother. She just gave him to Jolly's wife."

Dad gave Drew a sage nod. "You noticed the ex-Mrs. Marsh didn't take the little rugrat when she left." He directed that knowing expression at me. "That might explain how Rivers got cast in *Deadly Shadows*."

"And how he shot to the top so fast. He was shaking down everyone." I held out one of the journals. "*This* was his treasure."

"It fits. That was Rivers' kind of joke. But look at these names. They're either retired now or dead. We have nothing here to bargain with." Dad tossed the notebook he held onto a pile of ratty clothing.

I stretched out on the floor alongside the pooch and glared at the bastard on the poster. Maybe it was the angle or the dust-filed light streaming into the room—but I suddenly saw those intense eyes in a new way.

"Maybe not. But I know who we *should* be bargaining with."

TWENTY-SIX

"Look to the Light," Partytown Productions, 1970: Starring Martha Collins as Anne and Alec Grainger as Tom.

A couple cling to a tree in the center of a rising river.

TOM
The water's rising fast, Anne. Any idea how we get out of here?

Anne looks to the helicopter headlight that appears above.

ANNE
Sometimes, Tom, you just gotta look up.

DREW AND DAD slumped next to each other on the couch like bookends. They wouldn't get with the program, refusing to believe I knew who was behind our own little crime wave.

Still stretched out alongside the mutt on the floor, I said, "Look at the poster."

"I'd rather not," Dad insisted, turning away.

I raced to the poster so fast that, when the dog tried to follow me, his claws slipped on the varnished pine floor. I covered Rivers' dark hair with one hand and placed my other hand over the lower part of his face, framing his eyes between them.

"Look at him, both of you. Dad, visualize shaggy

blonde hair. Drew, remember the hole in your closet wall.''

"That looks like—Randy Barlow," Drew sputtered. "Alec, you really didn't know?"

"Oh, shit!" was all Dad said.

"So the reference in Rivers' journal to his angel wasn't generic at that," Drew concluded.

"Oh, shit!" Dad repeated.

"Dad...?"

"Martha's gonna be pissed," Dad said at last.

"Guess that means he didn't know," I muttered to Drew.

"Alec, was Angelique here that weekend?" Drew approached the poster, mesmerized.

Dad gave his head a sharp snap. "She was supposed to be. She was carrying Randy then, but she couldn't stop tumbling off the wagon. Martha hired a nurse to dry her out here, only the nurse felt a more confined setting was needed."

Did the nurse really make that choice? Maybe Mother knew Eddie was two-timing them and decided to knock out the competition. I hated that I always suspected her motives, but how often was I wrong?

Drew walked back to the pile of bones and stared as if he expected them to speak to him. "Why now, Trace? If Randy has always known who his father was, why would he start killing now? And how did he find out what happened that weekend?"

I smacked myself in the forehead. "I knew that stutter step was familiar to me. When Philly and I went to see Jolly, I heard a workman's scuffing footsteps outside the door. That had to be *Randy*. The construction at Beverly Vista was his other job. Jolly must have seen him and thought he was Eddie Rivers."

"Honey, I never suspected anything in all these years. Why would Jolly, as befuddled as he is now?" Dad asked.

"Trust me, Dad, Jolly's a lot more susceptible to ringers."

Drew paced among Rivers' rotting clothing. "So Jolly spilled his guts, and Randy decided to extract the treasure, that maybe his mom told him about, from the people who cheated him of it."

I rapped my knuckles against the poster to indicate Randy. "And when he heard me talking to Jolly and feared I was getting too close, he upped the stakes. He abandoned his letter harassment of Mother and took her hostage. Poor Philly happened to be at the wrong place at the wrong time."

"Philly's made a career of that," Drew muttered. "Where would he hide them? In Angelique's trailer?"

I joined Drew behind the bookcase, where I threw a smug glance at the bones that now looked so harmless. They weren't extracting their revenge. But they had left an ugly legacy we were all still living with. Or dying with.

"Drew, you know how Mother finds jobs for Randy. He oversees the L.A. homes of nearly every Hollywood legend who lives elsewhere now. They could be anyplace. Without a list of those houses, we'll never find them."

Dad climbed off the sofa. "Andrew, let's find that sombitch and beat the truth out of him."

Drew stared at his knuckles.

"Randy would pound the two of you into the ground without raising a sweat," I insisted.

They murmured protests and did a little male bonding shuffle right before my eyes. Okay, maybe I wasn't diplomatic, but I knew how it would go: Drew'd get beaten to a pulp, while Dad would take off again for Mexico.

I proposed a better plan. To my surprise, they both liked it. Drew found a pad in the desk, and we sketched out the details together. But we had to call Randy to put it in play.

Drew propped his feet up on the teakwood desk. "What if he's not at Beverly Vista?"

"Don't borrow trouble, okay? He's there, I know it," I insisted.

There was no working phone in that house anymore. I tried placing the call on Drew's cell phone, but in that hilly terrain, it wouldn't go through. Yet the little piece of crap Dad picked up in some Mexican bar did the trick just fine.

At Beverly Vista, when I asked for Randy, I was connected with the construction supervisor; he complained that Randy was gone from the site too much to allow him to take personal calls.

While I gave a vigorous nod to Dad and Drew to let them know we tracked him down, I commiserated insincerely with the supervisor. He hired that dolt—when his home looked like mine, we'd really talk. Eventually, he agreed to let me speak to Randy.

When Randy came on the line, I snapped, "Randy, when the hell are you gonna finish my closets?"

Randy's voice squeaked. "Trace. How did you find me?"

"Your mother told my mother, of course."

"Oh…right," he said vaguely.

While Randy and I debated *ad nauseam* the exact promises he made to me, in the background Dad and Drew went into the script they'd composed.

"Andrew, I don't know why you're fighting me," Dad snapped with believable anger. "I found a buyer in Mexico."

"If a jeweler in Mexico would pay that much, we could get more here," Drew insisted. Not a bad actor, either.

"Randy, are you listening to me?" I demanded, when he seemed to drop his end of the conversation.

"What about Martha and Philly?" Dad asked, as arranged.

Drew said, "When their captor realizes the treasure is gone, he'll let them go."

Randy could barely follow our conversation. But when Dad and Drew's script ran out, I asked if we had a deal.

"Huh?" Randy asked. "Oh, yeah—sure."

I slapped the little phone closed with a flourish. Only later did the unease set in. Something about that exchange troubled me. I just couldn't put my finger on what it was.

DREW AND I DECIDED to find a vantage point from which to watch the progress of our plan. We drove back to the south Valley and parked in a Sav-On drugstore lot on Ventura Boulevard. There we huddled in my truck, watching the world pass. Meanwhile, Dad arranged for a prop man to put together a "treasure" for him. We were all a little skeptical about that part of it. Randy was a show biz kid; would he be fooled as easily as others might? We had to hope. While Drew and I watched the passing cars, Dad went to pick up the pseudo-treasure.

After a while, Drew remarked, "I never realized there were so many teenagers driving BMW's—"

"All wearing more jewelry than Cleopatra," I added. The credit card rich—the Ferengi of planet Earth.

Randy's truck, with its oxidized red paint and the aqua surfboard propped on the tailgate, was easy to pick out in that parade. "Look, it's him." I bit my lip. "What if I just scared him? What if he's only going back to finish our closets?"

"Babe, trust me, you're not that scary."

No more than twenty minutes later, Randy's truck passed the other way. We waited there for Dad, till he returned with the so-called treasure he picked up from his friend. From a cardboard box, he removed a metal chest covered in red velvet.

"Not too hokey," I said.

"Never you mind, honey. Anyone foolish enough to want a treasure deserves to see a treasure chest," Dad insisted.

My jaw gaped when I saw what the chest contained. It looked like a fortune in antique jewelry—diamonds, rubies, emeralds, all elaborately set in what appeared to be gold and platinum. The phony stones even gave off a rainbow effect.

"Wow! If this is what paste looks like, who needs the real stuff?" I said.

"That's what I told Drew before he bought your ring, but he wouldn't listen," Dad muttered.

I did a double-take at my engagement ring.

We zipped back to our condo, watching all the while for Schuller's return. We stumbled over the note in the foyer. I checked first to see whether it was from our neighbors, suggesting a change of locale. But it was another anonymous demand for the treasure, just like the ones we found in Mother's desk. I assumed it had been shoved under the door till I noticed my computer was on. That bastard composed the note on my computer!

I was sure Randy wasn't smart enough to have installed listening devises in our condo, but this was still too weird for me. I whispered that we should read the note on the roof.

"I didn't know we had a roof key," Drew said as we climbed the stairs. "They must have given it to us when we bought the place, right?"

"Okay," I said.

On the roof, we gathered around the note. It instructed us to deposit the treasure in a Dumpster behind a North Hollywood Ralph's market. Later, we'd receive a call on the pay phone at the Wilshire Beverly Hills Starbucks telling us where to find the hostages.

It ended with, "Just the guy—leave the girl and the old man at home."

"Girl? I babysat that twerp," I said.

Dad whined, "Who's he calling an old man?"

"Don't gripe, either of you," Drew snapped. "I'm the only one he's not afraid of."

TWENTY-SEVEN

"From Babes and Fools," Oxford Productions, 1971: Starring Martha Collins as Joyce and Tory Holms as Sherry.

In an office filled with rows of desks, a woman rushes away from a coworker's desk, shouting excitedly over her shoulder.

JOYCE
Sherry, that's the first good idea you ever had.

SHERRY
(crying after her)
What did I say?

THE *GIRL* ENDED UP waiting at her mother's house, but not before she and the *old man* put up quite a fight.

Dad had said, "I'm following along behind you, Drew. She's my wife. I have to be there."

"Alec, you're crazy. If Randy doesn't spot you, some fan is sure to. Do you want your name shouted out at a critical moment?"

Dad just laughed knowingly. "Son, when an actor doesn't want to be recognized, he's not."

Dad had a theory that when a celebrity dimmed the light that seemed to glow inside, no one recognized him. He'd proven it many times, but never when the stakes were so high.

Drew had argued that more was called for than merely pulling a plug, and Dad finally agreed to make further modifications. He swiped a bottle of Yolanda's dark red hair rinse and applied it during a quick shower. A little makeup, a change of clothes—and he was a different man. Borrowing Yolanda's black Camaro completed the disguise. Drew admitted the change was dramatic, and he confessed that he liked the idea of someone watching his back.

But when I insisted I could do the same, neither of them would hear of it.

"Tracy, you can't extinguish your internal light—you proved that with Jolly."

"So the little woman waits at home," I growled.

"You're manning the base communications, honey," Dad said.

Same difference. Somehow, I'd show them.

I WAITED AT Mother's house till my nerves felt jagged enough to slash through my skin. I brought my cell phone in from the truck. Since I'd been keeping it connected to the cigarette lighter, the gizmo seemed to be fully charged. Who knew that would do it? But after two long hours of pacing, while I held it in my hand, the damn phone wouldn't ring.

When my legs grew weary, I sat. Only Dad's old lighter, still tucked in my pocket, dug into my hip. The lighter and phone changed places, and while I resumed pacing, I played with the top on the lighter. Well, I kept lighting it, too—I loved seeing the big spark it gave off before flaring. I strolled through room after room, striking the lighter and extinguishing it.

When the phone in my pocket finally jangled, I nearly dropped the burning lighter onto the plush cream living room carpet. I extinguished it carefully and answered the phone.

Skipping his greeting, Drew blurted, "Trace, it doesn't look good."

My blood froze.

"I did exactly what Randy wanted. I dropped the package in that Dumpster, then drove to the Starbucks phone, but he never called. Alec waited at the Dumpster till he picked up the package, and now he's followed Randy. The last time I heard from Alec, they were driving through south Orange County. Your dad thinks Randy is headed for the border."

"Mexico? What about Angelique? You said Mother checked her into the hospital yesterday. He's leaving her behind?"

"Looks like it," Drew went on. "Maybe he blames her for losing his treasure years ago. Or he's sick of being tied to a batty old woman."

I knew what that could do to you, though Randy never seemed to mind.

Drew's saga continued, "When I realized he was never going to call, I went to their trailer in Chatsworth to sniff around. I thought maybe I could get something out of Nan, that homeless woman who lives with them. But the trailer was empty."

"Nan has to be there, Drew. She needs Angelique or Randy to take her everywhere."

Drew sniffed impatiently, "Tracy, I looked through all the windows in that metal tube. No one was there."

Nan must have hidden in a place not visible from the windows. The way she babbled, she probably just didn't want to talk to him. They couldn't *all* change their spots at this point.

"Sit tight," Drew said. "Alec's heading home. He planned to alert the Border Patrol that Randy's carrying stolen jewelry, and he said he'd turn back afterward. We'll meet you at the house, and we'll strategize then." He signed off.

Sit tight, my ass—I'd strategize now. I knew I'd been right when I told Drew we couldn't find all the houses to which Randy held keys. But Angelique knew them. I remember having asked Drew which hospital Mother had checked Angelique into, but he hadn't answered. Why hadn't I pressed him?

I found a phone directory in the bottom of the mahogany TV armoire in the den. Turning to the hospital page, I balanced it open on one arm and strode through the house calling on my cell phone. I tried Cedars first; they had a lock on the biggest share of the sick celebrity market. No dice. One by one, I went down the list, my hate for voice mail growing with each call.

In between calls, my cell phone rang again.

"Drew?" I demanded with anxious hope.

"Did you misplace my son, dear?" my mother-in-law, Charlotte, asked in her syrupy sweet voice.

Jeez, does someone up there have it in for me? I had to get Caller ID. Used to be, I could avoid calls for so long that the people I didn't want to talk to grew tired of trying. Now they were always nabbing me.

"The reason I *keep* calling you, Tracy, is that I need a favor. My dear friend, Muffy—you've met Muffy, haven't you, Tracy? Well, Muffy's daughter, Buffy, is going to California, and the darling girl insists on seeing Disneyland. Why, I can't imagine. But I told Muffy you'd be happy to be her guide. Buffy is the youngest of Muffy's three girls, of course, and—"

When the phone book fell off my arm, I broke in, "What are the other two called? Boozy and Floozy?"

A gasp followed by some serious silence was Charlotte's only response.

"Charlotte, do you watch the news? My mother is on the verge of being indicted for murder." Not to mention that she was also misplaced.

With an exaggerated sigh, Charlotte said, "I always

change the channel when Martha comes on. Honestly, Tracy, I know she's your mother, but I can't imagine why you don't chain that old bitch in the basement.''

Not a bad idea, except for one thing. ''We don't have basements here. When the earth shakes a lot, it's not a good idea to be standing over a hole.''

''Nonsense, dear, I'm sure lots of people have basements in California.''

''Only lunatics and—'' The double-punch of *lunatics* and *basements* stunned me. ''Charlotte, you're a genius. You tell your friend, Fuzzy or Wuzzy, that I'll happily drag her brat, Huey or Dewey, to Disneyland.'' I cut the connection.

What was that Drew had said? Of course, that Angelique's trailer was in Chatsworth. I'd forgotten that. Randy had to be the caretaker of Mother's house on Windswept. Where better to stash his hostages than in a bomb shelter that no one ever entered.

The phone rang. ''Tracy, we were cut off—'' Charlotte started to say.

''Watch for it now—it's gonna happen again.'' I turned the phone off this time.

I wanted to dash to Windswept. But what if Randy booby-trapped the bomb shelter? He had unexpected skills—his having used my computer proved that. I still needed to talk to Angelique. I found the phone book where it had fallen. Since Charlotte was probably still dialing me, I decided to use the house phone.

I yanked the handset from the faux antique ivory phone on Mother's glitzy glass desk, but stopped at the sight of the redial button. In her own way, Mother did care for that clingy leech, Angelique. Could I possibly be that lucky?

I pressed the redial button. After two rings, a voice said, ''Beverly Vista.''

With my heart thudding in my ears, I asked for Angelique Barlow—and held my breath.

''One moment,'' the operator said.

I was surprised at Mother. While Beverly Vista was a chic place to be ill, intensive care was a joke there. Mother was nothing if not shallow, but she always expected excellent care. Maybe that was just for herself.

Instead of connecting me to Angelique's room, the operator rang the nurse's station. Didn't *any* call go directly through there?

When I identified myself, the nurse cut me off. "Oh, yes. I've been leaving updates on your mother's answering machine."

Jeez, you mean it was that easy? But why would I listen to her messages if I didn't play my own?

"Actually, I need to speak to Ms. Barlow about my mother. She's had an emergency."

"No, I can't permit that. Ms. Barlow is off the ventilator now, but she had a bad night. Her lungs are quite scarred, you know, and sometimes breathing gets too hard for her."

"So she can't talk?" I demanded. "Can she listen?"

In a chillier voice the nurse said, "She just drifted off to sleep. I looked in on her, and she was huddled in the fetal position with the covers up all the way to her white hair."

When Angelique could speak, she wouldn't thank her nurse. She considered her hair platinum.

"I won't disturb her," the nurse added with brisk efficiency.

I slammed the phone in her ear.

Booby-trapped or not, I'd have to risk it. I started for the door, but remembering Dad and Drew, I scratched a note on a yellow Post-it from the desk, telling them I'd gone to Windswept. I stuck the note to the kitchen table. Then I grabbed a flashlight from the kitchen and whistled for Lorenzo's dog.

ONCE I GLIDED to a stop outside the house on Windswept Lane, I looked into the pooch's soulful eyes before grabbing his head and planting a kiss on it.

"Wish me luck, boy," I whispered.

Rather than try the rusty key again, I went around to the back. The sliding glass door was still unlocked. I slipped through the door and went to the kitchen.

The trap door was closed. I lifted the handle, but once more, it caught. Shining the flashlight into the opening, I discovered that the door was tied from below with a piece of clothesline rope. I zipped to the other side of the island and found a sharp knife. On my return, I sliced through the rope. The door swung open in my hand.

When I shined the flashlight down the hole, I saw a dimly-lit set of narrow, concrete stairs. I stuffed the knife into my pocket along with the cell phone and crept down the stairs to a short concrete hall, lowering the trap door over my head. There were two built-in electric lights there, but they were lit with only minimum wattage. Somewhere within that underground space, I heard the muted hum of a generator.

At the end of the corridor was a closed door. I tried the knob. Locked. Next to the door, I spied a key hanging from a rusted cup hook. Man, if I came through this alive, I really needed to address precisely how much I'd picked up from my mother. I unlocked the door—much heavier than I expected; it seemed to be solid metal. I eased it open an inch or so and listened for the presence of anyone close by. Except for the generator, it was quiet there. I took the key with me.

I crept through the door and found myself in a small and rather basic Pullman kitchen. Instead of cabinets, deep pine shelves had been built over wheat-colored Formica counters. Food had been stacked on the shelves on one side and dishes and glasses on the other. But Dad was right. Most of the cans had exploded—Botulism Central here—leaving fossilized goo everywhere. The earthquake had made short work of the crockery. Broken pieces covered the counters, but it looked as if someone had swept the rubble from the dusty, brown linoleum floor.

Before moving on, I locked the outer door of the shelter from inside the kitchen and slipped the key into my pocket.

Another closed door blocked the rest of the shelter. This one was unlocked. I let myself into a cozy sitting room. The room contained all the basic necessities: Two yellowing white woven sofas, a collection of Parsons tables in a variety of primary colors, board games, a boxy thirty-year-old portable radio—and a fully stocked bar. Except for the lack of windows, I liked it better than my own living room in its present state.

I noticed there was a bathroom tucked behind the kitchen. But the rest of the rooms in this shelter were assembled railroad car style—the closed door to the next one was just ahead of me.

That door also proved to be unlocked. I stepped into what must have been intended to be my room come Armageddon. A pile of stuffed animals I'd never seen before topped a small white chest of drawers. The blue blanket covering a narrow bed was rumpled, and the impression of an adult-sized head remained in the yellowing pink-and-white pillowcase.

Who's been sleeping in my bed? Goldilocks—or Randy?

The rooms had begun under the house, but I felt sure the back patio was over this one. The next door stood an inch or two ajar. Like the others, it was solid metal and trimmed with a row of soft, rubbery gaskets along the side that made it fit tightly in its metal frame. I eased it open, figuring that had to be the room next to the pool, the one whose wall I'd seen through the crack.

Two things struck me at once: First, my mother had spent a fortune setting up what would have been her own room—compared to the utilitarian décor of the rest of the place—and, next, that I'd found the hostages. Mother and

Philly huddled together on the floor against the opposite wall, their hands and feet bound together with bright blue duct tape.

I yanked the knife from my pocket and took a few quick steps into that palace.

"Darling, go back!" Mother shouted.

From behind me, I heard the sound of an automatic weapon being cocked.

TWENTY-EIGHT

"The Ties That Bind," Prima Productions, 1972: Starring Martha Collins as Angela and Alec Grainger as Mike.

ANGELA
You took something from me, you bastard—now you owe me.

MIKE
I gave you something in exchange. Debts must be paid in this life, but not always with interest.

RANDY HAD PROBABLY hit the Mexican border by now. Who the hell was behind me holding a gun? I turned to face my miscalculation.

"Angelique!" I squeaked.

Her watery blue eyes looked sharper than usual—and angry. She wore the baggy denim overalls and the faded orange sweatshirt Nan had worn when they came to my condo. Her breathing seemed fine, though she was using her oxygen tank. She sure didn't act like a woman who had been in crisis only hours before. The hand holding the gun looked rock-steady.

So Drew was right—their trailer *was* empty. "You left Nan to fill your bed at Beverly Vista?" The white hair the nurse described should have told me; Angelique's platinum looked silver.

"My stand-in," Angelique said with exaggerated dignity.

"Jolly didn't tell Randy about Eddie's death—he told you," I guessed, speaking in half-sentences that I knew she'd understand.

Angelique just nodded.

"How did you get in to see Jolly? Your name wasn't in the register at Beverly Vista." Even as quickly as I read it, her name would have jumped out at me.

Angelique spat angrily, "The lousy nurse your mother hired for me years ago, so my poor boy wouldn't be as slow as he is—was Didi, the receptionist there. She never made *me* sign in."

No wonder Didi had given me that bug-eyed look—she must have thought her ex-employer had lived all these years in a vacuum. But wasn't Angelique confused about which of them guzzled the sauce while pregnant?

Another connection fell into place concerning the two murder methods used on Sperry. "*You* stabbed Vince Sperry." She wasn't home when I called to schedule Randy's work on my closets—he had to make the arrangement himself.

Talk about killer timing. At that moment, Angelique yanked the kitchen knife from my pocket. I held my breath till she tossed it into the other room. My cell phone followed it.

Feeling braver after the knife was gone, I asked, "What happened? Did Randy check on your handiwork the next morning and find Sperry wasn't dead yet? He shot Sperry to finish him off, huh?" Before showing up early at my place. With an inward groan, I remembered the red spatters on his painter's pants.

She gave me a shove that sent me reeling into the big brass bed, covered with a pumpkin-colored quilt, that filled the center of the room.

"What about Jolly?" I asked as she yanked me off the

bed. "You were both in Beverly Vista then, you as a patient, Randy as a worker."

She hurled me at the wall. "That was a family affair."

How wholesome. She ordered me to sit next to Mother on the floor. Mother's head was bent over her knees, denying me the chance to see her face. She still wore her royal Chanel suit. She must have been forced to put it on again when she was abducted. I looked past her to Philly. His blue-green eyes were as wide as dinner plates, but all the twinkle had been extinguished. And I promised he'd be in no danger. Poor, frightened man—I felt worse about him than anything else.

Angelique threw me a roll of that blue duct tape they must have bought on sale and ordered me to tape my ankles together. Then she told Mother to wrap it around my hands. "And it better be tight, Martha, or I'll snuff your kid now."

With her own hands bound and shaking, Mother did a piss-poor job—for which I was grateful. My mobility wasn't as limited as hers and Philly's.

"I knew you'd show up eventually, Tracy. You've always been such a little snoop. I hoped it would be before I joined my boy in Mexico. I know you all so well. I should, I've been crawling before you long enough."

What was that old saying? *Give a man a fish, and you feed him for a day; teach him to fish, and you feed him for a lifetime.* True, but not the whole truth. The other part was, *Keep giving him fish, and he'll blame you for his dependence.*

This scenario had been acted out so many times over the years, Mother playing Lady Bountiful, Angelique her appreciative slave—till Angelique's resentment built up and sparked in an angry little flare. After only a short cooling-off period, they always took up right where they left off. Didn't Mother realize Angelique had to be keeping some resentments in reserve?

I should have known it was her after seeing those threatening letters. There was obviously more than one killer, yet the letters all demanded that Mother hand over the treasure "to *me*." That was how Angelique referred to herself and her son.

Now I understood what troubled me when I called Randy at Beverly Vista. If he were smart enough to plan this vendetta, he wouldn't have fallen for Dad and Drew's vaudevillian routine. That bulb was just as dim as I always thought. Angelique was the one who'd hidden her glow all these years.

And I knew she was stronger than she seemed—I discovered that when she clutched my arms greeting me at my condo on Monday, when she and Nan came to deliver that wallpaper border. Her lungs were bad, but I bet they were better than anyone knew. She must have faked that attack and made Mother check her into Beverly Vista—so she and Randy had access to Jolly. I remembered the feathers that showed up afterward in our living room. From the pillow Jolly chewed? I bet Randy had planted them.

Angelique's pale blue eyes flared. "I've always hated you, Tracy. Attractive, smart, successful—everything Randy never had a chance to be. Thanks to her." She indicated Mother with a jut of her chin, knocking her long silvery hair over her face. She impatiently tossed it back. "Now Martha can watch you die at her side—before she and this old coot go, too."

Philly produced an audible gulp, and he seemed to shrink within his shabby clothes. Mother's arm, pressed to mine, trembled.

"You had Alec, Martha. Jesus, he adores you. I know, I've tried working my wiles on him more times than I can tell you. Why did you have to go after Eddie?"

In the throes of her ranting, her own irony seemed lost on Angelique. She paced the smooth maple floor, ably spinning her oxygen canister at each turn. It no longer squeaked.

Oxygen…? In that position, Dad's lighter dug into my hip again.

"But Eddie loved me best—me! For once I came out on top. You couldn't stand that, Martha."

Angelique glared across the bed. I followed her stare to a framed photo of the Earl of Rahway that rested on the mahogany nightstand on our side. Something had been inscribed across the corner in a black marker, but I couldn't read it.

Angelique read it to us. "'To my baby,'" she screeched. "He called you his baby."

His baby, his angel, his sugar—Dad was right, Eddie did favor generic names. I wondered at the photo's placement in a room Mother never intended to use. Had she and Eddie met here while Angelique writhed in withdrawal agony in the house? I hated the thought of Dad seeing that photo. But he probably wouldn't notice it—when he stumbled across our dead bodies.

Fear made me dizzy. Had Dad and Drew found my note yet? Why had I closed the trap door upstairs? They could be tearing the house apart at this moment and might never guess.

Angelique continued to scream at Mother while facing the photo. "You took my son's father—and my treasure. Eddie would have wanted me to have it."

With my hands only loosely bound, I was able to stuff them into my pocket and pull the lighter out. My playing with the lid had loosened it. It opened soundlessly now.

But *that* was when Mother decided to talk. All this time without uttering a peep—and she had to open her big yap precisely when I didn't want Angelique's attention on us. I hid the lighter between my hands.

"It's true, Angel. I deserve whatever you do to me. But Philly and Tracy don't. Especially Tracy. You know what she means to me." Mother turned to Philly, probably to issue a silent apology for kissing him off. He just stared at the floor.

To my surprise, instead of throwing out another threat on my life, Angelique twisted away. Through Nan's old rags, I saw the muscles of her back jerk as she began to sob.

I slipped my hands into position on the lighter. *Now!* I told myself. The sound of her sobbing covered the noise the wheel made when it lit. But I couldn't bring myself to use it. My brain ordered my hands to toss it at her back. Yet Angelique was such a victim, by her own choice, though her friends had aided and abetted. I couldn't deal the last blow.

She whirled around—and spotted what I held. Her eyes flared faster than the lighter had. Her foot, shod in Nan's dingy blue sneaker, shot out. When she kicked the lighter, it flew into her chest, lighting the sweatshirt on fire. It bounced onto the bed, flaring on the old, dry quilt.

The burning sweatshirt ignited her brittle hair. Instead of beating the fire out, she just screamed. She tossed her hands in the air, and the gun flew off and hit the floor. Still shrieking, Angelique ran into the other room, her oxygen tank trailing behind her. The door slammed shut.

While my brain-dead companions just sat there, I pulled myself onto the bed and rolled on the burning quilt.

"I swear, Mother," I muttered under my breath. "Every time I try to rescue you, I end up trapped in some awful place."

"You exaggerate, Tracy. It's not like it happens daily."

It *did* happen daily.

"It's not a trend," Mother insisted.

Not after today.

Mother looked past me to the door. "Angelique will be all right, won't she? Once she gets to the house, the sprinklers will go off. The fire department made me install them last year.''

After putting the fire out, I slipped from the bed. ''She won't make it to the house. The shelter door is locked; the key's in my pocket.''

''Oh, Tracy—you and your keys.'' Mother shook her head. ''The same key works all the doors. We have to get to Angel, darling.''

Right. Angelique first, then I'd get us all out of here. I scooted across the floor on my butt. When I reached the gun, I gave it a kick, sending it under the bed. Stuffing bound hands to the bottom of my pocket required a guru-level yoga twist. In my next life, I wanted to be in better shape.

I pulled myself to my knees and unlocked the door. But when I tugged at it, the door wouldn't budge.

''It's—stuck.'' I couldn't hear a sound from the other room. Maybe Angelique did find a way out. I pressed my ear to it—but jumped away when the door burned my ear. ''The fire's raging in there. The door expanded in the heat.''

''Poor, poor Angelique,'' Mother muttered.

''Poor Angelique?'' Philly shouted. ''That batty dame tried to kill us. Now she's locked in there with an oxygen tank. Martha, don't you know what that means?''

Smoke drifted in from under the door.

I looked into Mother's widening eyes. ''He's trying to tell you—we're toast.''

TWENTY-NINE

"Sins of the Mothers," Ordinal Pictures, 1973: Starring Martha Collins as Brett and Alan James as Sky.

A shocked woman stares when a young man in disco clothes enters.

> BRETT
> *But you're supposed to be—*

> SKY
> *Dead? That's right Brett, you cut my brake line—only Jill drove my car. You killed your own daughter.*

AFTER STUFFING THE QUILT below the door, I huddled with Mother and Philly on the far wall. The room was getting hotter, but the quilt seemed to be holding back the smoke.

After a long silence, I said, "I asked about this house once when I was little, but you said I imagined it. You know, Mother, I've dreamed of it ever since."

"Me, too. Only I don't call them *dreams*." Mother cleared her throat. "Eddie was…"

That sound itself was such an admission of pain, I cut in fast to spare her. "I know, Dad told me."

She recovered quickly. "Is his arm still in its socket? Angelique was right, darling, you are terribly nosy."

I blotted my face with my sleeve. "Maybe I wouldn't have to be nosy if you didn't lie." Nah, that wouldn't change it. "Explain something to me. Given the mess you make of your own life, where do you get off thinking you should control mine?''

"Uh…girls, is this really the time for that?'' Philly asked.

"Control? Is that how you see it, young lady? I don't want to control your life—I want to be part of it.''

That sucked the wind from my sails. ''But—you are part of it.''

"As what? An afterthought? A nuisance?'' She placed her bound hands on her knees and pressed her face against them. ''You love your child, but you always think you'll make time for her another day. Today you need to snag the next role or get ready for tonight's premier. Tomorrow will be her time. Only tomorrow you have to read what they wrote about the dress you wore last night, you have to be seen at the right lunch. Before you know it, you've run out of tomorrows. Your child doesn't need you anymore. Only then do you realize that none of the rest mattered, and you'd do anything to recover that lost time.''

So unexpected was the admission, I didn't know what to say. Feelings were just the coin we traded in, Mother and I; she on the screen, me in my writing. Our own emotions never saw the light. I swallowed hard and pressed my head to her shoulder.

"Of course, control isn't the same as *guidance*. No one could fault a mother for wanting to guide her child's life. Sometimes, Tracy, you really do need it.''

Even this late in the game, we couldn't bear to keep our deepest sentiments on display. But it was our way. Maybe that was *how* we expressed them. Despite the tears set to fall from my eyes, I started laughing. Mother joined in, and our laughter built to a rolling-on-the-floor level. It wasn't that hard to achieve here.

Fear had stiffened Philly's sweaty face. ''Get it together, you two. It's the time for action, not denial.''

Smoke filled the air now. I swallowed hard to stifle a

cough. "Look who's talking about denial. Philly, you wouldn't know the real world if it bit you on the fanny." Not that I was knocking his approach to life. But still, for me it's a choice.

Mother gave her forehead a dainty press with her Chanel suit sleeve; even in this heat, she glowed. And that suit—after three days—still looked great. Why didn't I get *those* genes?

"It's not denial, Philly—we're meeting...whatever happens...on our own terms," Mother said. "Only once in my life did I surrender to someone else's rules, and that's what put us here."

After Mother's rendition of "My Way." Philly just lowered his head.

The heat had risen so high now that the room felt like a simmering caldron. The air took on the translucency of the L.A. basin on a bad smog day. Wasn't there a certain irony in quitting smoking, only to die like this? A wracking cough shook me. It hit me, finally—this was the real thing. I longed for one more chance to experience the things that really mattered—making love, watching the sunset, chocolate. One more chance, *knowing* it was the last.

"I don't have your courage, Martha," Philly said, scarcely above a whisper.

Please God, I thought, let us live now, and I'll become anti-everything. Fat, food and especially—considering what was killing me—smoking. In case you think the world needs another asshole.

Though both their hands were bound, Mother managed to grasp Philly's fingertips with hers. "You do, my friend. You just have to find it inside yourself. It's been waiting there all along."

The faintest of sounds from the outside wall caught my attention.

Philly's fingers clutched at hers. "I wish—"

"Believe, dear man," Mother said.

"Can the conversion, willya! I'm trying to listen," I snapped.

"Now just a minute, kid. Don't you talk to your mom that way," Philly said.

I heard it again. "Yes, I'm right!" I brought my hands to my face and started chewing at the tape.

"Really, darling," Mother said, "we're all hungry, but it wouldn't hurt you to skip a meal."

Mid-chew, I stopped and glared at her. "Mother, open your ears, not your mouth. What do you hear?"

"Barking…"

The sound came and went. "It's Lorenzo's dog. He's alerting someone to where we are."

"Aw, Christ, Trace. How can someone so smart also be so dense? He's not Lorenzo's—he's *your* dog. I got him for you, so you could have a pooch in your truck."

"I knew that, Philly." I chewed at my tape as voraciously as a Type-A beaver.

"Yeah? Then how come you always call him that, kid?"

"I've been waiting for you to 'fess up. And for him to tell me his name. It's not Johnny O'Toole."

"How do you know?" Philly demanded.

"That he told me." I broke through the tape. The frantic barking started again. I freed my own ankles, and then pulled the tape from Mother's hands, leaving it to her to free Philly. "He's up on the patio. Come on, we have to help him attract attention."

I slid across the floor. Lying on my back, I pounded my feet against the wall. Mother joined me, though the tap her size five Ferragamos made couldn't have carried far.

"Help us, Philly," I grunted.

Philly didn't budge.

"Wait, Tracy. Do you hear something else?" Mother asked.

"An echo. They dropped something heavy into the pool."

"And an engine," Philly said, excitement finally engaging in his voice. "I hear a motor."

We lined up against the wall, the three of us now, set to resume our banging. But then, even through the sound deadening wall, the roar of an engine catapulted toward us.

"Get back!" I shouted.

We all slid away on the smooth wooden floor. Just in time. What felt like a tidal wave crashed into the pool, shattering it and pressing the pool's reinforcing steel through the wall of the bomb shelter.

I stared stupidly at the vision that appeared before me where a wall used to be. "That's my truck's grill." I was sure of it, even if the pool's steel bars were twisted into it. The grill seemed to be leaning at an odd angle, as if it flew down from the street level.

Dad's voice drifted in from outside. "Get in the cab, Drew. Back it up."

With the steel bars enmeshed in the grill, the engine strained. All at once, the truck broke loose. As the grill pulled away, I could see that it had twisted the closely spaced steel ribars away from each other, making a small space.

Dad's face appeared in the opening. "It won't be long now. The police are on their way with the Jaws of Life. We'll get you out of there soon."

"No time, Dad. There's a fire roaring in the other room, and Angelique's oxygen tank is in there. It's gotta be now."

Philly scurried over to the hole in the wall. As plump around the middle as he was, I didn't think he'd make it through the space, but I understood he had to try.

He surprised me. "Boys, I'll help from this side. Take

the women first. Start with Tracy." He looked to Mother to make sure she understood.

Children, sure—but normally, I don't go for this women-first shit. Still, I knew this was a step Philly had to take.

Drew jumped down into pool, along with a heavyset bearded man I didn't know. Rough hands reached into the shelter, grabbed my shoulders and pulled me through the twisted ropes of steel. But my jeans' pockets caught. Well, maybe my hips. I repeated my resolution: Next life, better shape.

Dad yelled, "Martha, you've got to pull off her shoes and her jeans."

While suspended between those steel bars, two pairs of hands tore at my clothes. I felt a moment of panic—not that I wouldn't make it, but over which undies had I worn. My tattered, dingy cotton ones, I remembered; worse than Drew's baggy court drawers. Mother would be furious. She always advised me to wear good underwear, "Because you never know what will happen." Sure, she meant an impromptu affair—but it's just as important when you're getting hurled through the side of a pool.

Once stripped, while rough steel scraped my skin raw, I made it through. My lungs sucked in the clean air. Drew short-circuited my breathing when he yanked me into a quick, bone-cracking hug before handing me off to the bearded man. He guided me through the slippery green goo filling the bottom of the shattered pool, to the stairs at the side, where a tall woman loaned me a pair of marigold silk Capri pants.

I looked at my benefactor. At dark hair and eyes and to-die-for cheekbones. Margery Cooper, the model, I realized. She lived around here, too? Lucky stiff. The Capri pants hung to my ankles, and I couldn't quite button them. Does this inexplicable spreading happen to everyone who quits smoking? Man, they oughta put *that* warning on the cigarette pack.

When I turned back to the opening in the pool, my tiny mother was being lifted out. Without the necessity of stripping, dammit. With sirens blazing, a caravan of police cars and a fire truck approached the house. When the fire truck slowed, one fireman jumped off the truck and rushed to the back of the knoll. He carried the Jaws of Life.

Everyone shouted at once to the racing fireman. I bet he couldn't understand anything beyond the urgency those garbled words conveyed. I clung to Margery and held my breath. The fireman and our heavyset helper, a neighbor I learned later, slowly spread the steel while Dad and Drew tugged at Philly's portly form. I didn't breathe again till his scuffed old tassel loafers made it out.

"It's hotter'n hell in there!" Philly shouted. "It's gonna blow."

Everyone scrambled from the pool and ran the length of the property.

Everyone but Mother—she took a few steps toward it. "Angel. We've got to go back for—"

For once, Dad didn't argue with her. He just swept her into his arms and carried her away. I hadn't seen anything that romantic since Rhett took Scarlett upstairs for a sound schtuping.

"Oh, Alec," Mother swooned.

I happened to glance at Philly, just as his face sagged with despair. Despite having shown more courage than most people ever have—the other guy still got the girl.

Before I could chase that thought, the longest three days of my life ended with a bang—the roof blew off the shelter. Drew knocked Philly and the dog down. And he threw his body over mine, crushing me to the ground as fragments of metal and mortar, and maybe flesh and bone, rained down on all of us.

THIRTY

"Mother Knows All: The Remake," Hargrove Pictures, 1974: Martha Collins reprises her first film, taking the role of Mother, with Lindsay Silver as Janet.

> ### MOTHER
> A mother always knows what's in her child's heart.
>
> ### JANET
> How can you say that? Everything that happened was your fault!
>
> ### MOTHER
> (shrugging cheerfully)
> All's well that ends well.

I SAT CROSS-LEGGED on the tiny part of the patio left intact after the explosion while the fire crew extinguished the last of the inferno that raged in the bomb shelter. In that position, I needed to slide the zipper down a smidge on my borrowed pants. As it appeared I might have a few years ahead of me, after all, maybe I should consider getting into better shape in *this* life.

The house didn't go up in flames, thanks to the sprinklers the fire department made Mother install. But the dusty furnishings were covered in a sheet of mud.

The pool looked worse than ever. Dad and Drew had placed the huge planks I'd seen spread across the back lawn into the pool. After wedging the accelerator, they let the truck race down those planks. The boards flew to the other side of the property during the explosion, but the truck was totaled.

Drew was pretty well totaled, too. His expression kept alternating between a silly little smile of relief and fierce anger at how close he had come to losing me. Or maybe over my leaving Mother's house without him. Whatever, he was a mess.

I clung to my dog. After the explosion, I grabbed his messy little head and planted a bunch of kisses on it, ending with a big one on his nose.

"You did it, my buddy. You saved our lives," I said.

He answered with a big doggie smile.

In surprise, I said, "Buddy. That's it—your name is Buddy!"

Before slapping his tongue all over my face, he gave me a look that seemed to say, *It took you long enough!*

The cops descended on us like locusts from every jurisdiction. L.A. city, L.A. County, even Ventura County and Beverly Hills. No one seemed certain which department covered that rocky ground, but they all wanted a piece of the action that was sure to get great play in the media during the weeks ahead. Even after the L.A. County Sheriff's Department won the toss, the others hung around, second-guessing.

Especially Schuller. The wonder in puce marched through the crime scene like he owned the joint—as always, shaking his pocket contents to his internal rhythm. For once my head was tuneless—a nice side-benefit to it being totally empty. And I wanted it to stay that way.

"Stop that!" I snapped. "Stop rattling those coins."

He looked dumbfounded. "I didn't know I was doing it."

If I ever display that little self-awareness, somebody shoot me.

"So—your old lady didn't kill Sperry," Schuller said. "She ever read my screenplay?"

Nothing like having priorities. "No, but I promise you she will." She deserved that for what she put me through.

His only answer was a satisfied snap of his head. At least he cancelled the coin concert.

Once the fire was extinguished, the coroner's crew showed up. It surprised me to see Angelique's body brought out in one piece. It seems she put considerable space between herself and the oxygen tank. She'd closeted the tank in the bathroom, while she took refuge under the bed in the little bedroom outside Mother's room. Despite having stuffed wet towels under that door, her lungs were too scarred; she died of smoke inhalation.

I figured Angelique just tried to distance herself from that volatile tank, and I didn't regard the exact place her body was found as significant. Mother took it as proof that Angelique had been trying to save her dear friend's life. More likely Angelique was trying to return to the one person she could count on to save *her* life. But there were limits to my forgiveness, if not Mother's.

"What's the statute of limitations on loyalty?" I asked Drew.

"Long over," he insisted.

Mother wouldn't budge in her belief. Somewhere I'd heard the definition of insanity: Doing the same thing over and over while expecting a different outcome. I'm still not sure which one of us that label applies to.

After my time at the Sperry and Marsh crime scenes, you'd think I'd be used to them. But this one was more chaotic and crowded than the first two combined. Dozens of cops crossed all over the property; endless numbers of crime scene techs seemed intent on classifying every bit of the mountains of debris. But though the scene buzzed with activity, Buddy and I just sat by ourselves, taking it all in.

Not everyone in my family was that passive. Once Mother identified Angelique's body, Dad and Drew gave the detective in charge an edited version of Randy's extortion scheme, and the fact that Randy had been on his way to Mexico. The detective reached the Border Patrol and had Randy brought to the crime scene.

Even after the cops found the treasure chest of faux jewels in his truck, Randy maintained his complete ignorance. Not a hard sell for him. But the wind went out of him when told that his mother had died. He didn't make a sound, he just lowered his head and let a steady flow of tears moisten the dirt beneath his feet. Mother elbowed a cop out of her way and ran to him. She and Randy embraced—bringing that whole insanity definition into sharper focus.

"Drew, you must represent this dear boy," she demanded as the cop she'd assaulted dragged her behind the crime-scene tapes.

When Drew finished choking, he reminded her that there might be a slight conflict of interest. Thereafter, she alternated between providing Randy with her own Miranda warning—and hounding Drew to find a top-notch criminal lawyer for him.

While Drew sought a spot on the mountainous property where he could place a cell phone call, he muttered many more synonyms for crazy than the brief number in Roget's little book. But I thought that craziness had little to do with it this time. Mother wasn't sure how much Randy knew about her past, and she still didn't want that coming out. To her dismay, Randy insisted on confessing to his role in his mother's crime spree. But Mother lucked out. All he knew was that Angelique blamed her old friends for the loss of his father's treasure. Beyond that, he just followed her orders.

But Mother still refused to bail when she learned she was in the clear. She insisted on following Randy to the

Sheriff's station. He clung to her as he had Angelique, even after Nan had been brought to the property from Beverly Vista. I couldn't help wondering whether, if Randy ever got paroled, he'd come gunning for me in resentment over the things Mother was doing for him now. The more things change...

Before the cops fully secured the scene, just as the lookie-loos flocked there, I spotted Philly slipping away. Buddy and I followed when he disappeared into a crowd of spectators and received a police escort off the property. Though the gravel hurt my bare feet, I ran to catch up with him on the main road.

"Philly, wait!"

He gave me a sheepish grin. "Clear things with the cops for me, willya, kid? This just isn't my scene."

"You're...leaving us?"

He nodded. "It's time I moved on. I'll get my stuff from the condo and be on my way."

I groped at the air before me, but my hand didn't reach him. "Where will you go?"

He shrugged. "Your pop seems to like Mexico. Maybe I'll try it. I hear you can sell crap to tourists right on the street."

How long had it been since we were at war with Mexico?

He started to turn away, but stopped. "She was just toying with me, honey. You tried to tell me, but I wouldn't listen."

"Look at it this way, Philly. When you were a boy, did you ever think Martha Collins would toy with *you?* None of the other kids can say that." Give or take a few thousand.

Philly gave his head a sad shake. It looked so final.

"Philly, we need you."

"Nah, honey, no one needs old Philly." With his head bent, he turned and walked out of our lives.

THIRTY-ONE

Darling, isn't it time we wrapped this production?

THE NUTTINESS CONTINUED over the weeks that followed as the media took hold of the crime and ran with it. But Mother's past never came up. If anything, talk-radio listeners seemed bent on canonizing her for her loyalty to Randy. She was shameless enough to agree with them. I'd say she was safe.

From the scandal, at least. As for the rest of her life, I couldn't say. We both read Schuller's screenplay, and we loved it. Man, it was tough to admit, but that puppy deserved production. Mother decided to give it a whirl.

Drew was aghast. "She's rewarding a bad cop. That guy solicited a bribe."

"He's not a bad cop yet, just one on the brink. The perfect time to get him out of the department." Besides, my sanity demanded that he carry more paper money.

I also figured, with the production, Mother wouldn't have time to tinker with my life. Fat chance. Since Hollywood sees no value in people over forty, she has endless numbers of bright old things to do the work for her. She might take an executive producer credit, but the only thing she seemed intent on producing was my future.

Despite her help, my life did look rosy. Once the dust settled, I read those emails Elijah Griffin copied from my publisher's files. They all discussed which writers they could safely drop and the reasons they could trump up to do it. It seems a merger was in the offing, and my publisher wanted to improve the balance sheet. I'd have thought it might be a better idea to publish books and make money. But that's not the way American business operates. Lock the doors and keep the customers out—so you don't have to pay the electric bill! That's why CEO's get the big bucks.

Elly leaked the rumor to an Internet news service, and that killed the merger. Now they're going ahead with the publication contracts they hadn't cancelled—fun for everyone involved, I'll bet. Lucky me, I wasn't among them.

Once word of our near deaths hit the fan, I had my pick of publishers. Just about perfect, huh? Not quite. Mother insisted on joint credit, since I used her story to write *Deadly Shadows*.

My decision flabbergasted Drew. "You're putting her name on the cover? You're going on a bookstore signing tour together? Are you out of your mind?"

"What can I say? The old bat threatened to sue me for plagiarism."

His eyes bore into mine. "Uh-huh. She risked spending the rest of her life in prison rather than let the secrets surrounding that film come out. Yet she'd hash it out in court."

"I'm telling you, Drew, she put the screws to me." I turned away from his probing eyes.

"So—that's your story, and you're sticking to it?"

When I didn't respond, he filled the silence with a knowing chuckle. I felt naked—and not the good kind, nooky naked.

A COUPLE OF MONTHS LATER, Drew and I returned to the house on Windswept Lane. After unlocking the door with a shiny new key, I let Buddy off his leash, and he dashed ahead. But I kept Harri Houdini in her case; no way was I letting the little minx loose in that labyrinth. Harri lived

with us again. Even after we cleared our condo of those
piles, she showed no interest in returning to Mother's
house. Drew chose to believe she missed us, while I felt
certain she just wouldn't leave Buddy. I made Drew close
his eyes when I led him through the door.

"Where are you taking me?" he demanded.

"Just keep 'em closed." We came to a stop at the glass
wall along the back of the house. "Okay, we're there. Ta
da!"

Drew's eyes bulged at what he saw. "The pool—it's
rebuilt."

"Not just rebuilt—restored to its former glory." I
pressed my nose to the glass and drooled.

"If that's what you call the gaudiest thing outside of
San Simeon." He had been revolted by William Randolph
Hearst's temple to himself, while I considered it a nifty
idea. "How did this happen?"

"Dad made it happen," I said. "Great, huh?"

"After everything he did at our place, Alec still had time
to find someone to do—this? Imagine that." His tone
sounded flat; Drew seemed to find the glitzy pool as in-
describable as I did.

When Randy got hauled off to the pokey, we needed to
address the holes he left in our condo. We realized too late
he was treasure hunting. That alone should have told us
he was no honor-roll student. But Dad came to the rescue.
He not only repaired the damage Randy did to the place,
using the plans Philly left, he redesigned our closets. Now
there was plenty of storage space, only the person we created it for was gone.

"What about the bomb shelter?" Drew asked.

I snorted. "He had that filled in with cement."

"Wise idea. But why fix the pool? No one lives here."
His face darkened. "Oh, I get it—they gave this place to
you."

When I shrugged, Drew stubbornly planted himself on

one of the white couches. But the knobby surface distracted him. Running his hands over it, he said, "Hey, no mud."

"What can I say? Dad's thorough."

Drew crossed his hands behind his head and smirked at me. "I don't know about you, Trace. You always insist you're so independent, but you're accepting a lot of gifts lately. Are you still going to let your dad buy you a new vehicle?"

When Harri started squawking about her confinement, I took the whiney little furball from the case and held her. Just so she wouldn't get lost. "Only fair. You said it was his idea to ruin my truck."

"What I said was—it was his idea to use it to save your life. Gonna get another truck?"

"Nah, you were right. I only bought it to annoy Mother. At my age, I shouldn't be that reactive to my parents."

"What are you going to get instead?" he asked.

"Some kind of sports car, I think. Something low to the ground. She'd hate climbing into that."

"Glad to see you've stopped being reactive," Drew deadpanned.

I nodded. "It really was time."

Drew gestured around the room, so much larger than what we were accustomed to. "And now this place."

I nuzzled the top of the tabby traitor's head with my nose. "It has to stay in the family, Drew. What with the Earl of Rahway lying in state behind the bookcase."

Drew bit his cheeks to keep from grinning when the furball started purring. "It's a shame no one thought to dump Rivers' bones into the shelter before they poured the cement."

"Yeah, a real tragedy," I said with a distinct lack of sincerity.

"Won't it bother you, knowing Rivers is there?"

I snorted in disbelief. "Are you kidding? I'm a mystery

writer with my own in-house skeleton. I'm fat, dumb and happy.'' My grin faded when I realized two of those traits—and arguably three—really were true.

Drew looked skeptical. "Does Martha agree?''

That had been my only hesitation when she suggested giving it to us. I would have razed the house I loved before I'd let it hurt her another day. But it seemed she'd finally grasped that she triumphed over Eddie Rivers decades ago. Those bones couldn't haunt her anymore.

"I think she's thrilled to have her favorite house back in her life,'' I concluded. "She really can't wait to help us decorate it.''

Drew's brown eyes bulged and his head spun from side to side. "Good God! You mean it could look worse than this?''

I love it when he turns that shade of green.

"Drew, you still take things too seriously.''

He frowned, and I thought he'd object. But he caught himself. With a grin, he said, "So I'm learning.'' He patted the sofa next to him. "You really want to live here? It'll mean a long commute for me.''

Harri and I sat beside him and snuggled close. "Sure, if you stay with SCREWED.''

He slapped his thigh. "So we're back to that again. I told you, Tracy, I still plan to make senior partner.''

I sighed. "That ship has sailed, Drew. Hell, it's taken a world cruise. You helped send one of their biggest clients to the slammer.'' The Feds were throwing the book at Benny Butler Marsh. It was only because Mother kept her legal business at SCREWED that Drew had a job at all. "Here's a thought: With so much space in this house, you could set up shop here.''

Drew seemed to consider it for a moment but gave his head a sharp shake. "No, I'm staying the course. I'll make partner next year. They're mad now, but they'll forget.''

Who knew he was such a dreamer? But how could it

hurt? So he waited six months before coming to his senses. It wasn't like Drew would go postal in the senior partner conference room.

Buddy charged into the room. He barked once and his brandy eyes glowed with excitement.

Drew laughed. "It seems I'm outnumbered." He wrapped Harri and me in his arms. "If you want it, babe, I want it."

The cat slipped away from me; she began to explore her new home. "You won't be sorry. You're gonna love it here."

He put his arm around me, and we propped our feet on the glass-and-brass coffee table. "Are you kidding? I won't be able to find my way around this place. What will we do with all the extra room? How about the dope-smoking room—what are we going to do with that?

"Convert it to a nursery?" I suggested.

We held each other's eyes for a moment—before bursting into laughter. "As if we needed kids with your parents," Drew said.

Mine? Wait till he heard the messages his mother had been leaving me. They'd scorch his ears. Now that I had Caller ID, I wondered how I'd ever lived without it.

But the idea of all the space we'd gained just reinforced what we'd lost. For both of us, it seemed, when our eyes met and acknowledged who was missing. Drew rose and walked to the window, where he stared in glum silence at our gaudy pool. I went and pressed my head against his shoulder.

Then we heard the sound of someone entering the house. Footsteps beat against the hall tiles with a jaunty beat.

Afraid to hope, I held my breath. But I knew that walk!

The footsteps stopped. "Which one's my room?" asked Philly.

Drew pulled me close and whispered into my ear, "Mrs. Eaton, it's a boy."

ACKNOWLEDGMENTS

I'm rich because I have so many generous, supportive friends. My deepest gratitude goes to:
• Judy and Joe Miller, who gave the "baby" its "shower," and to whom this book is dedicated;
• Gayle and Don Triolo, for hosting an enchanting book party for me at the Santa Lucia Preserve;
• Jamie Wallace, for designing my beautiful website;
• Terry Baker, of The Mystery Annex in Venice, California, and Linda Bivens, of Crime Time Books in Pasadena, California, for planning and hosting my magical, memorable book-launch parties;
• Bob and Debbie Levine, for their beautiful cake;
• Gayle McGary Partlow and Gayle Pfaught, for giving my book and signing schedule such fabulous coverage in *Ransom Notes;*
• Barbara Lakey, publisher of Futures, for the spectacular coverage she gave my book's publication in her magazine;
• Alexis and Tom Powers, who rallied much support for my signings;
• Gay Toltl-Kinman, who brought me to speak to her Soroptimist friends;
• Kathy Ptacek, publisher of *Gila Queen's Guide to the Markets,* and Margo Power, editor of *Murderous Intent Mystery Magazine,* for the promotional opportunities they gave me;

● Priscilla English, Lisa Seidman, and Mae Woods, editors of *Murder by Thirteen*, for choosing "L.A.Justice";

● The whine & dine gang: Susan Casmier, Claire Carmichael McNab, Gayle Partlow and Judy Smith, for all their encouragement;

● Kathleen Beaver, for giving me the lowdown on law firms;

● Ron Armstrong, for teaching me about bones;

● Serita Stevens, for answering my medical questions;

● Margery Cooper Flax, for lending me her name;

● Cathy Gallagher, the mystery guide for About.com, and Geraldine Galentree, editor of *Cozies, Capers & Crimes*, for their encouragement;

● My sisters and brothers in the Los Angeles chapter of Sisters in Crime, for their unparalleled support and the enthusiasm with which they embraced my first book;

● My sisters in the Central Coast chapter of Sisters in Crime, for always treating me like one of their own;

● My friends in the AOL mystery community and our wonderful HOSTs, especially Sherrill, Jacquelynn, and Pat;

● My cyber-pals on the Short Mystery Fiction Society digest, The Mystery Writers Forum, the Sisters in Crime digest and the readers of DorothyL;

● My tea-sipping friends who share the power of the purple;

● Betty Wright and Betsy Lampé, of Rainbow Books, Inc., who believed in both me and Tracy, and who made it all possible;

● and especially, my husband, Joe, for sharing the thrill of it all.

CONSIDER THE ALTERNATIVE

AN ANITA SERVI MYSTERY

Irene Marcuse

On the first day of her new job, Anita Servi arrives to find her boss dead, with a plastic bag tied around her head and a copy of the Hemlock Society's *Final Exit* nearby. Anita discovers three other suicides were committed using the recommendations found in *Final Exit,* and wonders if these suicides are "assisted" in a much more sinister way. Anita is soon traveling down several interconnected roads of murder, mercy and money—lots of it.

"Marcuse has perceptive things to say about geriatric foibles and abuses..."
—*Kirkus Reviews*

*Available
August 2003
at your favorite
retail outlet.*

WIM464

DEAD AND BREAKFAST

ROBERT NORDAN

A MAVIS LASHLEY MYSTERY

Arriving at her dearest friend's beautiful mountain farm,
Mavis Lashley senses immediately that something
is terribly wrong.

Eileen Hollowell has decided to turn her home into a bed-and-
breakfast. But when the body of a local teenager is found on
the property, suspicion falls on Eileen's mentally impaired
son. Mavis knows poor Claude wouldn't hurt a fly—but
she's beginning to suspect just who might be keeping
secrets that are worth killing to hide.

Available August 2003 at your favorite retail outlet.

The Hydrogen Murder

Camille Minichino

A Gloria Lamerino Mystery

Gloria Lamerino is called in to investigate the murder of her former colleague, physicist Eric Bensen. Her understanding of Bensen's breakthrough research on hydrogen convinces detective and almost-beau Matt Gennaro that this is a high-stakes crime with no shortage of suspects.

Bensen's research has enormous potential for big business. Gloria is determined to expose the data tampering, deception and fraud by members of Bensen's team. When the person with the most to gain from Bensen's death is murdered, as well, it takes her most brilliant analytical skills to identify a killer.

"...a stunning debut..."
—Janet Evanovich

Available September 2003 at your favorite retail outlet.